THE
KILLER SPEECH

THE
KILLER SPEECH

A
COLE HUEBSCH
NOVEL

KEVIN KLUESNER

LEVEL
BEST BOOKS

First published by Level Best Books 2023

Copyright © 2023 by Kevin Kluesner

All rights reserved. No part of this publication may be reproduced, stored or transmitted in any form or by any means, electronic, mechanical, photocopying, recording, scanning, or otherwise without written permission from the publisher. It is illegal to copy this book, post it to a website, or distribute it by any other means without permission.

This novel is entirely a work of fiction. The names, characters and incidents portrayed in it are the work of the author's imagination. Any resemblance to actual persons, living or dead, events or localities is entirely coincidental.

Kevin Kluesner asserts the moral right to be identified as the author of this work.

Author Photo Credit: Cole Kluesner

First edition

ISBN: 978-1-68512-295-9

Cover art by Original illustration and design – Cole Kluesner

This book was professionally typeset on Reedsy. Find out more at reedsy.com

To all of the strong and amazing women in my life, especially my wife of 42 years, Janet, my daughter, Karri, mom, Jeri, sisters, Kathleen, Michele, and Nichole, grandmothers, Alvina and Loretta, as well as friends, families, and colleagues. Together, you've taught me that true strength is made up of equal parts love and grit. Bless you all!

Fiction is the lie through which we tell the truth.

—Albert Camus

Praise for The Killer Speech

"It's a joy to follow Special Agent Cole Huebsch through the streets of Milwaukee in this fast-paced thriller. Kluesner exceeds the high standard he set with *The Killer Sermon* to deliver an exciting, humorous and thought-provoking story with a phenomenal sense of place."—Archer Parquette, *Milwaukee Magazine*

"In quick strokes, Kevin Kluesner vividly sets the scene—present-day Milwaukee—and introduces the protagonist, FBI agent Cole Huebsch, and the attempted political assassination he is tasked with investigating. The prose is strong and rhythmic, guiding the reader page to page as the story rapidly unfolds. Cole Huebsch is a character readers will want to meet again and again."—David Luhrssen, *Shepherd Express*

"Kevin Kluesner's second novel, *The Killer Speech*, intertwines politics, a complex murder investigation, and deftly written prose to create a must read mystery."—Melissa Collum, Morris Newspaper Corp.

Chapter One

If God ever created a more perfect daybreak, Eric Rhodes hadn't seen it. He ran up Milwaukee's 51st Boulevard in dappled early morning sunlight with the temperature hovering around sixty-eight degrees. He wore black nylon running shorts a couple shades darker than the deep cocoa color of his skin. Shirtless, he felt free and fluid. Even with the cooler air, he worked up a lather of sweat. Nearing the end of his weekday four-mile run, he held a steady six-minute per mile pace. He smiled. He earned this sweat.

His smile widened as he maintained his rhythmic breathing; two breaths in and one out. Two breaths in and one out. His lungs efficient bellows. It felt effortless. Funny how things went. Some days it was torture to crawl out of bed and lace up his shoes. Those days he literally pounded the pavement. This morning he floated.

This stretch of 51st was his favorite. He loved the big solid houses made of red brick, Lannon stone, and the milky brick that gave Milwaukee its Cream City nickname. Every house had its own distinct character and personality, like the diverse residents they sheltered. In arguably the most segregated city in the U.S., the broader Sherman Park neighborhood shined a beacon of hope and community. Towering mountain ash and maples touched leaves overhead while on the street below Muslims, Orthodox Jews, and Christians lived together in relative peace.

Rhodes wasn't wearing headphones or earbuds. The melodies he enjoyed this morning came from the songbirds that made their homes here. A lot of urban areas had to settle for nuisance birds like pigeons, but this neighborhood had enough trees and devoted gardeners to keep the songbirds content. Goldfinches serenaded him as he made his way on the empty sidewalks.

Rhodes was still on a high from the night before. Milwaukee landed the Democratic National Convention, and he was a surprise choice to address the raucous crowd during an early prime time slot on the event's penultimate night. Never one to go along to get along, the thirty-five-year-old Senator from Wisconsin spoke from his heart about his hopes and dreams for his community and his country. His message resonated with the crowd. It resonated with the country. He watched the national news afterward with his wife and kids, and he was crowned the Democrat's rising star. But he wasn't universally loved, even in his own party. A large contingent of the party's leaders had fought to keep him off the convention floor, since he openly disagreed with a third of the planks that formed his party's platform. He constantly pointed out it was their differences in opinions, backgrounds, and culture that made them stronger.

He was a block from his house and reliving the sustained ovation he'd received when he was shoved hard from behind. He might've heard a loud bang, but his focus was on trying to keep his balance. It felt like someone snuck up behind him and hit him in the back with a baseball bat. Someone like Aaron Judge or Christian Yelich. He stumbled headfirst and felt himself going down. He willed himself to his right and narrowly missed faceplanting on the sidewalk. He landed on a neighbor's lawn, unable to get his arms in front of him to soften the fall.

He tried to rise when a wave of pain broke over him like a cement wall. He screamed, but nothing came out. You can't scream if you can't breathe. The only sounds he heard were a car speeding away and the sucking noise of a lung that no longer functioned.

Chapter Two

A nurse led Cole Huebsch into St. Joseph Hospital's Intensive Care Unit and to the curtain that shielded the patient in bay number 16 from the bustle of the ICU's other 23 bays. He showed his badge to a uniformed Milwaukee Police Department officer on his way into the unit and flashed it again to the MPD officer who sat just outside bay number 16. When a U.S. Senator is gunned down on one of your streets, a city takes extra precautions. Cole approved.

He knocked on the metal doorframe and pulled the curtain aside when he heard a quiet "Come in." He slipped into the room and closed the curtain behind him, automatically pushing the lever on the hand sanitizer to make sure his hands were sterile. He stepped directly to the young woman who sat at the side of the bed, holding Senator Rhodes' hand. "Morning. I'm Cole Huebsch, Special Agent in Charge of the FBI's Milwaukee Field Office." He leaned down and offered his hand.

She shook his hand, then held it for an extra beat, looking directly into Cole's denim-blue eyes. "I'm Karri Rhodes," she said, letting go of his hand. "This unconscious man here in the bed next to me is my husband, Eric. Someone shot him in the back this morning. Are you going to find out who did it?"

"Yes, Ma'am. That's my goal. I promise I'll do everything I can to find and bring in the person or persons responsible for the attack on your husband."

"I don't want to hear that you'll try. I want you to tell me you *will* find out who did this and make sure they're put away. I can't lose my husband."

"I understand. And I'm very sorry you and your husband are going through this."

She shook her head side to side, and Cole was certain the Senator's wife was going to tell him she didn't want to hear "sorry" from him. She wanted results. But the large gentleman next to her reached out and took one of her hands in his. Alan Anderson, the hospital administrator, spoke to her. "Karri, I know what you're feeling right now. But I also know this man right here. Cole has lain in a bed at my hospital a couple times now, recovering from his own gunshot wounds. He's got more medals than anyone I know. He's earned my respect. If he tells you he's going to find the people who put Eric in that bed, then he will. Take it to the bank."

She rocked in place and kept shaking her head. Finally, she bent over as if in pain and buried her face in her hands. She cried softly and moaned. Alan touched her shoulder, and Cole stood there stiffly, unsure how to respond. After a minute, she sat up straight and wiped her eyes, brushing away the tears. She looked directly at Cole again and said, "I just never thought something like this would happen. Yesterday everything was amazing, all seashells and balloons. This morning I kissed Eric and teased him about his head getting big. He hugged me and went out on his run with a huge smile on his face. An hour or so later, I got a call that he's in surgery, maybe dying. How does anyone deal with that?"

"Nobody's dying," Alan reminded her. "Your husband's a strong and stubborn man. And he got lucky…if anyone who gets shot in the back can be called lucky. The bullet went through the right side of his back and out his chest. It was about as clean as it could be. It didn't hurt much of anything on the way in, and only broke two ribs on the way out. His heart wasn't touched, and neither were any other vital organs beyond his right lung. But they patched that up already. I won't lie to you; we aren't ready to hang victory banners on the aircraft carrier just yet. These next few hours are critical. But if we can get through that, everything should be okay. He'll have that chest tube in for a couple days, but he could be out of the hospital and recuperating at home within a week."

Karri looked at Alan. "Thanks to you and your team here at St. Joe's."

"And thanks to the paramedics that brought him in," he said, looking up at

CHAPTER TWO

Cole as he did. "They had just brought a neighbor to the hospital who was suffering from chest pain. They cleaned up their rig and were grabbing a juice from our break room when they got the call. They rolled in seconds and were at Eric's side in less than two minutes. It helped our cause that St. Joe's is just a block and a half from where Eric was lying. If those paramedics hadn't been so close, we might be talking about a different outcome."

"How'd they find out that Eric was shot?" Karri asked Cole.

"One of your neighbors a couple doors down was about to let her dog out to do his business when she heard two shots. She looked through her blinds and saw your husband stumble and fall into her yard, and she called 911. Then she ran outside and held her hand against his back to try to stop the blood flow. Her pressure on the wound made a difference too."

"Do you know the neighbor's name? The one who called 911 and helped Eric?" Karri asked.

Cole pulled his phone from the inside left pocket of his suit and checked, "Bina Twerski."

For the first time since hearing her husband had been shot, Karri Rhodes smiled. "We know Bina. We have children the same age. Her husband teaches at the Yeshiva school in our neighborhood. They're wonderful people."

Cole reassured her he would stay in contact and provide updates, and he gave the Senator's wife his card that listed both his cell phone and email address. He said goodbye and escaped the ICU. He was halfway down a long stretch of sunlight-splashed white hallway that would lead him to the main lobby. He took quick strides because this case would bring a lot of attention and a pile of work.

"Agent Huebsch! Agent Huebsch!"

Cole turned to see Karri jogging after him, her shoes clicking on the white tile. She stopped in front of him and took a second to catch her breath and compose herself. When she looked up at him, she did so with large, beautiful brown eyes tinged with grief and fatigue.

"I'm sorry if I was rude or cold just now," she said, shaking her head. "That's really not who I am. I just love my husband so much and I almost lost him.

I couldn't bear that. I just couldn't."

"It's okay. I understand. You don't need to apologize for loving your husband."

"But I do need to apologize, and even explain somehow. It might not make sense, but I need to. I know Alan. He's been a mentor to Eric for years. If he says you're one of the good guys, that says a lot. But I want you to know about Eric and me. Maybe it will be even more motivation for you."

They both stepped to the side of the hall to let a group of hospital staff members walk by; three wore colorful scrubs, and a fourth wore a navy t-shirt that read, *Nurses Inspire Nurses*. Their soft-soled shoes were noiseless, but their approach was announced by the swish of their scrub pants and their animated conversation about plans for the upcoming weekend.

Karri continued, "We grew up across the street from each other, a mile or so east of here. Eric was a year older than me, and best buddies with my brother Jim. From the time they were little, Jimmy and Eric were gonna' be ball players…make millions playing for the Bucks in the NBA. That was their dream. Eric was tall enough and quick enough to give him a chance, but Jimmy was naturally chubby, and he quit growing in eighth grade. They never stopped being friends, but when Eric kept moving on in basketball, Jimmy got sucked in by a gang. My brother was shot selling dope when he was in ninth grade. Shot in the leg. It should have been nothing more than a scratch. But they said the bullet hit an artery, and he bled out at the scene. By then, Eric was already becoming a star, and big-time colleges were talking to his coaches. He could have forgotten about the skinny girl across the street, but he never did. He always watched out for me.

"When I was a junior in high school, and he was a senior, something changed. Mostly it was me I guess. I filled out and some guys apparently thought I was kind of pretty. Anyway, Eric and I started to date. Eric took a full ride to play basketball at Marquette, partly to stay close to me. When I was a senior in high school, and Eric was a freshman at MU, I got pregnant."

She looked at him, her eyes even sadder. "I know. The same old story in the 'hood, right?"

Cole didn't know what to say, so he waited. Karri pursed her lips and

CHAPTER TWO

bobbed her head, and when their eyes met again, Cole saw her eyes welling, reflecting a mixture of fierce pride and love for her husband.

"The thing is," she continued. "Eric didn't turn his back on me. He didn't leave me. And he didn't offer to take me to a clinic to have the pregnancy terminated. Instead, he went to his coach and told him he had to quit the team and find a job so he could take care of the woman he loved and his baby." She was trembling, and her eyes were filling with tears. "That's what that man lying back in that ICU fighting for his life did for me."

She shook her head and wiped her tears, and her frown turned into the start of a smile. "That's why I'm kind of partial to him. Even though he's a big lug and drives me crazy sometimes, he's all I've ever wanted and all I've ever needed in a partner. We lost that baby, and Eric went on to be a Hall of Famer at Marquette. He would have made that dream of playing in the NBA too, I believe, if he hadn't torn his Achilles tendon his senior year."

Now Cole was smiling. "You don't need to convince me," he said. "I have two degrees from Marquette. I'm a huge fan of his. I remember your husband taking us to the Elite Eight his junior year, putting up twenty-nine points and pulling down nine rebounds against Duke. Ten assists, too, if I remember right. Losing in OT was a heartbreaker. I also remember the mock drafts had him going in the NBA middle first round. He gave up millions of dollars to come back for his senior year. I'm sorry about that."

"No need to be sorry. He earned his business degree with a philosophy minor and got a great job in marketing with Harley Davidson after graduation." She laughed. "He was making seventy thousand dollars a year, and you'd have thought we won the lottery. We were pretty naïve, I guess."

Cole put his hand on her shoulder and squeezed gently, looking directly into her eyes. "You two have come a long way together in a short period of time. I promise I'll do everything I can to catch whoever shot your husband so that the two of you and your family can grow together even more in the future. Let your husband know that when he wakes up."

He nodded once to make sure she felt the conviction of his words, then turned and headed down the hallway, hoping he could deliver on that promise.

Chapter Three

Cole sat at his desk facing east out on Lake Michigan. His blinds were half open, and he could see the brilliant diamonds of light sparkling off the gentle waves that followed each other up onto the shore. *Like lemmings to the sea,* he thought, or more *like lemmings from the sea* in this case.

The Milwaukee field office was a little south of Milwaukee, in the neighboring suburb of St. Francis. The 200,000-square-foot building sheathed in glass formerly housed a high-profile investment firm. Cole often wondered what the Bureau could sell it for and how much good could be done with that money.

He cracked his neck and rolled his shoulders, feeling the pinch and tightness in his left shoulder, a reminder of the bullet he'd taken there six months earlier while stopping a serial killer who targeted reproductive rights physicians. Cole was still rehabbing the shoulder, building its strength week by week, while the killer was six feet under.

He studied the *Milwaukee Journal Sentinel* story about Senator Rhodes' shooting on his computer. The accompanying photo showed a handsome, confident face that Cole was drawn to. He hadn't watched the Senator's speech, or any of the convention speeches for that matter. Like many of his fellow Americans, he'd become disillusioned, almost apolitical, turned off by the rabid polarization the nation's once proud two-party system had spawned.

But as Cole sipped hot black coffee from his favorite brown mug and read the story, he could tell that Rhodes was different. He didn't toe any party line; he considered not just both sides of every argument or issue, but also the nuanced middle where the truth usually lived. He avoided making personal attacks on his opposition, and worked to lift people up, instead of putting them down. From talking with Karri Rhodes and Alan Anderson, Cole felt like the senator was a good man: a decent human being.

Cole read the reviews of the Senator's speech in the print edition of the paper. He preferred newsprint to online, liked hearing the rustle of the pages as he turned them and the rough papery texture on his fingers. The reviews were mostly glowing. They cast Milwaukee in a brighter light, and its young senator as an inspiring leader willing to challenge the status quo. Not every review was positive. Cole read a piece by a national pundit from the *New York Times* who acknowledged Rhodes' charisma and called him a clever orator. But the writer labeled Rhodes naïve and questioned how the country would pay for his universal health care and other measures.

Cole sipped his coffee and leaned back in his chair to think when Li Song, his top analyst, stuck her head through his partially open door. "Can you spare a moment for Lane and me?"

Cole smiled and nodded, sweeping a hand toward the two chairs facing his desk. "Are you kidding? For my two favorite analysts in the whole world, *mi casa es su casa.*"

Li sat down and placed an open folder on the desk. She usually bantered with Cole, but she locked eyes with him now, all business. She adjusted the turquoise tortoiseshell glasses that framed her eyes, one chestnut and one sky blue. Most people never noticed, but once you did, it was hard not to stare at first…they were striking and pulled you in. The first time Cole met her, she said, "The condition is called heterochromia, and it's the only thing hetero about me." Cole couldn't help smiling when he thought of it.

Li said, "We're picking up a lot of chatter that white supremacists are behind the senator's shooting. Most of those hate groups' blogs and websites are echoing similar crap along the lines of, "an uppity 'n-word' got what was coming to him. They only wish the shot had been fatal."

"Anybody claim responsibility? Then we could just go arrest them and cage them like the animals they are."

CHAPTER THREE

"Not yet. Most of these groups talk big, but they don't have the guts to stand behind what they do. They're cowards," Li said.

"We've got agents deep in a couple of those groups. Have we heard from them yet?"

"We have," she confirmed. "But they didn't hear anything before the shooting and have only witnessed the celebrations going on...nothing that leads them to believe their groups are involved."

"We've got another problem," Lane said. Lane Becwar had just celebrated his thirtieth birthday. Six feet tall in his wingtips and athletic in a rangy kind of way, he'd worked full-time in the local offices of one of the "Big Four" accounting firms before joining the Bureau a year ago. He had short but thick black hair, deep brown eyes, and a nose a little big for his strong oval face. "At least two different protests are being organized for tonight, one near the hospital the senator is recovering in and one downtown at City Hall. Our guys who monitor the hate groups tell us the anarchists plan to be there in force. They think the white supremacists will show up too. Kind of like watching two Cat 5 hurricanes getting ready to collide over our city."

Cole stood and turned to face the lake, the waves almost on cue picking up in fury and purpose. "Sounds like Ty will have his hands full." Ty Igou was a detective with the Milwaukee Police Department who'd helped them track down the murderer in their last case that went national. They'd tried to talk him into joining the FBI permanently, but he'd been offered the chance to become an MPD Captain and felt he had to take it. Cole didn't want him in harm's way.

He turned back to Li and Lane, shaking his head. "The country's still recovering from George Floyd's murder. We've got to solve this shooting before things get out of hand. Alan and his team at the hospital better make sure Senator Rhodes pulls through, or it will be a disaster."

Cole's cell vibrated, and he slipped it out of his suit jacket, looking at the ID. "Speak of the angel," he said to both the caller and his analysts, his phone on speaker. "Alan! We were just talking about you. Please tell me you've got good news."

"I have good news, and I also have better news. You want the good news first, or the better news…"

"You mean good news or bad news?"

"No. Good news first, or better news first. No bad news here."

"I like the sound of that. Give me the better news first."

"Our distinguished senator is out of the woods. Completely. He won't be running marathons for a while, but he's on his way to a full recovery."

All three in Cole's office cheered. "Thank God!" Cole said. "I can't tell you what that means. Do me a favor and hold a press conference as soon as you can and tell the world what you just told us. Can you do that? It will take some of the wind out of the sails of the protests that are brewing right now."

There was a silence that grew uncomfortable before Alan said, "What makes you think I want to deflate the protests?"

Cole sighed. "Alan, I think you know where I stand when it comes to the fight for social justice. You and I have marched together more than once. I'm just trying to keep more people from getting hurt, maybe killed. Too many of the protests which you and I believe in have been hijacked by people on both sides who aren't interested in equality, but something more sinister."

From the phone, Alan's sigh echoed Cole's. "We'll hold that press conference. I'm pretty sure the protests will still go on, and I'm all for that, but maybe it will help keep things civil."

The relief was evident in Cole's voice, "Thank you."

"You ready for the good news?"

Cole brightened. "Absolutely."

"I think we found your shooters."

Chapter Four

Cole turned his ten-year-old Dodge Charger off Interstate 94, heading north on US 175 at five miles over the fifty-mph speed limit. He glanced at his odometer, watching it roll past 199,032 miles. He thought he should celebrate somehow when she passed the 200,000-mile mark.

"Thanks for bringing me," Li said from the front passenger seat. She had a law degree from the University of Michigan and worked three years in tax law at a big Detroit law firm before joining the Bureau as an analyst. She would turn thirty-five in a month and had told Cole she wanted to become a special agent. Since she wasn't a veteran, she didn't qualify for a waiver from the age thirty-seven cutoff, and Cole promised to help her make the transition over the next two years.

Some analysts have felt like outsiders or second-class citizens in the Bureau, like only the agents matter. Analysts don't carry weapons and aren't sworn law enforcement officers. But the modern FBI works to make its analysts feel like key members of an elite team, and Cole made that a focus of his leadership. Li was looking for a different career challenge, and he supported it.

Cole looked at her out of the corner of his eye. He knew she would be a great agent. It didn't take anyone long to see that she was brilliant, but if you didn't know her, you might think her fragile. You'd be wrong. She was lean because she ran distance and worked out fanatically. She loved judo and sparred three times a week. Over the past two years, she'd begun incorporating Krav Maga into her training, the self-defense and fighting system developed for Israeli security forces. It blended the simplest, most practical and efficient techniques of other fighting styles, and embraced aggression. She'd invited Cole to watch one of her workouts, and he was impressed. Her raven black, mid-length hair was pulled back in a ponytail, and it flipped from her left shoulder to her right when she turned to speak to Cole.

"I can tell you think highly of Mr. Anderson."

Cole nodded again as he turned off Lisbon and up 51st. "When a guy and his team patch you up a couple times and treat you like family, you start to like and respect them. His hospital's food isn't bad either."

"You think he's got something usable for us?"

"I do. Alan wouldn't have called otherwise," he said, slowing to maneuver around cars on the narrow city street. "On a personal note, how are you and Linda doing? Seems pretty serious."

Cole thought Li might be blushing, and she didn't try to hide the smile that lit up her face. She'd been dating Linda Puccini, a highly regarded freelance photographer, for almost a year. "It's pretty amazing," Li said. "She's so different from me in so many ways, but we just click."

Alan was waiting outside as they pulled under the massive canopy that shielded the main entrance. A valet took the keys to Cole's car as Alan stepped up to greet them. His deep voice carried to the attendant, "Maurice, don't dent this old can up too bad."

"Hey! The Charger's a classic. They don't make 'em quite like this anymore. And it's about the only thing around as dependable as me," Cole said, smiling, shaking the administrator's large hand and introducing Li.

Alan shook Li's hand and winked. "Cole tells me he's mentoring you. Hopefully, it won't derail your career." Li laughed.

They walked one at a time through a large, automatic revolving glass door and into an expansive lobby that rose several stories high. The receptionist and registration staff called out "good afternoon" as their footfalls echoed across the shiny marble floor made of beige tiles sixteen feet square.

Alan stopped at an unlabeled, non-descript door and paused, looking at his two guests. "Here's where I pull back the curtain to Oz." He opened the

CHAPTER FOUR

door, and they followed him down a sterile stairwell and into a basement corridor lined with painted white cinderblock walls.

"Reminds me of that part of Disney World the public never sees," Cole said, loud enough for Alan to hear ahead of them, as their heels clacked along the terrazzo floors that seemed to go on forever, stark, bare tunnels that branched off into a confounding maze. "If Alan starts cackling like a crazy warlock, run for your life."

"Funny man," Alan said, turning to rap on a door bearing the sign, *Switchboard*, before pushing it open with a swoosh. A low murmur, the hum of frenetic electrical white noise swarmed them as they stepped across the threshold. The room was dimly lit, with banks of black and white monitors stacked in front of two operators, almost touching the low ceiling. A young operator fresh out of high school was talking to someone on the phone while watching the feed from security cameras flash different scenes on the screens before her. The second operator looked to be in her early seventies, and her wrinkled face broke into a smile when Alan stepped into the room.

"Well. Well. The big guy came down to rub elbows with us cellar dwellers," she teased in a husky voice tuned through the years by nearly a million cigarettes. "We're humbled by his majesty's show of support."

Alan paused, holding up an index finger. "Jill, if you're trying to distract me, it's not working. I smell donuts." He tilted his head back and sniffed audibly, flaring his nostrils for show. "If I'm not mistaken, I smell Cranky Al's Donuts. If you have a cruller for me, I might keep you around a while longer."

She laughed and pulled open a metal file cabinet drawer, hauling out a box labeled Cranky Al's Donuts. "There are bloodhounds out there that envy your sense of smell." She handed Alan a cruller and napkin while he introduced Cole and Li. When she offered them donuts, Li declined. "Um, you wouldn't happen to have a maple-covered long john in there somewhere, would you?" Cole asked. She reached in and handed him one, along with a napkin.

"And to think some people say Jill's not much use to us anymore," Alan said with a mouthful of cruller, slipping a ten-dollar bill into a jar labeled, "Goodies."

Li interrupted, "Do you have something for us to look at, Mr. Anderson?"

"Ah, I'm working with her on the whole establishing a rapport thing," Cole said, trying to chew the long john instead of inhaling it. He licked a dab of sweet, sticky frosting from his lip.

"Nope. She's quite right," Alan said. "Jill, do you have those tapes queued up for us?"

"Indeed I do, Sir." She hit a button on one monitor, and a blurry SUV flashed on the screen, then off. She scrolled back and froze the frame with the SUV centered. "Two out of the 200 security cameras we have on our campus face 51st Street, and this is the best screenshot we have. The vehicle is traveling north, and the time stamp is 0624."

"That's six twenty-four a.m. for the uninitiated," Alan said.

"Yes, it is," Cole agreed, squinting at the screen. "This picture's not the best. It's grainy and black and white with, what, maybe five pixels? Does Walter Cronkite still come on and do the news at ten o'clock every night here?"

"Is Mr. Special Agent in Charge picking on us, Alan?" Jill asked.

"No. Not at all," he said, patting her shoulder. "You just don't understand FBI-speak. Let me translate; he just said the Bureau would like to outfit our humble nonprofit hospital with the latest and best security gear."

"Well, hallelujah. I've been asking for color monitors for like a hundred years," Jill said.

"That would be just after she started here," Alan said, earning a sharp elbow from Jill.

"You know, on second thought," Cole said. "I think we can use this. Yeah. A little lab work back at headquarters, and we should be able to make out the license plate, ID the vehicle, and maybe determine how many people are in it. This'll work just swell."

Jill harrumphed, and Li and Alan laughed out loud.

Chapter Five

Cole and Li drove back to the offices in St. Francis excited. The FBI had the best tech specialists in the world and all the latest toys at their disposal. If anyone could tease actionable information from the screenshot they'd downloaded to a thumb drive, they could. But as the afternoon melted into evening, Cole paced in his gloomy office, his mood darkening like the skies out his window. It was nine p.m., and the sun had set an hour before. The only light in the room came from his small desk lamp, the soft yellow glow spilling onto his laptop and papers and puddling on the carpet.

While they waited for the techs to do their thing, Cole and his team shared with local law enforcement everything they were picking up on the planned demonstrations. The protests had been peaceful at the beginning, but Cole was getting updates of windows broken and rocks and bottles thrown at police. He prayed it wouldn't get worse. Alan's press conference from his hospital's expansive lobby could not have gone better, in Cole's opinion. Alan resonated authority and integrity as he faced the horde of media, more than one hundred national, regional, and local cameras and microphones aimed at him like an overzealous firing squad. He praised the paramedics and his own team, cited the strength of Senator Rhodes and his wife, and asked the community to stay calm. He introduced A. J. Berg, the young trauma surgeon who operated on the Senator. Dr. Berg explained the surgery and confidently shared his prognosis; because of the Senator's relative youth and excellent health, he should be up and walking in a week or so, with a full recovery in six to eight weeks. The crowd of hardened journalists joined the gathered hospital staff in a loud, spontaneous burst of applause. Finally, Alan brought Karri to the podium. She thanked the paramedics, Alan, Dr. Berg, and everyone involved in her husband's care, and she thanked the public for their love and prayers. She promised to provide updates and concluded by echoing Alan's call for calm. But not everyone listened.

Cole's office wasn't bare, but close to it. He preferred to call it spartan. His two degrees from Marquette were at the bottom of a cardboard box somewhere in a closet at home. Instead, a forty-inch flat screen and a framed autographed poster of Olympic wrestling champion Dan Gable adorned two of his four walls. The only other thing besides electrical outlets on his walls was a fist-sized hole in the drywall. The hole had been created when the former head of the Chicago FBI office threw a chair a few months ago. Cole wanted to mark it for posterity, so he hung a small silver frame over it. He told Li and Lane it was his contribution to the art world, and his tongue was planted firmly in his cheek when he named the 'piece' *Leadership*.

A pair of Cole's old wrestling shoes hung from a peg behind his desk. He'd worn them when he won his own NCAA wrestling championship and had them autographed right after the meet with a borrowed black Sharpie. The guy who signed them was Cael Sanderson, a U.S. Olympic wrestling champ and the only Division one wrestler to win every one of his collegiate matches.

A large, round, faux-metal battery-powered clock snicked as it labored to keep time from its place above the door, its longest hand vibrating like a tuning fork as it ticked off the seconds. Ralph from maintenance had come in to replace it weeks ago, but Cole had shooed him away. He didn't like discarding things. He'd lost too much in his life already.

Cole had turned forty-five this past March. He was born and raised on the other side of the state in the small town of Prairie du Chien. An only child, he'd lost both parents in a car accident when he was 22, just before he graduated with his BA in English and Philosophy. He went into banking and earned his MBA but was fired from the bank he managed for ignoring bank policy and foiling an armed robbery attempt. He had taken a serial bank robber and killer off the streets, though, and the FBI recruited him.

CHAPTER FIVE

After scoring off the charts on the physical and written exams at Quantico, Virginia, he was sworn in. The FBI tried to steer him to DC, but he took a post back in Milwaukee and married his college sweetheart, Janet Stone, a local television reporter at the time. The demands of their jobs and inability to conceive a child pulled them apart; Janet was now his ex-wife and a Fox News anchor in New York, while Cole had risen through the ranks, taking charge of the Milwaukee FBI Field Office six years ago.

Cole sat down at his desk. He yawned deeply and rubbed his eyes. Each month he put out an internal newsletter for the staff under his command, summing up the most important of the official Bureau emails that tsunamied their inboxes. He noticed the August copy on his desk and picked it up. His assistant added historical and often inspiring FBI stories, and right now, he needed inspiration.

One story caught his attention. He knew it well, but it still troubled him. It also made him proud of the men and women who served before him. Nearly sixty years ago, three young civil rights workers were trying to increase black voter registration in Mississippi. They disappeared after being stopped for speeding by Neshoba County police. President Lyndon Johnson ordered the FBI to search for the men after their car was found stripped and burned two days later. Six weeks after that, the FBI found James Chaney, Andrew Goodman, and Michael Schwerner buried in an earthen dam.

Cole stretched his arms to the ceiling and yawned again, leaning back in his chair. He thought about the FBI agents overseeing the bodies being pulled from the mud and wondered how far his country had come in the area of civil rights over the past six decades. *Not far enough. Not nearly far enough*, he concluded.

He sat down at his computer and pulled up the Banana Republic factory outlet page. He was particular about his clothes but relished the challenge of finding a deal. He wore boxers, and the Banana Republic brand fit him best. They weren't too baggy or tight around the waist, and they gave the boys room to move about freely. He scrolled down the clearance page until he found three different pairs that were five dollars off the original price. If he typed in *BRfactory* at checkout, he'd get another forty percent off. He did the math in his head and liked the idea of paying seven bucks a pair. *Sweet!* One was navy with little yellow bananas; he couldn't overcome the phallic symbolism and passed. The second boxers were burgundy with little raccoon faces. He shook his head. *If only they'd been badgers.* The third was bright yellow with little blue eyeglasses, very close to Marquette's colors. *Hmmm.* He rubbed his chin. *Does it even matter? Nobody will ever see the boxers but me.*

His desk phone started chirping before he could decide, and he hit the speakerphone button, "Huebsch here."

"Cole. It's Gene Olson." Gene's voice boomed like a cannon. He was ten years older than Cole and calling from FBI Headquarters, the J. Edgar Hoover Building in Washington, DC. As a Deputy Director, he sat two spots below the agency's top position, and most thought he would head up the Bureau within the next few years.

"Hi, Gene. Seems like forever since I last saw you."

"You mean when I watched the president pin another medal on you, with half your hometown on hand to see it?"

Cole smiled, remembering. "Don't be jealous now. Some of my halo shines on you too."

Gene laughed. "I don't know about a halo, but you're sure in the spotlight again. We need to get Senator Rhodes' shooters soon. Protests are starting up again in cities across the country. The responsible party or parties need to be brought to justice now, and in a very public way."

"Amen, to that. Any chance you're calling with information on the image we sent?"

"Ah, maybe you know me too well. You took away the surprise. It was a Wisconsin plate, and we were able to make out two letters and two numbers, four of the seven characters in all. We ran the list against white Ford Broncos, and there's only one in the state. It's a '93, just like OJ Simpson's."

"That would be funny any other time."

"Yeah. And that Bronco belongs to James Harris. No way to tell for sure from the image you sent, but it could be Jim and his brother Robert "Bobby" Harris. They inherited a farm southwest of you, just above the Illinois border.

CHAPTER FIVE

I know this will take away from your beauty sleep, but I'm hoping you can put together a plan and pay the brothers a visit first thing in the morning."

"Sleep is overrated. And tell your guys they did nice work. I keep trying to tell the foot soldiers around here that HQ actually helps once in a while."

"Thanks, I think. You guys did some good work in getting that screenshot from the hospital's security camera so quickly. Let's wrap this up."

"Any other words of wisdom?"

"Just this," Gene said. "Don't get the boxers with the glasses. You'll end up making a spectacle of yourself!" His laugh bounced off the walls of the room before he dropped off.

Chapter Six

All 56 FBI field offices have their own *Special Weapons And Tactics* unit, and Cole's SWAT team was geared up and running in three black SUVs toward the Harris farm, a mile from the unincorporated community of Foxhollow, Wisconsin. Foxhollow was part of the town of Turtle, which boasted twenty-four hundred residents, a whopping one percent of whom were African American. The Harris farm sat less than a mile north of the Illinois border. Cole's team left the FBI offices in St. Francis before five a.m. and would make the normal one-hour drive in less than forty minutes. It was twilight, and they were ten minutes out.

Immediately after getting off the phone with Olson, Cole sent agents from the Madison office to watch the entrance to the farm and report on activity. He directed them to take their most beat-up unmarked vehicle down to Foxhollow and to park at least two miles out from the farm. They hoofed it in the dark through tall, wet cornfields and woodlots and set up in a dense oak grove across from the farm's entrance. They were in place and concealed by midnight, swatting mosquitos and watching the house and outbuildings through the latest night vision optics. Gene's people had traced the brothers' cell phones, and both were on; their GPS indicated they were inside the house.

The Madison team checked in with Li every fifteen minutes to provide an update, but also to let her know they were okay. So far, they hadn't registered any heat signatures at the farm aside from three deer and what they thought was either a coyote or a dog. Cole knew pretty much every

CHAPTER SIX

farm had at least one dog, and usually a couple. He didn't like the idea of one running loose, barking a warning to its owner. He also didn't relish shooting a dog if it turned on his team. Both brothers lived at the farm, and Cole hoped they could capture them while they were still sleep-addled; but his team prepared for the worst. A helicopter trailed two miles behind their convoy to avoid tipping the brothers with its rotor noise. It would remain overhead during the raid on the farm, alerting the team to squirters who might take off across the fields on ATVs or dirt bikes. Cole had asked the Illinois State Patrol to move squads nearby in case anyone tried crossing the border, which was marked by two lanes of blacktop aptly named State Line Road.

The SUVs were loaded with gear and Colectivo Coffee. The local java purveyor roasted every batch by hand, and its motto was "Strong coffee since 1993." That was just what the team needed since nobody had caught any sleep. They were together planning the raid by ten thirty p.m., Li and Lane feeding them incoming data from DC. Twenty of them crowded around a table in a spartan conference room. Cole leaned against a large whiteboard, and Li and Lane stood by easels, furiously filling up twenty-seven by thirty-four-inch white sheets and sticking them up on the bare walls. They spoke to the group as they worked.

"Jim Harris is forty-two, and brother Bobby is nineteen; same dad, different mothers," Li said loudly. Jim's clearly a bigot, based on his public posts we've seen, but he's not one of your 'sophisticated' white supremacists, if there is such a thing."

"Maybe in hell," Cole said.

"Right," Li continued. "What I mean is he hasn't used any of the sophisticated recruiting we've seen with white supremacists, things like targeting gamers who are into the most violent games, frequenting iffy online forums and chat rooms, no special apps, etc. He dropped out of high school after two lackluster years and leached off his dad until his dad passed a few years ago, and he inherited the farm."

"You're saying Jim got the farm when his dad bought the farm, so to speak?" Cole said.

Li shook her head and interrupted the chuckles. "Jim's a loner, no real friends that we can discern so far. Seems to have zero charisma, which is why he hasn't attracted any kind of a following. Bobby isn't the brightest from what we can see from his high school transcripts, and he may be following his brother, so he has a roof over his head. We don't think there will be more than the two of them, but we'll be ready if there are." She nodded to Lane.

"Jim's a big guy, six-four and maybe two eighty. Bobby's a beanpole, six one and one seventy. Neither has military or law enforcement in their background, so there's no special training to be concerned about. Jim's a brawler prone to violence. His rap sheet is littered with disorderly conduct and battery, some aggravated. He spent time in federal prison for attempted murder; appears he was winning one of his frequent bar fights and didn't want to stop. An off-duty cop kept him from kicking a patron's head in. The victim spent more than two months in an intensive care unit."

Cole broke in. "As a felon, he shouldn't have a weapon. But I doubt he cares about the rules of law. And there's good hunting land all around that area, some of which they own. You can bet they'll have shotguns and high-powered rifles in the house. At a minimum. This should be easy peasy but be prepared for everything and anything. We let our guard down, and one or more of us dies."

"Did you really say 'easy peasy?'" Li asked.

"We have a SWAT team here, and that doesn't inspire macho confidence," Lane added.

"You both missed the point I was making about keeping our guard up, so everyone makes it back in one piece."

They slowed and drove with their lights off the last mile, connecting with the Madison agents in front of the short gravel drive that led to the Harris farm. As they waited for five thirty and sunrise, Cole used the gloaming and the hint of light from a crescent moon to survey the house and outbuildings he'd only seen on maps and satellite images until now.

Facing south across the road, the short drive led to a gravel circle that connected three buildings. An old round milking barn on the left was attached to a scarred cement grain silo stretching eighty feet high, its metal

CHAPTER SIX

dome already catching the first hint of morning sun. To the right of that, in the middle of Cole's view, was an old wooden outbuilding they'd been told measured fifty feet wide and twenty-five feet high, not counting the peak. It might've held bales of hay at one time, but it was listing several degrees toward the two-story farmhouse that was another thirty yards or so to its right. Cole couldn't tell if the simple house was white or gray, but even from a distance, he could see paint was peeling off, and it needed a new roof. In the dim light, its missing shingles made the roof look like a haphazard checkerboard. A line of towering white pines a hundred feet tall crowded shoulder to shoulder to the right of the house. Without that windbreak, Cole wondered if the house would still be standing. A massive burr oak nearly twenty feet around at its base and sixty feet high guarded the front of the house, but its huge, gnarled, ancient limbs spread out above it, threatening to stave it in during the next big storm. No lights were on inside the house. The Bronco sat on the gravel drive.

It was another perfect morning, with the temperature in the high sixties. Cole and the others were wearing their FBI windbreakers over body armor, and he felt comfortable. A mild breeze ran through his hair, and Cole noticed the smell of wildflowers and dewy grass. He didn't smell cow manure or pig shit, no chickens, or even the smell of diesel fuel. The brothers leased out their tillable land to neighbors to grow crops on, but this was no longer a working farm. It was quiet. Eerily quiet. *Perhaps the calm before the storm*, Cole thought, before giving the word to move.

Chapter Seven

The barn and the middle building had no windows that faced the circle drive, so the team focused on the house first. That was where directed gunfire would most likely come from, and it was also where the brothers' cell phones were. The SWAT team had two agents in place behind the buildings, and the Madison agents had scoped rifles scanning the windows in the front of the house. Another SWAT member covered the west windows from the pines, while the main force was crouched low on that side, tight to the house, prepared to breach.

Cole called Jim Harris' cell. It rang repeatedly before going to voicemail. He tried Bobby's cell with the same results. No lights came on in the house, and nobody reported movement. Cole turned to Li, covering his mic momentarily while shaking his head. "It's never easy peasy." He took his hand away from his mic, all fourteen agents on-site on the same frequency, and he said simply and evenly, "Go."

His team slid around the house and went in on the backside. Cole couldn't see them enter, but he saw lights come on in a sequence through the first floor and then the second as they cleared the house room by room. No shots fired. They filed out and entered the second building in a choreographed manner meant to protect each man the best they could. Yellow light splashed through the door in front, with rays shooting through cracks and holes in the weathered wooden siding. They advanced to the barn with the same results. A staccato, "Clear. Clear. Clear. Clear," came over the earbuds. When the barn was deemed safe, the SWAT commander called for Cole to come to the middle building. The entire operation, from start to finish,

CHAPTER SEVEN

didn't take five minutes. Cole drove up the gravel drive and parked in front of the wooden structure. Its rightward lean gave it a sloppy drunk look, and Cole wondered how stable it was. The SWAT team stood outside its open door, pulling off their helmets and drinking water. He would have liked to breach with them, but that wasn't his role. He walked through the men and women, nodding and patting them on their shoulders, "Great job, you guys. Well done." The SWAT team hadn't encountered any resistance, but they hadn't known that going in. Each of them had put their life on the line without reservation. Li followed Cole into the building.

The inside was simple, with four high walls and a loft on the backside. Cole looked at Stan Adamson, his SWAT commander, with his eyes arched. "Yeah, boss, we cleared the hay loft."

Cole noticed rows of pruned marijuana plants hanging upside down under the loft, drying, he presumed. It didn't look like enough to earn the brothers much of a living, but certainly enough to keep them stoned. He turned to Li, "Maybe it was a bit of a working farm after all."

A twenty-foot square heavyweight blue poly tarp was spread in the middle of the room, tented in the middle in odd shapes. "We poked it to make sure nobody is hiding under there waiting to ambush us," Stan said, "but we wanted to preserve the scene, so we didn't lift the tarp up to see what was under it."

Cole nodded, "Good call." The outside light brightened and joined the yellow light of the building; the diffuse glow floodlit the walls. Two were bare wood, but two had been painted recently, the smell of enamel heavy in the air. The walls were tagged top to bottom in loud colors, letters, and symbols...what they all recognized as gang graffiti. Cole stepped back and looked up at the graffiti, taking in both walls, covering as much as one thousand square feet.

"What the hell?" Li said.

"My first thought was 'How the hell?'" Stan said. "How did someone find out the Harris brothers were involved? How did they beat us here? And how the hell did they get all this painted so fast?"

"The real question we need to answer," Cole said, stepping closer to get a better look, is "Who the hell? Who the hell pulled this off?"

Chapter Eight

Techs worked the scene, all three buildings and the grounds around them, collecting anything they thought had the potential to be evidence and taking high-resolution photos of everything. This was a lightning rod case with national media interest, and they couldn't afford to miss anything. Cole, Li, and three techs were the only feds left onsite five hours later. He'd sent everyone else home to get food and sleep. They would debrief at the end of the day. A Wisconsin State Patrol cruiser blocked the driveway, ensuring nobody would wander onto the scene and mess things up.

Cole stood inside the middle outbuilding with Li. The door was open, but little in the way of a breeze made its way inside. Cole had shed his armor and his windbreaker, but he still wiped sweat off his forehead as he directed the techs, "Let's do the unveiling."

Two of the techs grabbed separate corners of the blue tarp with gloved hands, while the third hit the record button on her camera. The two techs began walking back the tarp to reveal the lumpy objects underneath. Cole heard a slurping sound as part of the tarp peeled away from something beneath it. The techs paused, but Cole shook his head, stomach tightening with dawning recognition. "Keep going," he said. They began pulling again, and a severed leg came into view, then a shattered head. Blood congealed on the dirt floor. The tarp stalled again, and Cole said evenly, "Just keep moving; this is like ripping off a Band-Aid. Let's get it over with." Cole waited while one of the techs yelped, "Wait," and ran outside to clear his breakfast. To his credit, he came right back in, and a little shakily, he and his partner pulled the tarp away, exposing unconnected limbs, torsos, and the remains of two heads, neither recognizable. A sledgehammer and axe, both caked with blood, lay across the jumble of broken body parts.

Cole looked over and noticed Li had turned her head toward the exit. "When every part of me wants to run the other way, that's when I know I need to focus on what's in front of me."

"Who could do something like this?" she asked, biting her upper lip and facing the gore again.

"I don't know, but we'll find out." He watched silently as the techs shook off their horror and fatigue and got to work sampling and cataloguing and he repeated softly, "We'll find out."

Chapter Nine

Cole was back at his desk by one thirty, the early afternoon light streaming through the blinds causing him to squint and accelerating his sleep-deprived headache. He got up and closed the blinds, and pulled a bottle of Advil from his drawer, swallowing two with a hot coffee chaser. He encouraged Li to get some rest and after she resisted, he ordered her home. He told her she wouldn't be any good if she didn't catch some sleep. But he didn't heed his own advice. He leaned back in his chair, took in a deep breath, and let it out slowly, trying to focus. His cell phone rang, and he picked it up, his *roommate*, Michele Fields, on the line. Cole and the reporter had grown close chasing a killer down a few months ago. There was nothing physical between them after almost nine months, mostly because she was still trying to find her way back from being date raped shortly before they met. But Cole cared for her deeply.

"Hey," he said, trying to sound alert.

"Hey, yourself," Michele said. "When you didn't come home last night, I figured you were working the Senator Rhodes' shooting. How're you doing?"

"That's what makes you such an astute investigative reporter," Cole said, stifling a yawn. "And I'm doing okay. Kind of a grizzly scene this morning, but I'm not feeling much sympathy for the recently departed Harris brothers." He thought about the phrase, *departed*, and knew he could have said *deboned* just as easily. Bile rose in his throat, and he washed it down with another large sip of coffee.

"You sound tired."

"Lack of sleep has a way of doing that to you."

"When are you coming home? Maybe I could give you a massage after you wake up from a nap."

Cole cocked his head. Little things like that gave him hope their relationship could still move beyond friendship. "That sounds amazing, and I'm definitely taking a rain check, but I need to work through a mountain of evidence we recovered."

"You won't be any good to your team if you're a zombie."

Cole smiled, exhausted. "I gave similar advice to Li not too long ago."

"It was good advice then and still is…."

Cole's desk phone rang, jangling his frayed nerves. "Hopefully, we can connect tonight. I need to take this call from Gene. Thanks for checking in."

"Cole here!" He barked the greeting out in a failed attempt to sound alert.

"Wow! Did you wake up on the wrong side of the bed this morning?"

"Not a chance. I think you know I didn't lay my head on a pillow last night," Cole laughed.

"Not the takedown any of us expected this morning, but it'll do. Good work by you and the team. The president himself told the director to let you know he's very pleased with how fast and how well you handled this."

"What? The president's not calling personally to tell me that?" Cole ribbed. "I gotta hear it from his flunky?"

"Flunky?" Gene's laugh echoed. "You ungrateful bastard! Seriously, great work all around. Why don't you go home now and get some rest. Plenty of people smarter than both of us are sorting through the evidence. You'll be for shit to your team if you don't crash for a while."

"That's the third time that sentiment's been shared in the past hour, just not that succinctly."

"I do have a way with words," Gene said, pausing.

Cole massaged his eyelids and stifled a yawn. "There's more, isn't there?"

"Yeah. The president and the director are holding a press conference in a half hour from the White House. Some of the photos of the gang graffiti are already being leaked to key media. They think if the world knows that Senator Rhodes' shooters paid the price it'll suppress the civil unrest this

CHAPTER NINE

case sparked. They don't want more riots and mayhem in our city streets.

"Something's off about this whole deal, though," Cole said. "You get that, right? I think someone was waiting for the Harris brothers when they got back to the farm from shooting the Senator, maybe someone who put them up to it."

"Yeah. Nobody here has voiced that yet, but here's the thing… The powers that be don't want us to pick at that thread. They like the feeling of closure here. Two white supremacists shoot a black senator, and a group of blacks takes them off the board, balancing the scales of justice so to speak. The steam that was rising dissipates. The president likes that."

Cole sat forward in his chair, looking at the phone. "Are you telling me to stop investigating this?"

"Officially, I'm telling you to march the investigation into the swamp," Gene said, sighing. "But I know you can't do that, and that's not the way I taught you to work things anyway. Just do it with as much stealth as possible. Watch your horns and try not to knock any porcelain off the display cases."

Cole raised an eyebrow. "I'm a little groggy. Was that a 'bull in a china shop reference?"

"Even tired, you're my boy," Gene laughed. "Now, go home and catch some sleep and a good meal. And that's not a recommendation; that's an order!"

Chapter Ten

Even after eleven years of living on the third floor of the 10,000 square foot house Cole shared with its eighty-seven-year-old owner, Alvina Newhouse, he was in awe of the sheer size and staid beauty of the 1891 red brick and sandstone structure whenever he pulled up the driveway. But it was now almost six p.m., and nothing registered as he pulled into the six-car garage of what the locals called the "Castle Mansion" and trudged up the interior staircase.

A door opened as he made the first-floor landing, and Frau Newhouse held it wide. A bright blue apron covered most of her pale green housedress, and a kind smile filled her full face lined with wrinkles. Her white hair shook as she waved a wooden spatula at Cole. "And where do you think you are going, young man? Two beautiful women are right here making you a meal fit for a *Koenig!*"

"A king? Wow!" Cole couldn't help but smile as he gave her a quick hug and followed her into the kitchen. There were far more opulent dining options available in the house, but this small kitchen felt cozy. Cole joined Michele at the heavy oak table while Frau Newhouse went back to the stove. Michele would turn thirty-five next month, and she looked beautiful with her long, auburn hair cascading over the open collar of a simple white button-down shirt. "We thought we'd surprise you." Her deep brown eyes smiled.

She slid a hearty pour of a plum-colored cabernet in front of him. "I've been letting it breathe. That should go nicely with Frau's sauerbraten and spaetzle." He lifted the bowl of the crystal glass to his nose and breathed deep, sighing.

CHAPTER TEN

"Und red cabbage!" Frau chimed in without turning from the stove.

Cole brought the glass to his mouth and let the nectar sit on his tongue before swallowing. "It stands on its own pretty well, too," he said, smacking his lips.

After eating the big meal and helping with the dishes, Cole and Michele made their way upstairs. "Take a quick shower and slip into something more comfortable," Michele said. "I'll meet you on the couch in the library in ten."

The warm shower felt soothing, but Cole made quick work of it and threw on fresh boxers, a baggy pair of gray drawstring shorts, and a light blue v-neck tee shirt. When he entered the library, Michele was already seated in the middle of the deep, distressed leather couch, dressed in her own shorts and tee shirt. Her legs were pulled up beneath her, and she patted the couch, inviting him to sit right in front of her. "A promise is a promise."

He stood facing her for a moment, his denim blue eyes taking in Michele's dark brown, wondering where this might lead and surrendering himself to it. He turned and sank into the couch, facing away from her. She leaned into him and pulled him back against her, and he sensed only thin cotton layers between the skin of his back and her breasts. He felt himself stir and closed his eyes as her warm, slender fingers began to knead the knots in his shoulders. He felt the soft kiss of her breath on his neck and smelled her feminine scent, floral and vanilla. He'd gone without sleep for more than thirty-seven hours, and the massage and full meal had him sleepily wondering again where this was headed.

The sun streamed in through the library's tall eastern-facing windows, and Cole rubbed his eyes, squinting. He rolled over on the couch. He lifted his head from a pillow and threw off a blanket Michele must have covered him with. He sat up, yawning loudly, and checked the antique clock above the fireplace mantle. *Seven thirty.* "Shit," he said, jumping up and racing to get ready and back to the office.

Chapter Eleven

Cole called Li from his car, and she and Lane were seated at the round table in his office when he arrived. A Greek yogurt, plastic spoon, and napkin occupied an open spot on the table next to a manila folder and Cole's brown ceramic mug filled with black coffee. Cole could see the steam rising from it as he sat down. "How thoughtful. Thanks!"

"There's a domestic inside me just waiting to come out," Li deadpanned.

"Uh huh," Cole said, cradling the mug with both hands and breathing deep. The steam warmed his face, and he could almost feel the caffeine entering through his eyelids and the pores of his skin. "God, this is good. Can you guys fill me in on what's happened since I left last night?"

"Can do, Rumpelstiltskin," Lane blurted with a smirk.

"Rumpelstiltskin?" Cole knew he would catch some shit from his team for sleeping so long, but he scrunched his eyes at Lane. "You're calling me a little ogre who spins straw into gold in order to get a girl to give him her firstborn child. Really?" He took another sip of coffee and sat back in his chair, waiting.

"What? No! Rumpelstiltskin is the fairy tale about the person who falls asleep for a bunch of years."

"You mean, like, Sleeping Beauty?" Li said.

"No! No! Rumpelstiltskin!"

"You nitwit. Did you mean Rip Van Winkle?" Cole asked.

"Rip Van Winkle? Huh?" Lane had his phone out, scrolling. "Crap. You're right. Rip Van Winkle is the guy who fell asleep for years and woke up an older man. And here I've been emailing everyone around here to start

CHAPTER ELEVEN

calling you Rumpelstiltskin. Dammit!"

"My last name, Huebsch? That's German right there, pal. Don't get into a debate on the Brothers Grimm with me, or you're gonna lose. Every time. Now, you wanna start having everyone around here call me Rip, I'm all for it. I'll tell 'em it's short for ripped…as in my muscles."

Li looked at Cole over her glasses. "Nice to know your area of expertise is fairy tales, boss. I say we start calling Laney, 'Rump,' short for Rumpelstiltskin. Because the only way he's going to get a date is if he learns to spin straw into gold anyway."

Cole nodded. "Plus, he just made an ass of himself. So, 'Rump' it is!" He licked his spoon and pointed it at Lane. "Carry on, Rump!"

Lane blew out a big breath. "You saw the president's press conference before you went home, so you know they're playing up the gang angle one hundred percent. It's generated the intended response, because planned protests across the country have mostly been canceled. It's taken the wind out of their sails."

"There were a lot of talking heads planted on the evening news shows, and 'Poetic justice' is a term that's caught on to describe the Harris murders," Li added.

"You both know that DC doesn't really want us to look into this further?" Cole asked.

"We've heard," Li said. "But Rump and I know that won't work for you, and it doesn't work with us."

"Enough with the Rump already," Lane protested.

"Rumpus Aurelius," Cole said.

Lane just shook his head. "Meanwhile, back at the ranch. Or, in this case, the farm… Not sure you saw it before you left, but our guys searched the fields and found two dead dogs, a German Shepherd, and a mixed Lab, both shot multiple times. Also, neither of the brothers was tortured. They were both shot in the head while their bodies were intact. The mutilations took place afterward."

Cole rubbed his stubbled chin. "Somebody was waiting for them when they came back from shooting the Senator. They might've even come onto the property not long after the brothers took off for Milwaukee to do the deed. They killed the dogs and bided their time. When the brothers come back, they shoot them in the head, have some fun with the axe and sled, cover the remains with a tarp, and then take time to stick around and paint."

"That's your working theory?" Li asked, "Because it's not working for me. It's nonsensical."

"I know, right?" Cole said. "What do you think, Rump roast?"

"I think the rump thing is old already. Stick a fork in it! And I think someone else, not the Harris brothers' killers, did the painting. Murdering and painting are two very different skills. That gang graffiti is real. Someone came into that barn who knew what they were doing."

"I believe you're right," Cole said, sifting through the contents of the open file folder in front of him. "There were only two shots fired at the brothers, both point blank. So, the killers knew what they were doing too."

Li twirled her glasses absently, and Cole noted the faraway look in her amazing eyes. "I'm not seeing it," she said, sliding her glasses back on. "How did a gang or gangs find out who the killers were before we did? When they find out, they head to the farm and lay in wait, a mixed team of hitters and taggers? There's other stuff that doesn't add up either."

"Like?"

"How about the fact we didn't find a computer on the premises, and the phones were both wiped clean…cleaner than anyone but our techs can do. There's nothing usable on the phones. And you were right about the shotguns and rifles. We found two rifles and three shotguns in the house, just sitting in a corner of the basement in cloth cases. Boxes of ammo too. What gang members wouldn't grab that stuff on the way out the door?"

"Tell him about the weed," Li said.

"You know the weed you saw drying in that old hay barn?" Lane asked Cole. "I can see why they wouldn't take that, given the size of the plants and all. But we also found about four dozen mason jars in another corner of the basement filled with fully cured cannabis buds. Quality stuff, from what our guys can tell. What gang would leave that?"

"Maybe they took what they could without being conspicuous and left the

CHAPTER ELEVEN

rest," Cole said.

"That's the thing, though. These guys were low production, with maybe two harvests a season, given our climate, even with the faster-maturing plants. We think the fruit of their whole first crop was just left by the bangers. Curious, is what it is."

"What if the people who killed the brothers were the same ones who talked them into shooting the Senator in the first place? Maybe they even paid them. If you start from there, things fall into place. And maybe all the gang signs and graffiti are just an elaborate ruse to throw us off. If that's the case, they might have no use for the firearms or the weed."

Li nodded, "I like that angle."

"Anything special about the graffiti?" Cole asked.

"Whoever did it was fast and had some talent," Lane said, sorting through his notes. "Gang signs can say a lot of different things. The messages can be for their own gang members or for other gangs. They mark territory, notify people when one of their members dies, and more. Cross-outs are a big sign of disrespect, meaning a gang took over a territory or plans to, or that they killed or planned to kill someone. You don't want to see your name with a line through it; if you do, you're either dead or gonna die but don't know it. And the signs and symbols can vary from city to city, jurisdiction to jurisdiction."

Cole had enlarged photos of the graffiti spread in front of him. "A couple things seem to get emphasis here. First is this 241. What's that supposed to mean?"

"You hurt one of ours, and we kill two of yours. Two for one," Li explained.

"Okay, would you believe I thought that, but wanted to see if you guys had come to the same conclusion?"

"No," Li and Lane said, shaking their heads in unison.

"And I'm not going to ask what the big Harris with the big red line through it means. It tells the world the Harris boys are off the board."

"You would've been a good analyst, sir," Lane said.

Cole looked at him, "That means a lot coming from you, Rump." He stood up and stretched, finishing the last of his coffee. "You said something earlier,

39

Laney, that caught my ear."

"And to think 'Laney' used to bother me. I'll take it any day now."

"You said the signs and symbols can vary from city to city, jurisdiction to jurisdiction," Cole continued. "I'm wondering if there's any way to tell from these images who did the tagging. Anything stand out? Colors? Symbols? Etcetera? Maybe the tagger or taggers have a unique style or signature somebody might recognize." He turned to Lane. "Send the photos of the graffiti out to all the gang units in the state and the Midwest. See if anybody recognizes the work of any bangers in their area. Hell, get it out to the gang task forces across the country…city, county, state, and federal. Maybe something will shake loose."

"I'm going to have it come from you," Lane said. "I'm not worried about my name being on the request, but you're a bit of a legend in law enforcement circles, so they might pay more attention when it comes across their inbox."

"Whatever," Cole said, rolling his neck.

"I'm not sure how stealthy this is," Li said.

"I know," he answered. "But what can it hurt?"

Chapter Twelve

The next morning Cole was in the office by six thirty. Lane knocked on his doorframe and walked in at seven, failing to hold back a grin. "If I find someone who can ID the painters, will you drop the 'Rump' jokes?"

Cole pushed back from his desk and studied his analyst. "You're asking a lot here, Lane. Li and I are having beaucoup fun with it. I mean, come on, you just gift-wrapped it to me yesterday, and now you want to take it back?"

"It's a horrible nickname. Sherlock might be better."

"As in 'No shit, Sherlock?'"

Lane rolled his eyes.

"Just tell me what you've got, and I'll take the nickname under advisement."

"Okay," Lane said, excited again. "You're gonna like this. I just got off a call with a lieutenant from the Baltimore Police Department. He sits on something called the Baltimore Strike Force, which targets the area's drug gangs and their suppliers. The team was put together last year and besides BPD it includes Maryland State Police, DEA, FBI, and U.S. Marshalls. Ron Williams, the lieutenant who responded to your email, seems like a solid guy. He's been battling the gangs in his city for more than twenty years."

"What's he got?"

"He thinks he might recognize a signature on some of the work in the Harris barn. Said it looks like the work of a banger in his area."

"No shit? Wouldn't it be something if our Hail Mary was actually caught by this Baltimore lieutenant? You said his name was Williams? Call him back and tell him to bring the guy in for questioning. We need a virtual setup; let him know we plan to lead from here, but we'll double-team the guy with him."

Cole, Li, and Lane sat in the conference room four hours later, watching a lone black male in an interview room eight hundred miles to the east. Their camera and mic were off, so they watched and listened without giving anything away on their end. It was the slightly higher-tech equivalent of a one-way mirror. Each of them had read an updated rap sheet on Calvin *Weezy* Johnson while the man leaned back in his chair, looking bored. He was skinny, but still wore a muscle shirt, with every exposed inch of his arms, chest, neck and even the top of his bald head a canvas for bold, colored ink.

"He's not even thirty-two and he's been part of the Baltimore gang scene for at least twenty years," Li said.

Before anyone could reply to that, the camera caught BPD Lieutenant Ron Williams entering the room, carrying a stuffed manila folder. He sat down off camera, across the table from Johnson. Cole turned his mic and camera on, so Cal Johnson could see and hear him. He had spoken to Williams earlier, when they first put Johnson in the room to sweat a while, and their roles were loosely defined.

"Good afternoon, Mr. Johnson. I'm FBI agent Cole Huebsch. In the room with me off-camera are two FBI analysts. I believe you've already made the acquaintance of Lieutenant Williams. Thanks for making time for this chat."

A small smile appeared on Johnson's tired face. "Like I had a fuckin' choice in the matter." He nodded across the table. "The L.T. here can be a damn persuasive man."

Cole heard a soft chuckle from Williams. "I'm not going to waste your time, Cal. Can I call you Cal?" Cole asked

"Let's just jump to Weezy. We gonna be so tight and all."

"Weezy it is. That short for weasel or something?"

A scowl appeared on Weezy's face. "Hell, no. I ain't named after no fuckin' rodent. I got a touch of asthma. Plus, you ever heard of 'Lil Wayne? Weezy? He an artist. I'm an artist. Hence, Weezy."

Cole nodded. "Fair enough. So, Weezy, I won't waste your time here. I'm

CHAPTER TWELVE

going to quickly walk you through a story and then get your take. Sound simple enough?"

Weezy nodded, and Cole continued.

"A couple days ago, an African American U.S. Senator from Milwaukee was shot while out for an early morning run." Williams's hand came on camera, pushing an eight-by-eleven color photo of Senator Rhodes in his hospital bed across the table.

"The next morning, my team and I raided a farm southwest of Milwaukee, and we found this…" Williams pushed a pile of large, colorful photos of the gang graffiti found in the Harris barn in front of Weezy. Cole thought he saw a note of recognition as the gang member sifted through the photos. He continued.

"A big blue tarp lay in the middle of the hay barn." Williams slid a photo of the tarp, still covering the remains of the Harris brothers, in front of Weezy.

"And this is what we found under that tarp." Williams slid another stack of colorful photos in front of Weezy, these mostly red, showing the Harris's ruined bodies along with the axe and sledge.

Weezy shook his head back and forth slowly. "Nah. Nah."

Cole waited, allowing the discomfort to grow until it was a real thing, as real as the lights or the people in the rooms. "Lieutenant Williams. Would you share the last slide with Weezy, please?"

The final photo was pushed in front of the gang member, who seemed to shrink as the interview moved forward to its conclusion.

"B.M. Recognize that?" Cole asked. "That's your trademark. Your personal signature. Lieutenant Williams tells me it stands for 'Bodymore Murdaland.' Catchy. But more importantly, it's like your fingerprint. And you left it at the scene big as day."

Weezy's head was down now, and he had a hand over it, almost like he was protecting himself from a blow. "I'm not going to lie to you, Weezy," Cole said. "This isn't looking good. I don't see the weasel slinking away from this one. You put your signature on a huge piece of canvas with two fresh corpses lying there. Two Humpty Dumpties nobody can put back together."

He wondered how the Humpty Dumpty reference had popped into his head and spilled out of his mouth and was waiting for either Lane or Li to slip him a note about it when Weezy looked up, right at Cole. His dark eyes were huge. He started to open his mouth, but clamped a hand over it instead. Shaking his head harder, he said, "I need me a lawyer."

"That's the understatement of the year," Cole said in an even tone. "But here's the lifeline I'm throwing your way. I don't see you in that barn, all by your lonesome, like some Michelangelo in the Sistine Chapel."

Weezy smiled nervously at Cole, "Weren't solo."

"What?"

"Michelangelo didn't paint no damn Sistine Chapel solo. He had himself a posse. Fuckin' Sistine crib was twelve thousand square feet and change!"

Now Cole shook his head. "Thanks for the enlightenment. But it looks cold that you painted the inside of the barn, painted the livin' shit out of that barn, by the way, with two mangled bodies lying there. You don't tell us what the hell happened, and you'll be the fall guy. Now, you'll also be a cult hero of sorts, but you'll be in prison somewhere. Free rent and food, sure, but you'll be looking over your shoulder until one day you end up with a shiv or three in your skinny deadass, naked body on the shower floor." He shut off the mic and camera and had lunch brought in.

Williams texted Cole a half hour later, saying Weezy wanted to tell his side of the story. Cole cleared the table and refilled his coffee before sitting back down and turning the equipment back on. "I heard you're ready to talk."

Weezy leaned toward the camera and nodded. "I'm gonna be straight with you, but you gotta understand that I'm an artist. I run with gangsters, but I don't carry. The only thing in my hand when I'm workin' is a can of spray paint. I ain't never killed nobody around here, and I sure as hell didn't kill nobody in no Bumfuck, Wisconsin." He paused. "No offense meant by the 'Bumfuck' comment."

A small smile tugged at Cole's lips, and he shrugged, "None taken."

Weezy nodded. "Three days ago, I'm chillin' on the curb outside a joint called *Swills*. I'm drinkin' a beer, contemplatin' the mysteries of the universe, when a black SUV pulls up. Damn near rolls over my kicks. Baddest Air J's

CHAPTER TWELVE

you ever saw. Anyway, couple big dudes tell me about this whacky paint job they want done, and they show me a thick envelope with fifty 'K' inside. Told me there was another fifty 'K' for me when the job's done." He leaned back.

"One hundred thousand for painting a couple walls in a barn. You get that kind of request a lot?" Cole asked.

Weezy laughed out loud. "Hell no. It struck me as all kinda shady, but that's a lot of bacon. Now, I wanted that bank bad, but I'm thinking if they offerin' a hundred for the job, why not ask for two hundred? I barely say 'Double would get it done,' and one of the dudes shows me another envelope filled with cash and tells me I get the other hundred when the deed is done.

"I look at him cockeyed and say, 'And I don't hafta kill no fuckin' president or somethin?' And he just flashes me a creepy ass smile and says, 'No. You just need to pull a team together to do a little barn painting.'

"I round up three dawgs and the two dudes pick us up a couple hours later. We blindfolded, and they drive us to an airport and fly us God knows where and then we drive a while. Don't know how long. My boys almost pissin' they pants the whole time. Freakin' me out too. Then they take off the blindfolds and lead us into that rickety piece of shit barn. Leanin' like a mothafuckah. I like a nice canvas and what we got to paint was bullshit, but we do our jobs quick and nice. They tell us not to fuck with the tarp, and we don't. Say if we get done in two hours we get a bonus, and we got that bonus no sweat. It was big enough, but three hours is a fuckin' lifetime on a tag job. Then they put the blindfolds back on and reverse the process that got us there. When they pull the folds off next, we back outside *Swills*, like some fuck happy donkeys loaded down with all that cash."

"You wonder why they didn't just disappear you and clean up loose ends?" Cole asked.

Weezy smiled again, and Cole liked the smile. He didn't get conned often, and he didn't think he was getting conned here. Weezy answered, "Cause we ain't as stupid as they hoped. I wouldn't take the deal less they leave two of their guys behind with even more cash. I told 'em we don't come back safe n' sound, then they lose two homies and more greenery. The two shifty ass dudes didn't blink, and I could tell they could care less if they lost a couple boys and another bag of cash. So, I add on the fly that if we don't come back from they paint party, my boys would also go to the press and tell em we was hired to paint some fuckin' barn somewhere and disappeared. Said we'd go to the Baltimore Popo and the feds too, and let them sort it all out. They smooth and all, but that got they attention. Nice little life insurance policy."

Williams's low voice came over the speakers, "Anything else strike you about the two dudes?"

Weezy stroked his goatee. "Yeah. The way they dressed and all. They wore hoodies and jeans, but they was all so new I thought the tags might still be on em. Minnie fuckin' Pearl! And they hands weren't rough. Hard from liftin' a whole lotta iron maybe, but fuckin' manicured. These were polished mothafuckahs tryin' to slum it and not really pullin' it off."

"You need anything else from Weezy?" Williams asked Cole.

"No, I think we're good." He nodded at the gang member. "Weezy, I appreciate your cooperation. I believe your story, and if it holds up, I don't see any criminal activity on your part that I'm inclined to pursue. I'm assuming, of course, that you'll be claiming the income you mentioned on your tax return?" He was smiling.

Weezy laughed. "I got my 'countants workin' on that as we speak, sir."

"Last thing. The lieutenant is going to give you my cell phone number and I'd like yours. If you see the dudes who got you into this, let me know directly. Also, if we get a lead on them, I'd like to be able to text you their photos and have you confirm an ID if necessary."

"Can do."

Williams appeared on screen and led Weezy out of the room. He came back a moment later and sat down in the chair Weezy had just vacated. "Thanks for setting this up," Cole said. "We got as much from Weezy as we could have hoped for. I appreciate your help, Lieutenant."

"Not a problem, Agent Huebsch.

"Call me Cole. And can I ask another favor?"

"Shoot."

"Would you have someone check for security cameras at the hangout he

CHAPTER TWELVE

mentioned, *Swills*, I think it was? Maybe also check the adjoining blocks?"

"Sure, I'll do that. But I wouldn't get my hopes up. It's not really the kind of neighborhood that has security cameras. Security there comes in the form of cheap handguns. If we find any cameras, they'll likely have been smashed or shot up. But we'll give it a good look."

"Thanks. The guys who set this up sound like well-outfitted pros, so I doubt they'd be driving a traceable SUV with their own license plates anyway, but we don't have much else to go on at this point." Cole paused, ready to end the interview, before asking, "You know Weezy way better than us. Do you find his story credible?"

Williams nodded. "Yeah, I tend to believe him. He's never been violent, that we know of, and he takes his art seriously. Probably why he couldn't keep from adding his signature at your site. We got an alley here in Baltimore, used to be a place to shoot heroin or get a cheap blowjob. Now it's in an arts and entertainment district and it's set aside just for graffiti. Everyone calls it 'Graffiti Alley,' and Weezy is royalty there. So, yeah, I believe him. Is there anything Weezy said that leaves you with more questions?"

"Just one," Cole said. "How the hell does he know about Minnie Pearl?"

Chapter Thirteen

Later that evening, a woman stood facing out a bank of tall, floor-to-ceiling windows, while her assistant waited nervously a few steps behind her. Streaks of lightning leapt from one brooding cloud to another and stabbed daggers of electricity into the earth's flesh, the violence muted by the thick glass panes. She wore a classic navy Michael Kors suit. A seamstress she'd found at the Kennedy Center for the Performing Arts had fit it perfectly to her lithe body. She owned a dozen suits by the same designer, all in dark shades, and each priced north of two thousand dollars. She was tall at five foot nine and added to her stature with precisely three-and one-half inch heels. Flats or lower heels would have been more comfortable, but she liked looking down on others. She kept her lustrous black hair long, to the bottom of her shoulder blades. If you asked people off the street to describe her in a word, they might say 'chic' or 'powerful.' If you asked someone who knew her better, like her assistant, they might use the word *scary*. Heart-stopping scary. If they had the balls to be forthright.

Her steel gray eyes couldn't discern the U.S. Capitol, but she gazed in the direction she knew it stood, less than two miles distant. She tapped a long, slender fingernail against the window. She turned to her assistant, eyes penetrating. He blinked and yearned to turn away but knew better. She turned back to the windows and faced the storm, walking to her right and tapping her finger against the glass again. She felt she could almost touch the White House, a scant quarter mile in the distance. "I guess not all the pompous pricks in this city realize they work for me yet," she said. She spun on a heel then, "What shall we do about it?" No response was expected

CHAPTER THIRTEEN

or given, and after a beat, she walked behind her heavy granite, chrome, and glass desk and sat abruptly in her Aresline Xten chair. The sleek black chair was made by Pininfarina, the Italian design house that produced for supercars Ferrari, Maserati, and Lamborghini. It featured advanced comfort gel, a synchronized tilting system, and fabric designed to cover the bodies of Olympic athletes. The advanced ergonomics, comfort, and style came at a price associated with oceanfront luxury homes and typically reserved for the Middle East luxury market. Her board of directors allowed such indulgences, because she delivered the results they expected, insane profits that fueled their own individual excesses. The executive leaned back and said dismissively, "Get Carter in here now."

Dexter Carter entered a moment later and pulled the large door shut behind him. He tried not to fidget while he waited. The woman's fingertip rubbed her bottom lip in a distracted motion. Carter knew she was deep in thought, but it still aroused him. Her lips were full, and she'd let him taste them on occasion, but always on her terms and timetable. He knew he was no more than a beast of burden to her, but he'd do whatever needed to be done to stay in her inner circle. The pay was twice what he could make as Chief Security Officer at any comparable size employer, and he craved the rare moments when she gave him her attention. He wasn't proud of that, maybe even embarrassed by it, but she was a potent drug to him.

"It seems like someone's gotten to our painters," she said. "I thought the right people all agreed it was in our nation's best interests to make the Senator's shooting go away."

Carter nodded. "True. But apparently, the SAC of the Milwaukee FBI field office didn't get the message. Or he ignored it. He sent an email out with photos of the graffiti to gang units across the country. He got lucky; a Baltimore cop recognized some of the tagging as the handiwork of a local gang member."

"The SAC…Cole Huebsch. You don't have to do a deep background profile to know that name. He was the toast of the city, even the country, a few months ago. His fifteen minutes of fame petered out. Maybe he wants more. Is he *lucky* or good?"

THE KILLER SPEECH

"Definitely good. Maybe the best in the Bureau," Carter admitted. "I'm told he's in Milwaukee by choice; grew up in Wisconsin and likes serving there. The current director and others have tried to move him around their chess board to more strategic locations like here, New York, or LA, but he's politely stayed put."

"What should we do about him then? Sounds like someone who won't walk away from this." Her finger trailed from her lip, down her neck, and came to rest on her chest."

"What do you mean?" Carter said, his eyes following the path of her hand like a serpent following the sway of a snake charmer's pungi.

Her fingers found the smooth porcelain melo melo pearl that hung from her neck by a simple strand of platinum and small but nearly flawless diamonds. The pearl was the size of a large gumball. A natural pattern of flame fanned across its hard, intense orange surface. She'd spent more than three hundred thousand dollars on the unmounted pearl at a Christie's auction, and nearly the same amount for the setting from Tiffany. She rolled the pearl in her fingers, and her eyes grew wider, drawing him in. "What I mean is this; he needs to stop meddling. Immediately."

Carter blinked. His Adam's apple rose slowly before plummeting back down as he swallowed hard. "Are you asking me to tell Huebsch to back off? You want me to threaten a decorated federal agent?"

She shook her head, her long locks dancing on her shoulders, as she rose and leaned across the desk. Her full, red lips nearly brushed his. Her eyes were still wide and unblinking. He swore he could see the swirling clouds reflected in those eyes, complete with brilliant flashes that mirrored the fury of the storm. He felt heat coming to him and wondered if it was from the tease of sex, the flame from the melo melo pearl, or maybe the gates of hell. Her lips turned into a sinister smile. "No, I don't want you to threaten a federal agent," she said, drawing out the words slowly, tracing a finger along *his* lips. "I want you to kill him."

Chapter Fourteen

The Milwaukee FBI Field Office doesn't have the amount of crime and corruption to root out as its LA or New York counterparts, but it also only has a fraction of their man and womanpower. A week passed since the Weezy interview, and nothing new developed in the case. Meanwhile, Cole and his team were busy investigating a sex trafficking pipeline that followed Wisconsin's interstate system, counterfeit goods coming in through the Milwaukee harbor, a murder-for-hire allegation, and evidence of rampant police corruption in a local suburb. The case of Senator Rhodes' shooting and who was ultimately behind it grew colder.

It was a little after noon as Cole and Li stepped out of their office building, crossed the parking lot, and walked west down the blacktop Oak Leaf Trail. The traffic on Lake Drive to their right and jets from nearby Mitchell International airport generated white noise, almost comforting in its familiarity. A brilliant sun followed directly overhead in a cloudless sky. White contrails, some tight and some billowing, etched the sky above. The temperature was in the mid-eighties and Cole was grateful for the cool breeze coming off Lake Michigan on their left. The *lake effect* moderated temperatures on the lake and a few blocks inland, keeping them as much as ten degrees cooler than further west during the height of summer and that much warmer during the cold winter months.

Cole and Li were headed to La Finca Coffee House, a short third of a mile southwest of their offices. They walked there at least once a week when the weather cooperated. Lane would have been with them, but he was taking a rare PTO day. Cole was glad he'd left his suit jacket draped over the back of his chair. He walked with the sleeves of his white dress shirt rolled up to his elbows and his tie loosened. He would've left his Glock nine-millimeter tucked in his desk drawer, but agents were required to always carry their firearms while on duty; it rode in the compact holster on his hip. His black Wayfarers kept him from squinting as he took in the shimmering vastness of Lake Michigan. The Mississippi and Wisconsin Rivers were his constant companions growing up on the western side of the state, but the sheer size of the Great Lake always took his breath away…beckoning to the horizon and beyond. Sailboats with brilliant canvases bobbed on the lake's surface, while the occasional powerboat threw up white plumes of water as it charged across the waves. Cole wondered how many people knew that world-record brown trout and salmon were pulled from the lake almost in the shadows of the city's tallest office buildings.

They left the trail and crossed Lake Drive on Packard Avenue. A brick and stone monument sign announced the beginning of the Packard Gardens Retail District, but at this point, the proclamation seemed more hopeful than descriptive. Acres of land on their left were undeveloped and listed for sale. They passed a tattoo parlor and yoga business on their right, followed by a single-family home and a large two-story brick and vinyl apartment building with a metal sign in front that read: *Stop. Look. Lease.* La Finca was next, sharing a newer building with an insurance agency, financial advisor, and direct mail company.

Most of the agents, analysts, and other FBI staff frequented La Finca, and Cole and Li knew the two sisters who owned the coffee shop. Janeth and Lizeth were as much a draw as the exquisite coffee and food. They imported beans from their grandfather in Oaxaca, Mexico, and roasted them locally for fresh flavor. La Finca was Spanish for *the estate* and referred to the Oaxaca spread their family had grown coffee on for five generations. Cole and Li went inside. Rich wooden beams broke up the high white ceiling, and potted palms and strings of soft lights overhead created a cozy ambience. They sat at a table for two, and Cole ordered a Cubano sandwich and Poblano soup. Li opted for the Sinconizada quesadilla, with its Monterey Jack, ham, mayo, and tomato.

CHAPTER FOURTEEN

They surrendered their menus to the waitress, and Cole said, "You sure you don't want the hummus and walnut toast?"

She took a sip of salted caramel and chocolate latte from a vibrant, handmade mug and winked. "I like my meat as much as you do."

Cole almost choked on his black coffee and knew better than to respond directly. "Okay, then."

A huge blackboard on the wall near them featured a quote in both English and Spanish that changed weekly. This week's quote was from Pablo Neruda and read, *There is a certain pleasure in madness that only the madman knows.*

Cole nodded to the board and said, "Kinda reminds me of the Senator's shooting."

"I know. The case bothers me. It doesn't feel right that we don't have much to go on there, and nobody in DC seems to care. I mean, a U.S. Senator was shot! I thought when we sent them the report on Weezy's interview, it would cause some excitement. Instead…crickets."

"I know. I don't get it. But I'm not sure where we go from here."

Li held her mug close to her face and felt the steam warm her cheeks. "What did they pound into all of us during our training back at Quantico?"

"Always wear clean underwear?"

"No." Li smiled and shook her head.

"Got it. Be prepared!"

Li laughed out loud. "Um, I think that would be the Boy Scouts. Stay with me! We were always told, 'When in doubt, follow the money.'"

Cole took a sip of his coffee as the waitress served their food on colorful plates that matched their mugs and saucers. "Follow the money," he mused. "You might have something there. If Senator Rhodes became more powerful and his ideas became reality, who has the most to lose?"

Li nodded, smirking. "If the Senator's popular ideas became law, whose boat would be rocked?"

"Whose applecart would be upset?"

"Whose ox would be gored the deepest?"

Cole's mouth was open, and after a pause, he said, "Enough already; you win that round. We need to review the Senator's speech to really understand what he's proposing and who might be adversely affected. I like it. At least it's something."

They finished their lunches and headed back to the office. A block away from the coffee house, they came upon a big guy in jeans and a plain gray t-shirt kneeling by the passenger side of a car. He held a small air compressor and looked like he'd just finished putting air in a tire. He stood up and nodded at them as they passed, wiping his hands on a rag. Another man in a brown delivery uniform walked toward them, and Cole and Li moved to the right to allow him to pass. When he was a few feet away, he stepped to his right off the sidewalk, and Cole whirled around and back, knifing his right elbow through the air. He hit the extended arm of the man who had quietly fallen in behind them, and the gun he'd pulled flew out of his hand. Without slowing, Cole lowered his center of gravity, bear-hugged the man, lifting him in the air as he pivoted before pile-driving him headfirst into the cement sidewalk. He thought he registered the sound of the man's skull cracking, but he was already moving forward, launching himself to tackle the man who'd stepped into the grass as he pulled his own handgun. Cole slammed his shoulder into the big guy's muscled stomach and drove him onto his back. The guy let out an "ooof," but the turf wasn't hard-baked, and he fought back, trying to bludgeon Cole's face with his gun. Cole tucked his chin in tight and winced as a glancing blow struck him on the back of his head. But Cole was on top of him now. He ripped the gun from the guy's hand, snapping a finger in the process, and at that point, it was over. Even though he was two decades removed from being a world-class wrestler, there were only a handful of men on the planet who would've been able to escape Cole in this position. He forced the guy over onto his stomach and wrenched his arms behind his back. Cole might've heard tendons or ligaments snapping, and he damn well heard the guy's scream. He held the man there with his face in the dirt and looked over at Li. She was standing on the sidewalk, mouth agape, eyes as large as the painted saucers back at La Finca.

"Li," he said. "Li!"

She turned to him and shook her head, "Yes?"

CHAPTER FOURTEEN

"Call the office and get someone over here with cuffs. And call an ambulance. I'm pretty sure that guy by you is going to need medical attention; this guy might also. Get any available techs over here too. We need to secure this crime scene, bag their guns and impound their car. I'm guessing it's the one that guy by your feet was pretending to work on. And take a couple of photos of these two with your phone and forward them to me. I want to get them to Weezy to see if these were the same guys that paid him and his crew to paint the Harris barn."

She pulled out her phone and made the calls while Cole kept his eyes on one of the assailants and his hands on the other.

Chapter Fifteen

Cole didn't settle back into the chair behind his desk until nearly five p.m. He'd stayed on the scene for three long hours, first making sure the bad guys were secure before the first responders whisked them away to the nearest hospital; an MPD officer accompanying each rig. Then he walked through everything he could think of with the techs. After that, he and Li hoofed it back to the office and filed their separate incident reports.

Now he leaned back, facing away from his desk and out onto the lake. The sun was on the other side of the building, but still shimmered on the gentle waves. It was soothing, almost hypnotic. A knock on the door jamb brought him upright, and he turned to find Li framed in his doorway. "May I come in?"

"Now we're going to get formal?" he smiled, "After everything we've been through together?"

"It's about that," she said, moving into the room and sinking into one of the desk chairs. Her words came out in a rush. "I keep playing out what happened in my head. Over and over. When it came time for a fight or flight response, I froze. It was over before it even occurred to me to react." She looked him in the eye, and her bottom lip quivered. "I'm wondering if I'm cut out to be an agent. Maybe it's better I just stay an analyst. I'm okay at that."

Cole wondered from the moment he had the second bad guy on the ground if Li would react this way. He leaned forward, resting his forearms on his desk and keeping direct eye contact. He wanted, no needed, her to know he

CHAPTER FIFTEEN

was sincere. "You are way better than an okay analyst. You know that. And *maybe* it would be better if you stayed an analyst, but I don't believe that for a minute. I think it would be a mistake. You've got everything you need to be a great agent and more."

She shook her head and looked down. "What the hell even happened back there? How did you know to respond so fast?"

Cole pulled back in his chair and took a moment to think. He ran his hand through his hair and let out a breath. "I didn't have any alarm bells going off in my head when we passed the guy with the air compressor. Nothing registered, to be honest. I was thinking about how great the meal was and how it was such a beautiful day." He smiled and arched his eyebrows. "I was even daydreaming about visiting Oaxaca, maybe riding in the Sierra Madres on a horse with no name. But when we were almost to the guy in the delivery suit, he stepped to his right off the sidewalk. It was instinct; I just knew he was stepping out of the line of fire and that there must be someone behind us getting ready to shoot me in the back. That delivery guy stepped off the sidewalk to make sure the shooter's round didn't hit him after passing through me…and maybe some of my vital organs."

"So, any time someone steps off a sidewalk, I should go berserk and launch a counterattack against someone who might be behind me?"

"No," Cole said. He wanted to laugh but knew better than to make light of her reaction. "You just need to be in those situations a time or two, and you develop a feel for things. And then instinct takes over."

"What if I don't develop like that? If I freeze up again, I could get a partner or someone I'm supposed to protect killed. I'm not sure I could live with that."

"You're being too hard on yourself. Neither of us was really prepared. We were walking back to the office on a beautiful day, sun shining, birds chirping, and all that. We aren't expected to be on high alert twenty-four seven. If we were, we couldn't survive. We'd wear down and be useless in a matter of days or weeks."

"Yeah, but the fact remains you reacted to the situation, and I didn't." She looked down again.

He waved her off. "Jesus! Quit beating yourself up. I've been there before, maybe not that exact situation, but similar. I guarantee you it'll be different for you next time too." He got up and came around the desk to stand next to her. He looked into her rare, beautiful eyes that had turned insufferably sad and said, "Let it go. You have everything you need to be not just an acceptable agent, but an exceptional one. You're smart, strong, wicked athletic, and you're ferocious. I've seen it." He let his words sink in as a smirk claimed his face. "And you've got the world's best mentor!"

She laughed out loud then, and the room brightened. Cole turned serious again. "You know what happened to us today is rare, right? I mean, like Halley's Comet rare almost. If you have to protect yourself or someone else, you'll know it. People typically don't set out to gun down federal agents. And now no matter who tries to quash our investigation into the Rhodes' shooting, even the president himself, it ain't gonna happen."

Cole pointed to his computer. "My inbox is blowing up. I'll bet yours is too. You attack one of us, you attack us all. I'm getting notes of support from all over the country, and not just friends inside the Bureau. U.S. Marshalls, DEA, ATF, state guys, local police…every brand of law enforcement. Ty wants to know what he can do, and my buddy, Fwam, wants to take a leave as Crawford County Sheriff so he can be my personal bodyguard. A certain sheriff from Red Stick, Louisiana, offered me the same deal. Whoever attacked us today made a mistake, not only because they failed to take us off the board…."

"You mean kill us," Li interrupted.

Cole dodged, "Yeah, that. But they also stirred up a hornet's nest when our case was basically dead in the water."

"You seem pretty sure that today's attack on us was tied to Senator Rhodes' shooting. Couldn't it be tied to your bust of the Raging Disciples gang last year or us tracking down the guy who was killing reproductive health physicians?"

"Wow. You must be a little shook up. Those weren't gang bangers today, and I don't think it's anybody trying to avenge the death of Deputy Hubbard either. No matter how the old saying goes, I don't really believe 'revenge

CHAPTER FIFTEEN

is a dish best served cold.' The human animal can almost never delay gratification. No, I think whoever had the Senator shot put out a hit on us with even less luck. And thank God for that!"

Three hours later, the sun had set, but Cole could still see the lake in the twilight. His stomach growled as he peeled an orange, the only thing he'd found in his mini fridge and the first thing he would eat since lunch. Watching the lake descend slowly into darkness changed the mood in the office, and Cole was glad the ringing of his desk phone pulled him away from the view.

"Cole here!"

"It's Gene, Cole. How're you and Li doing?" Gene's loud voice always broke the silence like a Ming vase thrown against a concrete wall. Cole smiled.

"We're both good." Cole felt the knot on the back of his head, but it wasn't much. "I might've gotten a grass stain or two on my pants, so watch for a dry-cleaning bill to come through."

"Right. I'll be on the lookout for it. You ever think about using that black plastic and metal thing on your hip?"

"No time for the Glock, Gene. Plus, if I'd used it, you would've taken my gun and badge and put me on leave. I love my job too much for that."

"Well, the one guy is in pretty bad shape. Nobody's raised the issue of excessive force, but…."

"Christ, Gene!" Cole exploded. "Are you kidding me? We were up against two pros with guns drawn and intent to kill. No warning. No chance to prepare. And Li was right by my side. They would've killed her too. And you're worried one of the assholes has a bump on his head?" The emotions he'd been burying the past few hours all leapt out of their shallow grave at once.

"Easy, big fella. And yes, I know they wouldn't have let Li go, since they made no attempt to hide their identities. But that asshole you mentioned doesn't have a simple bump on the noggin. His skull is cracked. Your government has already paid for one surgery to relieve the swelling on his brain. It looks like more surgeries are in his future. He may not survive, or he may live with the IQ of an acorn squash, and that's okay, because he got what's coming to him. Karma's a bitch and all that. I just want to make sure as a friend now, not as a boss, that you're okay and watching yourself.

Cole shook his head. "So, you really do love me after all."

"Fuck you."

Cole softened. "It just happened a few hours ago, but I've been thinking about it. Everything went down so fast. I did take the first guy down hard. I needed him out of the game so I could focus on the other threat. If I was any gentler in taking down the first guy, I'm pretty sure his buddy would've shot me before I could've reached him. It was close the way it was."

"How did Li respond?"

Cole hesitated. "A lot like an analyst working to become an agent. She followed my lead and called in the cavalry."

"Did she draw her gun or respond physically to the threat?"

This time the pause was longer. "No. She did neither. But we were walking back from lunch. We had no reason to believe we were going to be ambushed like that. She reacted the way any agent would've."

"But not you."

Cole let that go. "I think she'll be a fine agent, Gene. I wouldn't tell her or you that if I didn't."

"Good enough for me, brother." Now it was Gene who paused. "There's one more thing I want to bring up with you. It's about a Milwaukee sports reporter who got a similar beatdown to that first guy you took out today. MPD said it was an old homeless guy who did it. Hard to believe...."

Cole went rigid. A few months ago, he'd disguised himself as a homeless person and goaded the sports reporter, Dan Rippa, into a fight behind a local bar, and then planted him face-first on the asphalt. Weeks before that Rippa had slipped Michele a roofie, raped her, and gotten her pregnant. It would've been hard to prove legally, so Cole had taken matters into his own hands. "Are you fishing, Gene? Or do you have a question you can ask me straight out, man to man?"

Now Gene's voice rose. "No. I don't have a question I can ask you straight out, because if I did, I think you'd be dumb enough to answer truthfully, and

CHAPTER FIFTEEN

I'd be duty bound to follow up on it!"

Cole waited, and it seemed like Gene was trying to compose himself on the other end of the line. "You're not the only one who wanted to find out what happened to Michele. I was grateful for the help she gave us. I wanted it checked out but knew you were too close to her for me to call on. It didn't take much looking to figure out the reporter took advantage of her. When we saw he'd had his face broken open like a watermelon dropped from the roof of a skyscraper, we interviewed the reporter's pals. They described what happened, and it sounds an awful lot like what happened to that guy who snuck up behind you today, intent to blow out your heart."

Cole stared at the speakerphone, wondering if this man he revered was going to tell him that the career he loved was coming to a premature end.

Gene read the pause and said, "I don't want your badge, Cole. Dan Rippa drugged and raped women. He's despicable. You stopped him. Today your actions prevented two professional hitmen from killing my best agent and a damn good analyst. We'd be giving you another medal if you didn't already have every one we award. But here's the thing… There's a line between having to use extreme force to put down a bad guy. And it's not a fine line like some of our critics in the media and Congress might think; it's a squishy, fuzzy line. I just want to make sure you don't start to like using force, not even a little. Every time you need to hurt someone to get the job done, I want you to wrestle over that, to worry about it, and then to keep moving forward. We've both known guys in our careers who start to like using force; it happens over time, and it happens on the local level and with feds too. But those guys invariably become hard, jaded, and then rotten. And you're too good for that. Just watch it is all I'm asking."

Cole let out a deep breath he didn't even realize he'd been holding and blinked away tears he hadn't felt welling up. The realization that he and Li could have died that afternoon washed over him like a dark wave from the big lake, threatening to pull him to the depths. And the thought that he could've killed a man without remorse threatened to hold him under.

Chapter Sixteen

The sun had set an hour ago, but the lights from nearby Ford's Theater fused with those from nearby federal buildings, retail, corporate headquarters, and condos to light up the night outside the tall windows. In the heart of the district, the nation's capital was wide awake, and the real business of running the country and shaping world politics was being conducted. The woman in the charcoal Michael Kors suit looked down on the scene, bathed in a kaleidoscope of shifting lights, holding a slight remote control in the long, slender fingers of her perfectly manicured right hand. Her face was blank; you wouldn't know it to look at her that she worked to keep from hurling the remote against a wall. Power and control had gotten her to this point, and she didn't plan to lose either any time soon. The thick glass and soundproofed walls and ceiling cocooned her in silence, broken when her security chief knocked and entered the room. He stopped in the middle of the office and waited.

He could hear her sigh as she turned from the window and depressed buttons on the remote; the clear windows immediately shifting to an opaque white, while the door eased shut. Dexter Carter almost jumped at the sound of the deadbolt locking in place behind him. The woman pressed another button, and the office lights dimmed, but he could still make out her slight, crooked grin and her large, unblinking eyes. He thought of a saltwater crocodile, only its head above still waters, gliding toward its prey. He blinked and steeled himself as she moved forward. Carter couldn't tell if it was the walk of a temptress or a predator. Maybe both. She stopped when she was almost on top of him, so near he felt the crease of her slacks nudging the

CHAPTER SIXTEEN

wool of his pants against the hairs on his thighs. A current moved upward, follicle by follicle like electricity through relay switches, until it settled into his groin, throwing a switch. Turning it on. Turning *him* on. He felt himself hardening, and his face mottled with crimson. He didn't know if she could see him blush, but he knew she could sense it. *What the fuck? Are you fourteen? You stupid mother fucker*, he thought. Embarrassed. Ashamed. But mostly aroused. Her chest brushed his, and she looked slightly down into his eyes and shook her head in disapproval. This close, he felt her heat and smelled her. Strong, yet feminine. She slid her left hand in the scant space between them and grabbed him through the thin material of his suit pants and silk boxers.

"You *are* a man," she said, holding him. "I needed to check after the day's events." She began massaging him, eyes at once flat and devouring. "It wasn't that long ago; we women were considered the weaker sex. Hard to believe, right?" She stopped and tightened her grip, and a moan escaped him. He closed his eyes, and she released him, her voice hardening. "Look at me when I'm talking to you." His eyes flew open, and her fingers slid around him again over his pants and began moving, rhythmically along with her words.

"I've heard reports that your attempt to remove agent Huebsch went poorly. An utter failure. Not only did he walk away unscathed, but your henchmen are in custody. I know one of them is unlikely to talk." She leaned in and whispered in Carter's ear, continuing to move her hand, the silk sheathing him. "It seems your fellow is really *fucked* up. If he lives, he'll have an IQ like my resting heart rate. Seems this Huebsch is a *real* man." She shifted to face him again. "Your other man is a different story altogether. It seems he's in fine fettle, able to sing like Pavarotti given the chance." She stared into his eyes. "Do you think he'll sing?"

Carter struggled with his breathing, "Um, no...."

She stroked him faster. "Do you think he can identify you?"

"I, um, I...." He bit his lower lip. "I don't...I don't think so."

"What about your painter friend. Can he be traced back to you...to us?"

"I...I doubt..."

She brought her right hand up, cupping the remote, and she placed her index finger over her lips.

"Ssssshhhh. All this 'afraid' and 'doubt' business is making me lose confidence in you. You don't want that to happen, do you?"

Sweat had broken out on his forehead and upper lip. He shook his head. "No." His mind was a mess. He didn't fully understand the *hold* she had on him. He never thought of himself as weak, or a masochist. *Why did it feel so good to be dominated?* She mashed the remote against his lips, grinding it against his teeth and splitting the skin. He tasted his own blood and willed her to keep going.

She painted his cheek with the bloody remote and picked up the pace with her left hand. More insistent. They were so close he could taste her mouth if he just darted his tongue out. But he held it, afraid to break the spell. She leaned into him again, her lips touching his ear, a new deeper current of lust and fear traveling south at the speed of sound, the soft sound of her words. "You and I are in this together. For better or worse. Richer or richer." She shifted forward, and her pelvis covered his. "You could say, 'we're joined at the hips.'" She felt as much as watched his knees quake and his body tremor. Guttural sounds he could no longer suppress escaped his lips. He shuddered.

She stepped back and released him, looking down at the front of his pants. Her gray eyes lifted, locking back onto his. Then she turned away from him and moved to her desk, speaking over her shoulder, her voice cold as death. "Looks like you've got quite a mess to clean up. I suggest you get to it."

Chapter Seventeen

Cole shoved aside his hunger and fatigue when he got home, making a beeline for the en suite shower off his bedroom. He didn't bother turning on a light in the bathroom; the soft, warm light that spilled in from his bedroom and a night light was enough as he tried to scrub away the day's tension and confusion. He worked the shampoo into a lather and felt the knot on his head, thinking for the hundredth time about what he could have done differently during the attack. The answer he kept coming back to was, *not much*. He'd been fast and hard with the first gunman because he needed to get to the second guy before he could pull his weapon and open fire. That realization helped a little, and the warm water calmed him even more. With his eyes closed and his head back, he let the soothing spray take him to a better place.

Cole finally turned off the water and opened the shower door. He'd forgotten to turn on the fan and he stepped out of the shower into a heavy fog. He stood on the bathmat, grabbed the big cotton bath towel from its hook, and dried off. He finished wrapping the towel around his waist just as Michele materialized through the mist in front of him.

"Oops. Sorry! I knocked a bunch of times, and when you didn't answer, I came in. You don't typically shower this late."

"No. I don't. But then, not much about my day was typical, after lunch anyway."

"I heard about the attack. Are you and Li okay?"

Cole rubbed the bump on the back of his head. "Other than a knock on my thick skull, I'm okay. Li's fine physically, but she's questioning whether she has what it takes to be an agent."

"Maybe she needs some time. It has to shake you up when someone tries to kill you." She paused, reaching forward and touching his cheek. "Even someone like you."

She turned to walk out, but stopped, "When you're dressed, meet me in the TV room. I've got an idea I want to run by you." She smiled, "And I've also got three-quarters of a stuffed pizza from Tenuta's left, along with a growler I picked up from Good City."

At that Cole's stomach growled loud enough for Michele to hear, and they both laughed.

Fifteen minutes later, Cole sat on the carpeted floor in the TV room, his legs tucked under him like a pretzel. He'd reheated the pizza in the microwave and had two of the large sausage and pepperoni slices on the walnut coffee table in front of him, along with a pint of Good City Brewery's Reward double India pale ale. The thick head of foam promised cold, hoppy goodness, and Cole took a big swallow before cutting off a generous bite of the pie with his fork. Michele was sprawled out on the middle piece of the large sectional behind Cole, remote control in hand.

Michele watched him as he ate, and she teed up the speech. "The senator was shot the morning after his speech, but it had to have been planned in advance. I think the Harris brothers got the go-ahead after Senator Rhodes gave his speech."

"It *was* planned. Someone had to know the time of morning he typically ran, his route, his pace…. They also planned the Harris brothers' murder, and there was nothing simple about that. It was elaborate, with lots of moving parts. But nothing happened until after the Senator's speech. You think that was the trigger?" He looked over his shoulder at Michele while he took another swig of the IPA. He licked the delicious foam off his top lip, and Michele smiled at him. He fought the urge to crawl up on the couch with her.

"I do think the speech was the trigger, kind of like how Father Wagner's Christmas sermon set crazy things in motion a few months ago. Words matter, and sometimes they're a catalyst. I DVR'd the Senator's speech and

CHAPTER SEVENTEEN

watched it. It was electric. He has some bold ideas for the country, and he sold them hard that night. He was larger than life and very convincing. Think of the best halftime speech you ever heard and the way it inspired you to be your best. It was that kind of speech. I think if you watch it, you'll understand the direction he wants to take the country and also the industries and people who might not support the new direction."

"It's funny you say that," Cole said. "Li and I said the same thing at lunch. Whose ox would be gored if the Senator had his way? That sort of thing. Li said, 'Follow the money.'" He picked up his phone and texted Li and Lane and told them to watch the Senator's speech if they could find it on YouTube or on demand.

"Maybe when we're done watching this, you'll have a list of suspects," Michele said, arching her eyebrows and hitting the play button.

Chapter Eighteen

(TWO WEEKS EARLIER)

U.S. Senator Eric Rhodes sat at a small table in the large, brightly lit conference room inside Fiserv Forum that served as a staging area for Convention organizers and speakers. He tried to ignore the flat screens that ringed the room, flashing the image of an East Coast governor at the podium inside, banging the lectern repeatedly, hammering home her demands for equal rights for women and minorities. NBA legend Kareem Abdul-Jabbar stared at him through his trademark goggles from a towering portrait mounted nearby. Eric thought Kareem had looked mighty good in that green Milwaukee Bucks jersey with the red thirty-three on his chest, lifting the city and the team to a world championship before heading west to join the Lakers. There was a large spread of food at a nearby table, but Eric had barely picked at it. He didn't have butterflies in his stomach; something more like full-grown American eagles were swooping around in there. He sipped from an icy bottle of Nicolet natural artesian water and shuffled through his notecards for the hundredth time. He wouldn't use them or a teleprompter during his speech; he didn't want to be tethered to the podium or a set speech. He felt more confident free, and on the move, reading the crowd and taking advantage of opportunities as they presented themselves. He glanced at one of the wall-mounted HD screens and saw he had ten minutes or so before he'd be called on stage. Just like before a big game, tension and excitement fought for control. *Why does that make me feel*

CHAPTER EIGHTEEN

like I have to pee, he wondered. He felt a hand on his shoulder and looked up into the smile of President Barack Obama. "Good luck, Senator Rhodes. I know you'll hit it out of the park. Or, maybe in this venue and with your background, I should say, 'I'm sure you'll sink the winning bucket for us.'"

Eric nodded. "I'll, ah…I'll sure try, sir," was all he could think to say.

Obama patted him on the back and went to graze at the food tables. Eric watched starstruck as the country's forty-fourth president put an arm around fellow former president Bill Clinton and the two shared a laugh. He pulled his phone out and FaceTimed Karri. She picked up on the third ring. Karri held their youngest, three-year-old Rosa, and Eric couldn't help thinking about how much he loved his wife and three children. They had their arguments, setbacks, and troubles like anyone else, but he and Karri both knew how blessed they were.

"Hey! What's up? Aren't you about to go on?"

Eric nodded, answering quietly, "Yup. About to give the biggest speech of my life, maybe the one that determines how far I'll go in life."

Karri gave him a big smile that warmed his heart. "Don't make it bigger than it is. You have great ideas on how we can heal this country, and this is just one more chance to tell people about them. If you give the worst speech ever, your life won't end. You'll still have at least four members in your fan club." She turned the phone's camera on Rosa and their two boys, who were rolling around on the floor in front of the television at their home, waiting for their dad to come on. Their squeals of delight made him grin. "And if you give the speech of your life, maybe you can make the world better, or at least our corner of it." She smiled even bigger. "Haven't you always been the guy who wanted to take the big shot or make the big assist? Here's your opportunity!"

He nodded, returning her smile. His voice dropped to a hush, and Karri strained to hear his words through the arena noise and her children's giggles. "Guess who just chatted with President Obama? That's right, yours truly. Who's your man?"

"You are," Karri said. "Now go out and knock 'em dead."

Eric stood off stage five minutes later, hidden from the audience. Fiserv

THE KILLER SPEECH

Forum opened four years ago, and its sound, lights, and other electronics were cutting-edge. The stage was lit but empty. Eric waited for the attendant at his side to give him the *go* sign. The young woman had her hand on his forearm, and Eric figured it was to keep him from heading out prematurely and spoiling the choreography; everything timed to the second. She wore a headset and a genuine smile as she listened for a hidden maestro to give her the word that the last television commercial had run. Though Eric couldn't see the commercial, he thought it was probably for a new prescription drug that promised the world. On the rare occasions he had a chance to watch television for pleasure, it seemed like every other ad was from a drug company. He shook his head at that. Eric had an earbud tucked discreetly into his right ear, put there so they could help him keep track of time. He tried to relax and go with the flow, and he listened to the words coming at him crystal clear from the building's myriad speakers. Ray Charles sang "America the Beautiful," and it sounded so pure, Eric thought maybe Ray was performing live from heaven. The words and melody flowed into Eric's ears and through his whole body, the power of them etching goosebumps on his arms.

"*You know, I wish I had somebody to help me sing this,*" Ray crooned, and the audience joined him, slow at first and building…

America, America, God shed his grace on thee
America, I love you America, you see
My God he done shed his grace on thee
And you oughta love him for it
'Cause he, he, he, he crowned thy good
He told me he would, with brotherhood
From sea to shining Sea
Oh Lord, oh Lord, I thank you Lord

The young woman by his side patted Eric's arm, nodded, and smiled, and mouthed, "Good luck."

Eric strode to center stage in front of seventeen thousand people on their feet, screaming, reveling in the sense of pride and togetherness Ray Charles had conjured. In that moment, Eric decided to change his opening remarks.

CHAPTER EIGHTEEN

An announcement came overhead and was carried on every network, "And now, here's our host State of Wisconsin's favorite son, U.S. Senator Eric Rhodes!"

Eric waited while everyone sat down and grew quiet. A hoot and a "Give 'em hell, Eric," echoed in the stillness.

"Wow," Eric said, slowly turning to look all around the mammoth facility, packed to the rafters. "Just wow." Both the Forum's mega screens and the television screens at home showed a close-up of Eric winking conspiratorially as he said, "If you listened to that rendition of America the Beautiful and didn't get goosebumps on your arms or tears in your eyes, well, think about getting a checkup…either your ears or your heart might need a tune-up."

The audience laughed its agreement, and Eric continued, revising the opening of his speech on the fly. "America the Beautiful was sung for the first time more than one hundred years ago, and it still resonates with us today. We all felt it just now. We rallied around it and it brought us together. You know, there are a couple of lines from that song that I want to repeat, because when I hear them I want to be a better person, a better citizen."

He paced the stage now and you could sense his athleticism and his energy. He stopped and raised a finger, "First are the words, 'Who more than self, their country loved.'" He paused and repeated, "Who more than self, their country loved…

"But I am asking you here. Tonight. Right now…, Do you see this 'love of country more than self' in our leaders?"

A smattering of people in the crowd shouted, "No!"

Eric knitted his brow and shook his head, "What was that? I need you with me here." His voice rose, "We all need to get engaged tonight and every day moving forward. I'm gonna ask you again, and I want to hear your response this time, "Do our nation's leaders love their country more than they love themselves?" He shouted the question.

"No!" came the answer in unison.

"Is that what you see?" Eric screamed

"No!" the audience roared.

THE KILLER SPEECH

"Hell no!" Eric yelled, stalking the stage again like a panther. "Hell no!

"Love this country? Nah. No way. I'm not seein' it. And more than themselves? No. Not in a long, long time. That's the hard truth," he said, his voice low and even again.

"The second line from America the Beautiful that strikes me is the one where God 'crowned thy good with brotherhood, from sea to shining sea.'"

Eric's voice dipped even lower, and the crowd leaned forward in their seats to hear him say, "Brotherhood." The word seemed to sour his expression. "You want to talk about brotherhood?" Eric's voice rose again. "Well, if brotherhood ain't dead, it's on life support! And '"Sea to shining sea?"' he yelled. "No way! No how! We don't have brotherhood from city to suburb, let alone sea to shining sea! Today we're all about Black versus White and Red versus Blue. We're more divided than at any time in our history, except for maybe, and I repeat maybe, during the Civil War.

I look in the mirror, and I know," he nodded. "I know I've got to do better." He slowly pivoted three hundred and sixty degrees and said, "I look around this arena, and we all know that we've got to do better. We've got to *be* better." He raised his hands to the sky. "We have to get better as a party, as a people, and as a nation." The crowd stood and shouted their approval. He had them.

Eric prowled the stage again. "They told me before I came out here tonight that I could talk about my ideas for improving health care. What I'm about to share are my views, and not necessarily the views of my party. And I'd like to thank our presumptive nominee, the next president of these United States, for giving me this chance. I endorsed the Governor not because we see eye to eye on every issue, but because she's a leader who listens, to the people and her colleagues. Maybe most importantly, she listens to the opposition. And she listens not to formulate a counterargument; she listens to understand. Governor Nancy Barrett is exactly the leader our country needs right now!" The audience was on its feet again, roaring its agreement.

Eric rubbed his forehead, wiping away the beads of sweat caused by the millions of watts of light focused on him. "When I talk about health care, I like to ask a few questions." The cameras loved his grin. "Now this is gonna

CHAPTER EIGHTEEN

feel familiar. First, does health care work?" A smattering of *Nos* rang out, but the audience seemed conflicted. "Trick question. I think the answer for almost all of us in this room is, 'yeah,' it works okay. Most of us here tonight, and probably most watching on television, have health insurance. If you've got a government plan like I do, that insurance is tight…you've got access to any care with little worries about the cost.

"There are lots of other people with insurance, but if you get through the fine print…and there's pages and pages of fine print…that coverage has holes big enough for the entire World Champion Green Bay Packers football team to run through."

He held his hands up in mock surrender. "Sorry, I couldn't resist."

The crowd laughed, blowing off nervous tension, and Eric grew serious again. "More and more health insurance plans sold these days are so-called 'catastrophic' plans; I guess because if you come down with anything more than the common cold with those insurance plans, it's a catastrophe! The coverage is about as good as the coverage you get with most hospital gowns. Way too much exposure for my way of thinking!

"You have a heart attack, cancer, need major surgery…you might just lose your car, your house, or your life savings…maybe all of the above." He paused and nodded, "Catastrophic coverage? Yeah, they got that right. And how many people have no coverage at all?" He waited in silence until the pause grew uncomfortable, then his voice boomed, a change of direction as devastating as the crossover dribble he'd used countless times on the hardwood. "Forty-four million people in the U.S. have no health insurance! And another thirty-eight million Americans have inadequate health insurance coverage! That means every day, one-third of our fellow Americans wake up without the security of knowing medical care will be there for them if they need it. They worry themselves sick, worrying about getting sick!"

He took a deep breath and dropped his voice. "Now, that's certainly not the case for most of us in the Forum here tonight. He looked directly into the lens of the nearest camera, eye to eye with the people watching at home, "And that may not be the case for most of you watching across the country tonight.

But remember those words Ray sang, those words about caring more for our country than for ourselves. He wasn't talking about nationalism; he wasn't asking you to care more about the red, white, and blue than you do yourself." He looked around the entire arena again, and his voice shook with emotion and echoed throughout the building. "He was talking about patriotism, calling us to care more about our fellow Americans, be they black, white, brown, red, or yellow, than we care for ourselves." The audience rose to its feet as one, screaming their support. When they settled back down, Eric continued.

"I asked earlier if our health care system works. I hope we can all agree that with one-third of us on the brink or completely left on the outside looking in, that it definitely does not work…not for all of us. It's broken! And when it comes to the cost of that broken healthcare system, well, it's breaking us. Other countries around the world, even those that have now surpassed us in wealth, spend far less on health care than we do. Switzerland spends twelve percent of its Gross Domestic Product on health care. Germany, Sweden, France, and Canada spend about eleven percent. The rest of the world spends ten percent or less." He paused and shook his head, raising his voice again. "Here in the U.S., we spend more than *seventeen* percent of our GDP on health care! More than seventeen percent! And the average life expectancy for people living in those countries I called out by name? Every single one is higher than the life expectancy of U.S. residents. People in Switzerland live more than five years longer on average than we do! So, we pay fifty percent or more for our health care, and what do we have to show for it? The truth is, nothing. We pay more, and we die earlier. Economists call us an outlier when it comes to the cost of our care, but the rest of the world just calls us *stupid*." He almost spat the last word.

Eric walked to the center of the stage and to the stairs that led down to the arena floor. He sat on the top step and wiped his brow again. He looked out at the audience and said, "Are you still with me?"

"Yes!" they shouted back.

Eric nodded. "So, let's keep digging into this deeper…just a group of Americans concerned that maybe we're not gettin' what we're payin' for

CHAPTER EIGHTEEN

when it comes to our health care. The next thing we need to do is to take a look at the factors that drive our cost of care up so high. And the first one on my list is our health insurance industry."

Eric licked his top lip. "Did you know that five companies control close to half of the health insurance policies written in the U.S.? The names, if I read them off here, would sound familiar to you." He cocked his head and winked again. "They've mostly got a nice patriotic ring to them." He shook his head. "These are for-profit companies, and they do a darn good job of making profits...over thirty-five billion dollars in profits in a year. Even more in a big year. In addition, their CEOs *earn* twenty million dollars a year on average." The word earn came out of Eric's mouth like it had a bitter taste to it. "Those CEOs and their similarly highly paid executive teams *earn* those ginormous salaries by adding layers and layers of complexity to our health care system that run up the cost and detract from its overall value."

Eric stood and stared into the camera, and his voice rose again. "The health insurance companies make staggering profits, and their CEOs make monopoly money while rural hospitals and urban safety net hospitals struggle just to keep their doors open." He shook out his shoulders and waved a hand in the air, his voice dropping a couple levels. "I know. I know. I need to settle down a little, right? But this stuff gets my blood pressure up and makes me a little crazy. I've got a friend who runs a hospital here in town. Now, I'm not a little guy, but my friend Alan is a great big guy, like to blot out the sun. Thing about Alan, and I can't tell *him* this, but his brain and his heart are even bigger than the rest of him. He keeps telling me to look deeper into things, keep peelin' away the layers of the onion. You see, the power five health insurance companies drive a lot of extra cost. But they're just the tip of the iceberg, and our health care is that cruise ship, you know, the Titanic. Alan points out there are more than nine hundred health insurance companies in the U.S. right now, each of them adding waste and complexity to our system. Think about that! Close to a thousand health insurance companies, and every one of them puts their own demands on our hospitals and physicians in terms of what hoops they need to jump through in order to get paid for their services. A whole industry has sprung up around claims denials. The more the insurance companies deny claims and the longer they deny claims, the more money they make. We've got costly armies of people on the insurance side denying claims and costly armies on the physician and hospital side fighting to get paid for the care they've delivered." He's shouting now. "And who's caught in the middle? That's right, we are! The patients. Are you starting to see how a single payer system could simplify things for everyone and also maybe save us a ton of money…upwards of a trillion dollars a year?"

Eric paced the stage again. "A lot of my colleagues in Congress quietly share my feelings, but they don't like it when people ask, 'How are we going to be able to afford that single payer system,' or, 'Are you going to raise my taxes?' But I think these are softball questions, like sending a guy to the free throw line who sinks twenty-five in a row every day before he leaves the gym. The question isn't 'How can we afford a single payer system.' The question is, 'How can we afford to not have a single payer system?' If we're spending fifty to seventy-five percent more on our healthcare system than countries with single payer systems, then let's face it, we need to change. And 'will I raise your taxes to pay for it?' My answer is, 'You bet I'll raise your taxes!' But the thing is, you won't be seeing all that money taken out of your check anymore to pay your share of your crummy insurance. And your employer won't have to pay for that crummy insurance, so they can invest more in their operations and their people, and they can compete on a more equal footing with companies based in other parts of the world."

Eric pursed his lips, and heard *twenty minutes* in his earbud. "Sorry. That's enough about the insurance industry. I know I'm getting into the weeds, but I need you to understand this stuff. So, let's spend a couple minutes on another key driver of healthcare costs…the pharmaceutical industry." He shook his head and looked down for a beat before looking back up into the cameras. "Let's talk about big pharma!"

Chapter Nineteen

The screen froze with Senator Rhodes in the middle of the stage with his mouth open. Cole shook his head and stretched his arms above his head. He let out a deep breath. He'd been engrossed in the Senator's speech. He looked down at his clean plate and empty pint glass and couldn't remember anything but the first exquisite bite and sip.

"What do you think so far?" Michele asked, gazing at Cole from her perch on the sectional.

"He had me at hello. He's taking complex issues and making them almost understandable. And it's easy to see how the health insurance industry wouldn't want to see his ideas gain traction. If Senator Rhodes has his way, the industry will soon be a memory, like pay phones and camera film; it just won't be a fond memory for most."

Cole's stomach growled again, and they both laughed. Michele said, "Why don't you get another slice and fill up your glass. Then we'll watch the rest."

When Cole came back, his glass was full of cold beer, and his plate held two more big slices of the stuffed pizza, the cheese bubbling from its spin in the microwave. The mozzarella, tomato paste, and garlic scents drifted back to Michele. "Did you leave any pizza?" she asked as Cole tore into a slice.

He wiped his mouth with a napkin, "There's one slice left."

"Crap," she said, getting up and heading for the kitchen. "I've got no willpower these days." She came back a few minutes later and joined Cole on the floor, her knees touching his. She lifted the big slice of pizza with two hands and bit off a mouthful, grabbing the string of mozzarella that hung from the slice and sliding that in her mouth too. The tip of her tongue circled her lips to catch every morsel. Then she borrowed Cole's napkin, wiped her hands, and hit the play button on the remote…

Chapter Twenty

"Big pharma," Eric repeated, putting his left hand in his pocket, while wagging his right index finger in the air. He shook his head side to side. "Mmmm. Mmmm. What I've got to say here is gonna' shock you, and you aren't gonna like it one bit. You see, in the U.S., we pay more than three times what the residents of other prosperous nations spend on the same prescription drugs. Think about that for a minute." He started to leisurely walk around the stage, at the pace you might walk in a garden if you wanted to stop and look at the different blooms now and again. He spoke as if talking to a buddy. "Now, if I walk up to a candy counter with one friend who's German and another who's from Ireland, I wouldn't like it much if the owner charged me a buck fifty for the same kind of candy bar he charged my friends fifty cents for. That wouldn't sit well with me. If my buddies and I went to a Best Buy and the cashier tried to charge me a thousand dollars for a television that my friends bought for three hundred, I would be irate. But that's what's happening when we in the U.S. need to buy prescription drugs; we pay more than three times as much for the exact same pills! And this isn't a little bit of money I'm talking about here; big pharma rakes in more than a trillion dollars a year! Now, you gotta be asking yourself why in the world we're paying so much more for our medicines than they are in Canada, Germany, England, France, etc. The answer is because all those countries, and pretty much every other country on planet earth, set limits on what they'll pay for their drugs. We don't. It's that simple. So, we get stuck paying for the world's research and development and the huge profits the drug companies make. Now, I'm a free market guy as much as anybody, but if nobody else in the world is on the same page, then it's anything but a free market. When it comes to the medicines we need to treat the sick, the whole world has walked away from the table and stuck us with the tab. This has been going on for years, and it's absolutely bankrupting our health care system."

Eric reached into his suit jacket and pulled out a small prescription bottle. He held it high over his head, with his hand covering part of the label. Close-ups of the bottle filled the screens in the Forum and in homes across America. Eric brought the bottle down and shook it by his right ear. The speakers in the arena and televisions picked up the rattle of pills like maracas. "What I'm holding in my hand here is just one of the latest and worst examples of what's wrong with how we pay for our medicines in the U.S. This isn't a new, cutting-edge drug, by the way; it's an old drug that's been on the market for a long time. It helps fight certain parasites. The manufacturer recently increased the price of this drug in the U.S., upped it from thirteen dollars a pill to almost eight hundred dollars a pill. Overnight! Why? The answer is, why not? These are for-profit companies, and there's nothing stopping this in the U.S. What's worse, though, is I've got an old college buddy who's still hangin' on playing basketball over in England. He's not getting rich, but he makes a living, and he's having fun. You want to know how much this same drug would cost him in the United Kingdom?"

A few yeses came from the crowd. Eric cocked his head and raised his voice, "I said, do you want to know how much this same drug costs in the UK?"

"Yes!" the audience shouted.

Eric nodded in satisfaction. "Better. I just told you that we pay almost eight hundred dollars a pill for this drug here in the U.S. But in Britain? In Britain, they pay forty-three pence a pill for this same medicine. That's sixty-six cents, by the way. Can you imagine that?" He stretched on his tiptoes and reached the pill bottle as high as he could. "We pay almost eight hundred dollars for a pill," he said, then switched the bottle to his other hand and squatted on stage, holding the bottle just off the floor. "While they pay just sixty-six cents for the same pill across the Atlantic."

CHAPTER TWENTY

He paced again. "I would recommend to Governor Barrett that as soon as she wins the coming election...that she hold a world pharmaceutical summit and tell all the other leaders in the world that we are mad as hell and we're not gonna take it anymore. We are done paying three times more for our prescriptions as everyone else. We will no longer be taken advantage of. That will rock the pharmaceutical industry, but we need to come up with answers together. We're not rich enough anymore to pay for everyone else."

Ten minutes, said his earbud.

"We're almost home," Eric said. "We've talked about the problems with health insurance and prescription drugs; now let's spend just a couple minutes talking about our hospitals and our physicians and other providers. I spoke earlier about my buddy, Alan, who runs a hospital in town. I'm incredibly proud of our doctors, nurses, therapists, pharmacists, aids, housekeepers, food service workers...everyone who works so hard to keep us healthy and fix our bodies when we break down. We've got far and away the best physicians and hospitals in the world. I think we're all willing to pay a little more in order to access care like that. And these aren't part-time, nine-to-five kinds of fields. Our hospitals operate round the clock, open nights, weekends, holidays...ever vigilant. But because of the way we pay for health care, things have been getting more and more mucked up along the way. The hospital systems, even the nonprofits, keep building more and more hospitals in the suburbs, while closing rural and urban safety net hospitals. They're just following the money, of course. It's hard to pay your staff on Medicaid and the uninsured.

"Here in Milwaukee, we used to have a dozen hospitals in the city. We had a county hospital, too, a hospital whose sole reason for existence was to care for the poor. Today, we're down to just five hospitals in our city, and that county hospital was shuttered twenty years ago. It's getting harder and harder for people in our city to get access to health care. And the most sinful part about this is, these are the people who most need access to care. The people in our city are the sickest, with the most co-morbidities, yet they can't find access to care. Their diabetes, asthma, COPD, high blood pressure...controllable diseases...rage out of control, and contribute to their early demise. People at Alan's hospital experience their first stroke or heart attack twenty years earlier than the white people just a few miles away in the suburbs. Black infants in the cities in my state are dying at a rate three times higher than white infants! Can you hear what I'm saying!"

"Yes!" The audience roared.

"Can you live with this?"

"No," came the response, shaking the building.

Eric massaged his forehead, and the cameras could see his eyes welling up. He slowly nodded his head up and down. "You know, more than fifty-five years ago, the Reverend Martin Luther King, Jr. gave a speech on health care. In his remarks, he said, 'Of all the forms of inequality, injustice in health is the most shocking and inhuman.' Now, I ask you today, more than a half-century after he called out health care in the U.S., how far have we come? How far have we come when black infants die at a rate three times higher than white kids and city folks are having strokes and heart attacks twenty years earlier than suburban folk? And the answer must be, not very far. Not very far at all."

He walked back to the center of the stage. *One minute*, came over the earbud. "And now, here we are. We're back, literally and figuratively, to where I started tonight. And I want to know if you think there's a chance, even a small chance, that we can put aside our differences and work together?"

"Yes!" yelled the crowd.

Eric nodded, his smile wide. His voice grew louder. "I want to know if you're willing to work on these health care issues, to make important and maybe difficult changes, to rebuild that brotherhood Ray Charles sang about from heaven."

"Yes!" yelled the crowd more loudly.

"Do you think you can try to love our country and your fellow man more than you do yourself?" he shouted.

"Yes!" screamed the crowd.

"Well, alright then," Eric said with a megawatt smile. "Let's get on with it! God bless you, and God bless America!"

CHAPTER TWENTY

Aaaand done, came through his earbud. Eric waved and trotted off the stage to a thunderous ovation, everyone on their feet stomping and whistling their approval. He was off stage and still jogging, heart hammering in his chest, people lined up clapping for him behind the curtain, high-fiving him, when someone caught him by the arm, bringing him to an abrupt halt, his smile still plastered to his face. He looked to see who grabbed him and turned into the weathered smile of Bill Clinton. The former president's face crinkled. "Nice job, Senator Rhodes. But tell me how the hell I'm supposed to follow that." He pointed to the crowd screaming its approval, and brought Eric back on stage with him for a curtain call. Maestro be damned.

Chapter Twenty-One

Cole's eyes blinked open. He tried willing them shut again, but something was niggling him to consciousness, whether he was ready to get up or not. He was burning up, his body trying to work off all the calories he'd eaten and drank so late in the evening. He kicked off his comforter but kept the sheet around him. He must have been lying on his left arm for a long time, because it was in the state he wanted to be in…. Asleep! He rolled onto his back, alone in the king-size bed, his left arm dead and useless. After a while, he felt little pinpricks as circulation began flowing through the arm, and then a fiery sensation. *It's alive*, he said to himself, as he flexed it a few times.

His tongue felt thick. He had cottonmouth, tumbleweeds running down the back of his throat. He groaned and swung his legs out of bed, and padded to his bathroom, relieving himself and washing his hands. He shuffled to the kitchen, left arm still semi-useless, pulled a glass out of a cupboard, and filled it from the fridge's water dispenser. He would have liked ice, but he didn't want to wake Michele. He tipped the glass to his lips and drained it. He reached forward and refilled it. He stood there with pale moonlight streaming through the window, wearing only the yellow boxers with the blue eyeglasses he'd bought online. Maybe he should've stopped after two slices of pizza. Maybe one pint of ale would have been enough, given its eight-and-a-half percent alcohol content. Lite beers had less than half the alcohol and maybe a third of the calories. Even in the dim moonlight, his hindsight was twenty/twenty. *Bullshit*, he thought; the Reward IPA had ten times the taste of the lite beers.

CHAPTER TWENTY-ONE

His body had been trying to digest the extra calories and alcohol while his mind tried to digest the events of the day and the Senator's speech. His whole being was on overload, and all he wanted to do was shut down. He remained there, dazed, registering the ghostly 3:22 on the oven clock. Too early even for him to get up and start the day. He yawned and scratched himself and turned just as Michele stepped soundlessly into the kitchen. She appraised him, spending an exaggerated amount of time on his boxers. She lifted her head and smiled at him. "Go to bed. You're making a spectacle of yourself."

He looked down at his boxers and laughed. "I get that a lot." He went back to bed and pulled the sheet over him. He felt more settled and yawned again, hoping sleep would take him. His eyes closed, and he felt himself drifting. He was almost out when he sat up in bed and shook his head. "Weezy!" He rolled over and grabbed his cell phone and texted, "Cole Huebsch, FBI Milwaukee here. Do these two guys look familiar to you? Let me know either way. Thanks." He attached the two photos and heard a zipping sound when he hit send. He lay back down and took a couple of deep breaths. Closing his eyes, he gave himself up to his dreams and demons.

Eight hundred miles to the southeast, it was four-thirty in the morning, and the crowd at *Swills* had been gone for more than an hour. The bartenders and wait staff had cleaned up and headed home, and only the new proprietor remained. The exterior lights were off, and so were most of the interior ones. Weezy sipped from an icy bottle of National Bohemian beer. The lager was born in Baltimore over one hundred thirty-five years ago, and ninety percent of its sales were in Baltimore. The "Natty Boh," as they called it, would be Weezy's first and only beer of the day. He studied the bottle between sips, "Why you only got one eye, little white boy?" He enjoyed his first moment of quiet since he'd opened for the night almost twelve hours ago. Disjointed light thrown from a muted television behind the bar strobed the news. Weezy was content, thinking maybe, just maybe, he'd found a way out of the haphazard life he'd been sucked into when he was just a kid. He thought about making an honest living from the bar and working on his art, maybe fixing the place up and turning it into his personal gallery.

Something on the television caught his eye, and he looked up to see the face of the FBI agent, Cole Huebsch, on the screen. Scrolling across the bottom of the television, he read, *Decorated Milwaukee FBI agent thwarts apparent attack. Two assailants in custody, one in critical condition.*

Now what the fuck is that all about, Weezy wondered. He didn't trust anybody from the law enforcement side of things, but so far, the FBI agent had been true to his word and hadn't come after him. He'd looked the other way and let him keep the money he'd earned from painting the barn, too. That had been the stake he'd used to buy *Swills*. He pulled out his phone and noticed the text from Cole, and looked at the photos. "Mothafuckah," he said aloud. He thought about calling the agent back but noted the time and thought better about it. *It can wait*, he thought, as he got up to check the beer coolers behind the bar. He was tired, but they needed topping off, and he'd rather do it now than right before he opened later in the day.

Dexter Carter was set up a half block away. *You want something done right*, he thought, *you fuckin do it yourself.* He had boosted a Toyota pickup and backed it into the dark alley a couple hours earlier. He waited until he was fairly certain Weezy was alone, but he needed to move now, before the little shit left the building. When he exited the vehicle, the interior lights stayed off; he'd broken them as soon as he'd taken the truck. He wore gloves as he pulled the rocket launcher from the back seat, shut the door, and pointed it at *Swills'* front door. He flicked the safety off and held the open site up to his right eye. No fancy guidance system on this bazooka, but he wouldn't need it at this distance. He set himself and eased the trigger back. A loud *whooooshhhh* filled the early morning, followed by a tremendous explosion. The windows and part of a wall blew outward from the bar, and a fireball lit up the sky. Carter could feel the reverberation on his chest. He dropped the hot weapon, hustled back to the pickup, and drove out of the alley and away from the burning building, keeping his headlights off for the first two blocks. When he turned the headlights on, he also turned on the radio. He'd purchased the RPG off the books, but he thought as he drove that it was funny that any adult with a clean record could legally own such a device.

On the radio, John Mellencamp sang about his younger, reckless days.

CHAPTER TWENTY-ONE

Outside the club Cherry Bomb, our hearts were really thumpin... Carter laughed out loud, thinking, *My heart was just thumpin outside the club Swills. Just about the same time, a nobody named Weezy's heart thumped for the last time.* He didn't know all the words to *Cherry Bomb,* but he sang along the best he could.

Chapter Twenty-Two

Cole drove to the office in St. Francis the next morning in a downpour, his wipers whup, whap, whup, whapping fast as they could go. The storm was coming from the south and bringing higher temps along with heavy rain. It promised a steamy afternoon. The sun was up somewhere over the lake, but it could've been midnight from Cole's perspective. A gust of wind tried to shove the little Dodge off the Hoan Bridge, but the stubborn Charger hugged the concrete like a billy goat. Another gust hit as he drove through the thin veil of clouds on the bridge's apex, 120 feet above the lake water below, and Cole gripped the wheel tighter. High winds always set him on edge. He had a fuzzy memory of riding out a tornado in the basement with his parents early in his life, but he wasn't sure, and they were no longer alive to ask.

Cole glanced at his clock when he entered his office moments later and flipped on the overhead lights. The slim second hand quivered in place as the clock showed twelve-fifteen. Cole sighed, draped his suit coat off the back of his desk chair, and rolled up the sleeves of his white dress shirt. He fumbled through his desk drawers and came away with a small screwdriver and a double A battery. He dragged a chair from his table over to the open door and stepped up onto its seat. It wobbled, and he grabbed the doorframe to keep from falling. Li ducked under his arm, followed closely by Lane.

They sat at the table while Cole lifted the clock off the nail it rested on and pulled it off the wall. The chair rattled and wobbled again as he hopped off and joined the analysts at the table.

"A mechanic too?" Li asked. "You truly are a renaissance man."

CHAPTER TWENTY-TWO

"You might need to do CPR on that thing," Lane said. "Not sure there's much life left in that old clock."

"Ah, you kids and your throwaway society," Cole replied as he unscrewed the clock's plastic cover and pried out the old battery. "The soaring landfills in our country are built one clock at a time."

"Thank you, Captain Planet!" Li said as Cole seated the new battery and replaced the cover. He wound the clock correctly for seven-ten. When he stepped back up on the chair, it shuddered.

"I'm not sure you should be standing on a chair with wheels," Lane said. "I'm pretty sure that's in the FBI handbook."

Cole ignored the comment, replaced the clock on the wall, and made it back down without incident. He watched the second-hand quiver and twitch as it stumbled drunkenly around the clock's face. He bowed to Li and Lane, "Voila! Good as new." They shook their heads and rolled their eyes clockwise as the clock snicked at them like an angry squirrel.

"Shoulda just replaced it," Lane said.

Cole shook his head, "Not on my watch." Then his eyes widened, and he added, "Pun intended!"

"What? No way! You didn't call that!" Lane objected.

Cole leaned back in his chair. "Admit it, Lane. That was an awesome pun."

"You didn't call it. It's like making a crazy bank shot in pool. You have to call the pun, or it doesn't count."

"I said pun intended."

"Plus," Lane said. "It's a clock, not a watch!"

"Ah, you're so literal, Lane. Hmmm. Literal Lane. As alliterative as it is illustrative. You may become the man of a thousand nicknames."

"God, no. Just no." Lane said.

Cole snapped his fingers and pointed at the clock. "I just had another brilliant thought. From this moment on, that clock right there…we'll call him 'Timer…'"

"Him?" Li interrupted. "The clock is a him? As in masculine?"

"No. Wait. I don't want you to get all *wound up*." He nodded to Lane, "Pun intended. "You're right, though, Li. Timer could also be a she or an it. Makes it even more inclusive and genius probably. Regardless, Timer is now the Milwaukee FBI field office's unofficial mascot. Gritty. Takes a lickin, keeps on tickin kind of thing. That's us in a nutshell.

"I think the licking and ticking thing's already taken," Lane said. "We might get sued by Timex."

"An inanimate object as a mascot? I'm not sure I'm feelin it," Li added.

Cole nodded to himself. "No, it's wicked good. Think 'Ohio State Buckeyes' or San Antonio Spurs.' They're both freaking dynasties. I'm onto something. Speaking of which, I'm hoping you had a chance to watch the Senator's speech, and you've developed some theories."

"Well, I watched it last night for the first time after you texted us," Li said. "And my first thought was, 'This is the person who should be running for president.' Rhodes is an amazing orator. He's got big, dreamy brown eyes with whites as pure as new snow. And what an emotive face! He pulled me in with the wink, the scowl, and how he raised his eyebrows. He was humble and compassionate one moment and filled with righteous anger the next. I was trying to watch dispassionately, but I felt those same strong feelings right along with him and the crowd."

"Ditto," Lane said. "He has a way of breaking complex issues down to simple concepts we can all understand. But it's more than that. I know it's a big deal, but I've never thought much about health care before. No offense, but I'm a lot younger than you guys, don't have any chronic health issues, and we've got maybe the best insurance anyone can have. But I not only understood what he was trying to convey, I felt it deep inside. Somewhere in the first couple minutes, I stopped taking notes. I was just listening. Really listening. He pinged something inside me and pulled me along with him. I gotta believe a lot of people in the crowd at the Forum and watching at home felt the same way."

"I agree," Cole said. "He's damn handsome, too, and his voice commands attention without seeming to even try. Listening to that speech, I thought that's what you'd get if you put the voices of James Earl Jones and Denzel Washington in a blender."

"Put their voices in a blender?" Lane asked.

CHAPTER TWENTY-TWO

"Not literally, Lane Man. The other thing I noticed is that he doesn't talk with his hands in an annoying way, like some do. But when he needs to make a point, his whole body helps tell the story. It's like Tiger Woods sinking a winning putt."

"He didn't hide behind the podium or read from a teleprompter either," Li said. "I'll bet he didn't even know *America the Beautiful* was going to be played before he went on. He just went with it. I think almost everyone who watched it thought it wasn't the typical canned speech; it was original and from the heart. If he faked all that, then it's even more remarkable and frightening as hell."

"He really went after the health insurance industry and big pharma hard," Cole said. "Can you imagine if Senator Rhodes took that speech on the road?"

"And if the Senator's electability scores go up after the speech, other politicians might start to take notice and they might begin parroting his views," Li said. "Hell, they'll steal liberally from his speech in order to improve their own numbers and their reelection chances."

"Anything else?" Cole asked.

"I did some of my analyzing magic last night," Lane said. "I checked to see how the stock market reacted the day after the Senator's speech. I know Rhodes wasn't the only speaker, but it seemed he was the only one people talked about afterward."

"What'd you find out?" Cole asked.

"One of the big five health insurance companies was down eight percent overnight. Another down seven. Another nine. One five. The last would've been down the most, but they announced their quarterly results earlier in the day. Their earnings beat analysts' projections, and the value of their stock still dropped five percent!"

"Ouch," Cole said.

"Big ouch," Lane agreed. "The largest has almost a billion shares outstanding, and they started yesterday at three hundred and fifty dollars a share. That eight percent drop cost them twenty-eight billion."

"So, we've got at least five companies that wouldn't want Senator Rhodes to become the Pied Piper of health care reform."

"Five companies?" Lane replied. "No! You've got almost nine hundred suspects. Rhodes was right that there are nine hundred health insurance companies operating in the U.S., and none of those with stock did well following the Senator's speech. And, if Rhodes' ideas become policy or law, they'll all be finished as far as I can see."

Cole was in the middle of letting out a big sigh when his cell phone rang. He answered, putting it on speaker and setting it down in the middle of the table. "Morning, Lieutenant Williams," he said. "How are you?"

"Morning, Agent Huebsch," the Baltimore PD officer said. "I'm doing just fine, but a mutual friend of ours isn't so hot this morning."

"Weezy?"

"The one and only. He turned his recent payday into ownership of the bar he hung out at, and in the wee hours of this morning, someone shot a rocket-propelled grenade through the front door. The whole place was mostly leveled."

Cole stood up and looked at the phone, feeling guilty for not calling Weezy yesterday. He paused. "Is he dead?"

"No. Turns out he's as lucky as he is artistic. Just before the bomb liquidated his investment, Weezy stepped into the walk-in cooler to get a couple cases of Natty Boh to refill the mini fridges behind the bar."

"What's Natty Boh?" Lane asked.

"Just a second," Cole said, muting the phone. He turned to Lane. "National Bohemian. It's a popular Baltimore lager; been around more than a hundred and fifty years." He wagged a finger at the younger analyst. "I'm surprised you didn't know that." He turned and unmuted the phone. "Sorry, Lieutenant. Please continue."

"Anyway, Weezy won't be dangling from a ladder like some modern-day Michelangelo any time soon. He's got a pretty good concussion, more contusions than you can count, and a broken arm from where a metal shelf fell on him. But it coulda been a lot worse. The walls of that walk-in cooler were double-sided steel, with thick insulation in between. A mini bomb shelter. If Weezy was anywhere else when the shell went off, he'd be a

CHAPTER TWENTY-TWO

memory."

"Someone didn't want him talking with us," Cole said. "This is serious shit. You see RPGs used by bad guys on U.S. soil all the time in the movies, but that's just not real life. ATF and the FBI have both confiscated RPGs during raids a few times, but this could be the first time one was actually fired with bad intent here."

"Everything keeps adding to the fact that we're dealing with really bad people with really good access to resources," Li said.

Cole talked aloud as he thought it through. "Yeah, these aren't your common thugs," he agreed. "Thugs, for damned sure, but uncommon. What are you doing with Weezy?"

"He's at our city hospital right now. We checked him in as a John Doe. I'm going to do everything I can to make sure the people who did this think he's dead."

"Perfect," Cole said. "You need help, anything, just let me know, and we'll throw resources your way. Weezy might've bent or even broken a few laws along the way, but I like him. I needed to talk to him, but even so, I feel bad for putting him in harm's way. Early this morning, I texted Weezy photos of the guys who tried to kill Li and me yesterday. I was hoping he could tell us if they're the same guys who hired him and his crew for the barn painting."

"Better text them to me, and I'll show them to Weezy," the lieutenant said. "Weezy's phone came out of that blast this morning in worse shape than he did."

"Will do. And thanks for calling. Let's keep in touch," Cole said.

"Wouldn't have it any other way," Williams answered. "My life is a whole lot more exciting since you entered it."

Everyone laughed as the call ended. "What now, boss?" Lane asked.

"Me and my sidekick here…" he pointed at Li, "are gonna go visit us a U.S. Senator."

"Sidekick?" Lane smiled.

"Don't start, Rump," Li said as they got up to leave.

Chapter Twenty-Three

"Have you been to Summerfest yet?" Cole asked Li, as he drove toward Senator Rhodes' home in the Sherman Park area of Milwaukee. The annual week-long music festival on Milwaukee's lakefront hosts a thousand acts of all genres on twelve stages that draw nearly a million people.

Li smiled. She liked the fact that her boss knew she loved the fest. "It just started yesterday. Linda and I talked about going at least a couple times for sure."

"Do me a favor and take the afternoon off," Cole said. "You had a crazy day yesterday, and you did your homework on the speech last night. You and Linda make a day of it."

"For real?"

"Why not? You deserve it," he said, turning onto historic Grant Boulevard.

Li texted a message and got a reply back almost immediately. "She's *into* it!"

"Alrighty then," Cole laughed, pulling up in front of a beautiful, large yellow Colonial-style two-story house with white trim. He parked behind a non-descript gray sedan with two big men inside. He knew there would be another sedan with two more men in the alley behind the house, agents put in place to ensure a recently targeted U.S. Senator's protection. As he stepped out of the car, he noticed Eric and Karri Rhodes sitting in comfortable white Adirondack chairs on the wide porch that ran the length of the house. Cole took in the lush landscaping and waved on his way up the walk, Li at his side. "Hello," he called. "I was hoping we might catch you at home."

CHAPTER TWENTY-THREE

The sun had broken through, and the humidity was up after the morning storm. The porch was mostly uncovered, but the shade of two large maples made it both inviting and comfortable. They walked up six elegant steps and between two stately tapered pillars and made it to Senator Rhodes just as he pushed himself out of his chair. They shook hands all around and introduced themselves. The Senator grabbed a wooden cane from the porch railing. "Li, why don't you grab a seat next to Karri and get acquainted. Cole can help me get the pitcher of homemade lemonade we've got chilling in the fridge."

Cole followed Eric through the stout wooden door and inside. Caramel-colored oak flooring reflected the light streaming into the entryway from all sides. The walls were a light shade of ochre, offset by white trim and crown molding. To their right, large French doors led to a beautiful dining room, and to their left, matching French doors showcased a spacious family room. Both rooms featured unique, hand-crafted fireplaces. As they walked down the wide hall, Cole whistled. "Your house is beautiful, Senator. They don't make them like this anymore."

"Thanks, Cole. And call me Eric," he said as they entered the kitchen. "The house was built in 1930. We bought it move-in ready two years ago for two hundred and thirty thousand. You put it on a flatbed and move it a few miles east or west of here, and it would cost three or four times what we paid for it. But Karri and I grew up just a few blocks from here. We won't run from our roots. We don't like the fact that some of the houses on our old block are boarded up, and you could buy them for a buck from the city. But that's why I ran for public office in the first place; to try to fix things that are broke."

"Speaking of which, that was a helluva speech you gave at the convention. You think someone who works for the government would pay attention to politics more, but I typically don't. Too much bullshit, corruption, and narcissism...." He caught himself. "I'm sorry. I didn't mean to imply anything. I was speaking more in general."

Eric leaned back against a large butcher-block island and smiled. "Don't worry. I felt the same way. But I saw three choices. I could bitch about it, ignore it, or try to do something about it. I chose option number three."

"That's where I was going with my comment about politics. It was obvious from your speech that you don't fit the self-serving politician mold. Either that, or you're the greatest con artist ever. I've got a pretty good bullshit detector, and I think you meant every word you said in your speech. I also think something you said put a target on your back."

"What do you mean?"

Cole saw a pot of coffee warming. "Do you mind if I skip the lemo and have a cup of coffee? I didn't get my full caffeine intake yet this morning."

Eric pointed to a cupboard with his cane. "Grab a cup and help yourself."

Cole selected a cup and filled it with coffee. "I know speeches like the one you gave aren't written on a blank sheet of paper. I'm pretty sure you've never given that exact speech before, but I'd bet you've made the same points over and over in different settings. When you see the funniest comedian do a killer standup routine, you feel like he's just talking out loud, making random observations. But the truth is he or she has told those jokes a hundred times in small clubs in dozens of cities, finding out what works and discarding what doesn't. And in the end, it just seems natural."

"That's right. I've talked about health care in nearly every town hall and political forum I've attended. I can tell when my point is going over the head of my audience or when I've dumbed it down to the point it holds no meaning. I can also tell when I nail it; when I connect with someone on the fence and win them over." He stopped and smiled broadly. "My wife said you know Alan Anderson."

"I do. He's a good man."

"He says the same about you. Alan's the one who talked me into running for office in the first place. He thought I could make a difference, and he also thought it might help the kids in cities like Milwaukee to see another person in power who looks like them. One of the many quotes I attribute to Alan is this, 'A line well received is a line oft delivered.'"

"That's what I mean. I think someone in the healthcare industry has been following your career. They've been reading your opinion pieces, watching your voting record, and listening to your speeches. Your convention speech made it clear that you're a threat to them...a very real threat. The health

CHAPTER TWENTY-THREE

insurance industry alone lost tens of billions of dollars in stock value overnight following your speech. And we haven't looked at the impact on big pharma's pocketbook yet or explored other angles."

"You're saying it wasn't white supremacists who shot Eric?" Karri asked from the kitchen's entryway. Cole and Eric had been lost in the conversation, and neither noticed the women come in.

Li stood next to Karri, "We weren't sure what you two were up to, so we came back to find you."

"Agent Huebsch," Karri said, more forcefully. "Are you saying someone other than the Harris brothers shot Eric?"

"No. We're pretty sure they shot your husband. But we also believe now that they were paid to do it by someone else, someone a whole lot more sophisticated and resourceful."

"Well, shit," Eric said. "I was kind of hoping this whole thing was behind us."

"I don't think they'd be stupid enough to make another attempt on your life," Cole said. "But that's why we still have the protective detail around you. Better safe than sorry."

Karri's whole body seemed to stiffen. She clenched her jaw and shook her head.

"Hey," Cole said, his voice soft. "That's why we're here. I want you two to know everything we know. I also want you to know that we're in this together." He nodded at Li. "You might have read or seen on the news that Li and I were attacked yesterday. We think it was to stop us from digging further into the attempt on Eric's life. It seems a lot of people would like to let this drop, including powerful people in Washington. But we know now that it wasn't gang members who killed the Harris brothers. It was someone else. Likely the people who paid them to murder you, and paid someone to murder us." Karri seemed to soften a bit, and Cole took another sip of his coffee. "That's another reason why we're here, to see if you can help us sift through some of the potential suspects."

"We'll do whatever we can," Eric said.

"The kids will be here soon," Karri said. "I don't want them around when you discuss this."

"I thought the house was awful quiet," Cole said.

Eric nodded. "My parents still live nearby. The kids are with my mom and dad this morning. I'm sure grandpa's making them the same smiley face pancakes he made for me and my brother growing up." He paused, turning to Karri. "Are you okay waiting for the kids while I go with Cole and Li to talk with Alan at the hospital?"

"As long as you tell me everything you discuss, no secrets between us."

Eric nodded and pulled his wife close for a hug. "No problem. Partners for life, right?"

"Partners for life," Karri responded. Then she turned to Cole and hugged him tight before stepping back and looking him in the eyes. "Thank you for putting your life on the line and for not turning your back on this. It means a lot to us." She hugged Li then, too and the Senator followed the agents to Cole's car. Li held the door for Eric and shut it for him when he was settled in, while Cole told the agents watching the house to stay there and keep an eye on the Senator's wife and kids when they got home. He told them he'd take responsibility for Senator Rhodes' safety for the next hour or two. Then they made the short drive to the hospital.

Cole pulled under the hospital's huge canopy three minutes later and left the car with the valet. He led them through the main lobby, and they rode the elevator up a flight to get to the administration offices. Alan's assistant, Nicole, told them that Alan had a hole open on his calendar, so he would likely be found on the third floor, in the neonatal intensive care unit. "That's where we take care of our most fragile newborns," she explained. "It's one of his favorite places in the hospital." They followed Nicole's directions to the third-floor NICU, where they were buzzed into the locked unit.

A nursing assistant led them down to a dimly lit room where Alan gently rocked a newborn. The tiny baby looked content in Alan's massive arms.

"Can you talk?" Eric asked quietly.

"Sure. As long as you all keep your voices low and comforting. This is our NAS unit, where we care for infants born to opioid-dependent moms. They experience withdrawal symptoms that make their days more painful

CHAPTER TWENTY-THREE

and even life-threatening. The quiet and soft lighting help them heal. We also have a volunteer group who rock these youngsters when no parent is available. We've got a waiting list for this but holding little guys like Tyrone here is a perk of the job for me. I can watch his heart stop racing on the monitor when I hold him. It calms me too. Now, what can I help you with?"

Cole started. "We're pretty sure that the Harris brothers shot Eric, but we also believe that someone with a lot more brains and resources paid them to do it. Then they murdered the Harris boys and tried to make it look like a revenge killing by one or more African American gangs. We were able to track down one of the guys who tagged the barn; he and a couple of his buddies were flown in from Baltimore to do the paint job. I should learn today whether the guys who paid the artist are the same ones who tried to kill Li and me yesterday. Li thinks we should follow the money. After watching the speech last night, it seems there are a lot of people in the health insurance and pharmaceutical industries in particular that could be suspects. You think that makes any sense?"

Alan looked up from the baby and directly at Cole. "You're not making it easy to keep my voice under control. I've seen kids brought into our emergency department who were shot because another kid wanted their tennis shoes. So, do I think a rich white guy would kill someone to protect millions or billions of income annually? Yes. I'd say that's certainly plausible."

Alan continued to rock and gently patted the baby's back with his fingertips. He looked back up at Cole. "You've been following the money by looking at how much the different industries and individual companies have to lose if Eric's ideas become reality. That's a good start. But you said there are people in Washington that don't want this investigation to go anywhere. You could follow the money in a different direction. See how much money those same industries Eric went after in his speech throw at our politicians. I haven't looked for a while, but it seems to me that the health insurers and the pharmaceutical companies are both in the top five when it comes to contributing to the political campaigns of Congress and the president. I would focus there too. There are also plenty of real-life examples out there of companies in both of those industries behaving badly. You might have a hard time narrowing the field."

"I like that," Cole said. "We'll follow that thread. Anything else?"

The big man looked back down at Tyrone nestled on his chest and sighed. "Not now. But if I think of anything else, I'll ring your cell." He nodded at Eric. "Hard to admit it, but I'd like to see that tall drink of water next to you have a long life as much as I want that for little Tyrone here."

Cole called Lane from the car and asked him to start digging into how much money the pharmaceutical and health insurance industries pump into their lobbying efforts. A call came to his cell phone after they dropped Eric at his house, and Cole put it on the car's speaker system so Li could take part in the conversation. "Huebsch here!" he answered.

"Agent Huebsch. This is Lieutenant Williams from Baltimore PD. I'm in Weezy's hospital room, and I've got you on speaker."

"Great. I'm with Li, and we're driving back to the office right now. We have you on speaker as well."

"Okay," Williams said. "Weezy's got something to say."

"Damn straight, I got somethin to say! I almost got planted in the ground thanks to you. Someone sent a muthafuckin missile into my bar, and now it's wrecked!" Weezy's voice was loud and pitched with emotion.

Cole turned the volume down. "Hopefully, you took out insurance on the building when you bought it."

"You think I'm mothafuckin stupid!" Weezy was almost screaming. "Course I bought me insurance. But now I gotta start over."

"Is that all bad?" Cole asked. "Maybe this is a chance to build a bar from scratch that matches your personality. It might take longer before you open, but it'll really be yours when you're all done."

There was a pause, and Cole and Li could almost hear Weezy thinking. "Yeah," he said, his voice under control. "Maybe so. I already ordered new signage for the place. Custom made, so it ain't been delivered yet. I'm calling the place, 'Weezy's on Goul.' Neon signs are comin in a few weeks and they be fuckin lit!"

"Goul?" Cole asked. "Is that like the safe place when you're playing tag? Safe on goul?"

CHAPTER TWENTY-THREE

"Damn straight. I didn't know you all had goul in Bumfuck. But you right. I talked to some of the, uh, businessmen I deal with in the city and they agreed it would be good to have a place where everyone, no matter what colors they wear, could feel safe for a bit."

"Makes sense. You don't limit your clientele that way."

"Fuckin right. I had a room I was gonna call the 'Goul Hall,' steada pool hall, but that's all blown to shit and cinders now. I got insurance on the building and the rest, but I ain't got no health insurance. This little stay in the hospital could wipe me out."

"Maybe we can help with those expenses," Cole said. "Did you look at the photos of the two gentlemen that tried to kill Li and me?"

"I did. They's the same ones paid me and my boys to tag that rickety ol barn. No question."

Cole let out a sigh. "That's something. I'm not sure what at this point, but it's another thread to pull on. Thanks for the help, Weezy. And I'm sorry they came after you." He paused. "Lieutenant Williams?"

"Yes, Cole…"

"Please keep Weezy safe until we get to the bottom of this."

"Got it. We'll do our best," he said. Before he could click off, Weezy came back on. "Agent Huebsch?"

"Yes?"

"I heard you fucked those two boys up pretty good that came for you. I been around long enough to know that there are good guys doin bad and evil motherfuckers doin worse. Those two fuckheads you trashed were in that last camp." The call ended.

"What's next?" Li asked.

"I'll check in with Lane on the lobbying angle and see if we can connect the two guys who tried to kill us with anyone else further up the food chain. You need to get changed and head to Summerfest with Linda. It's a little warm, but the lake breeze will feel good. Should be a perfect day for it!"

Chapter Twenty-Four

At six-thirty that evening, Li and Linda Puccini rode the Summerfest Skyglider in a light blue chair that matched the cloudless skies. They floated high above the festival grounds. The popular ride was like a chairlift without the skis and ran nearly the length of the Big Gig's park. They had sampled a few bands and a couple of local beers; jumping on the Skyglider was a nice way to get above the crowd and catch even more of the lake breeze. Both women wore white sleeveless blouses that seemed to reflect the mainsails of the sailboats sharing the same breeze just outside the harbor. Li kicked her legs under the chair. She felt carefree when she was with Linda. She looked at her partner's porcelain skin and her big smile, the year-round freckles splashed across her nose. A gust of wind blew Linda's straight black hair across her face, and she caught Li's gaze as she tucked it behind her ear. Her smile grew. "What? You've got a look about you."

"Interesting way of putting that. I just like being with you is all. I realize that more all the time."

Linda rested her head on Li's shoulder and took her hands in hers. As they swayed forward, bright chairs the colors of the rainbow passed by on their right, carrying other couples holding hands and parents hugging kids. Throngs of people milled below. Children's squeals of delight joined country and hip-hop, music of every kind, blending together in the unique harmony of summer. The flashing lights of stages, food, and beverage vendors clawed the night sky, vying for attention with bright logo signs from Miller, Harley Davidson, and other Milwaukee icons. The city had no skyscrapers to compete with those in Chicago or New York, but the U.S. Bank building at

CHAPTER TWENTY-FOUR

forty-two stories and the Northwestern Mutual Insurance tower at thirty-two floors seemed more than big enough in the distance. The brilliant white of the Santiago Calatrava-designed Milwaukee Art Museum and the Discovery World Museum drew their gaze to the seeming infinity of Lake Michigan. As they came to the end of the ride, the breeze carried the buttery smell of roasted sweet corn to them, and Linda said, "I'm starving. The corn on the cob is on me!" They skipped off the chair, laughing.

A half-hour later, they sat across from each other at a metal picnic table, each with a large roasted ear of sweet corn slathered in butter and a plastic cup filled with icy, fresh-squeezed lemonade. Linda took a sip of the tart drink, and her lips puckered. She smacked them. "I'm pretty psyched about the Halsey concert," she said. "I love her voice and how she's turned the pain of her early years into something beautiful."

Li leaned on her elbows and wiped butter from the corner of her mouth. "Her early years? These are still her early years. She's what, ten years younger than us? You planning to leave me and rob the cradle?"

Halsey might still be young, but she'd been early and strong in her support for the LGBT community. The singer was openly bisexual, and both Linda and Li connected with her alt-music and her social activism. Linda's eyes crinkled with mischief. "I'm not under oath, am I?" They both laughed.

"Seriously," Linda said. "Thanks for getting the tickets. I love the amphitheater, and the lawn seats are the best. I checked the weather for Friday, and it's supposed to be perfect. I can't wait. I owe you, big!"

"You did spring for these," Li said, pointing to her matching temporary blue tattoo Linda had bought online that said *Linda + Li* inside a heart. They applied them to their bare shoulders with moisture from their cups. "Although it does kinda look a little like prison ink," Li teased. "And why is Linda on top of Li?" They both laughed at the unintended double entendre. "What I meant to say," Li blushed, "is how did you get top billing? It's close, but I'm pretty sure Li comes before Linda in the alphabetical order thing."

"It's the only way I could get our names to fit in the heart right," Linda said, nibbling on her ear of corn. "It's the thought that counts." The couple next to them at the table left, and a shadow passed over as two men took their place.

"Hey, girls." Li turned and looked at the speaker now sitting next to her. His sweaty knee touched her thigh under the table, and she cringed. She figured the man was in his late forties or early fifties, with a receding hairline shaved to stubble. He had a fat, gray mustache and blue eyes that might've been attractive once, but now looked dull and mean. Ropy muscles flexed inside a dirty white t-shirt with the sleeves torn off. The shirt featured a blocky red cross and the words *BONER DONER* in red. The guy next to Linda had broad, sloping shoulders. His blond crew cut framed his piggish face. He was young enough to be the other guy's son. His sunburned face matched his red, sleeveless t-shirt with the words, *I DIDN'T FART MY ASS BLEW YOU A KISS*. Li looked at Linda and saw she had pulled her hands into her lap and was looking down. She reminded Li of a beautiful flower that closes its petals into itself before a storm.

"You two look like you could use some company," the older man leered. "A little male companionship." He took a slug of Lite beer and licked his lips.

If that was meant to be sensuous, it missed the mark, Li thought.

"Kenny," he said. "Why don't you buy these two hot women a couple beers?"

"That's okay. We're good." Li said.

The guy put a wet arm around Li's shoulders and leaned into her. She could smell his foul breath and sour body odor. "We insist," he said, rubbing her arm. Li wanted to punch him in the face, but she felt a cold and paralyzing terror. She looked across at Linda and saw her trembling. Despite the heat and humidity, she felt the same chill. Cold fear. But also a glint of anger. Deep inside. Broad daylight in front of tens of thousands of people, and this shit was happening. *Do something*, she shouted inside her head. An elbow strike to the man's face would probably be all it would take, she thought. She could get plenty of torque up in the small space between them. The people around them would notice a flicker of movement and then his head snapping back, blood spurting from his ruined nose. Li felt the man's hand sliding off her shoulder and onto her ribcage, then ranging higher. She shook off his hand as she stood up, knocking his beer over. The cold amber

CHAPTER TWENTY-FOUR

liquid doused the front of his jean shorts. "The fuck!" he yelled, reaching for her again, but Li had already rounded the small table and pulled Linda out of her seat. "Come on."

It was slow going through the crowd, and within thirty strides, Li felt a strong hand grip her shoulder and turn her around. She let go of Linda's hand and naturally adopted a fighting stance, when a uniformed MPD officer stepped in. She had a hand on her baton. She looked at Li and then Linda. "Everything okay here?"

"Peachy," the older man said, answering for them. "Just enjoying a nice evening with the ladies."

"That right?" the officer asked Li and Linda. Linda wasn't making eye contact, and Li's throat felt constricted. *What the fuck is wrong with me?* The officer shrugged and turned to leave when Li blurted, "No, officer; it's not okay. We don't know these two. They're making us uncomfortable as hell." It came out in a rush, and her heart hammered.

"You want to press charges?" the officer asked, her fingers sliding to the microphone button on her shoulder. "Say the word. It's been kind of slow so far."

"Can you charge guys for being assholes?" Li asked, her voice firmer.

"Not sure there's a statute for that."

"Then maybe it was more of a misunderstanding, if these guys can take a hint," Li said.

Li flinched as the older guy flashed her a barracuda grin. "Darlin, we were just leavin'. Maybe we'll see y'all around sometime." The three women watched as the men melted into the slithering mass of people. Li shook her head to try to shake the sense of stink and repulsion. She reached for Linda's hand, but Linda just shrunk more into herself. The officer took off her sunglasses and slipped them into her shirt pocket. When Linda still wouldn't make eye contact, she looked directly at Li. "I'll repeat myself. Everything okay? I got a bad vibe from those guys."

"You've got good instincts, then," Li said, rolling her shoulders in a futile attempt to ease her stress. "I don't know what they could have been charged with, unless being creepy is a felony now. We're glad you came by when you did, though. Thank you."

The officer nodded. "Maybe I'll see if I can catch up to them. If they're going around making more women uncomfortable, I'll find something to write them up on. Take care." The officer moved off with the flow.

"We need to go," Linda blurted. She was shivering, and Li was afraid maybe she was in shock.

"Hey," Li said, trying to catch Linda's eyes. "Those guys freaked me out too. I'm embarrassed to admit it. But I wonder if we should wait a while to make sure they aren't still hanging around."

Linda's face was pinched, and tears started to spill down her face. "Please. I just want to go."

Li's heart sank. It had been such a beautiful afternoon. And now it was ruined. She looked around to see if the men who'd harassed them were still in the area. When she didn't pick them out of the crowd, she said, "Okay. I'm sorry. Let's go." They walked to the exit gate. They'd parked at a Tosa shopping mall and taken the freeway flyer to Summerfest so they wouldn't have to worry about fighting traffic or drinking and driving. They found the bus that would take them back to the mall and settled in toward the back; Linda huddled against the window, trying to make herself small and invisible. Li was thinking about how best to console her when the *BONER DONOR* and his friend *MY ASS BLEW YOU A KISS* shuffled noisily down the aisle along with a tall, scrawny guy with long, greasy brown hair tucked under a tattered baseball cap that read, *Titties & Beer, That's why I'm here.*

Linda's eyes fluttered open, and she saw them coming down the aisle. Something between a moan and a sob escaped her lips, and she squeezed her eyes shut, hoping it was a bad dream. Li's heart rate picked up, and she turned to follow the men's movement. The older guy dropped into the seat across the aisle from Li, and his two buddies sat down in the seat right behind her and Linda. A fourth guy got onto the bus and sat directly behind the driver. He pulled something from his pocket and held it down by his thigh. Li couldn't see what it was, and she couldn't make out what he said to the bus driver, but she heard the door close with a hiss and felt the bus shudder and begin to move.

CHAPTER TWENTY-FOUR

"Missed you, girlfriend," the older guy said to Li, with a sick smile that wasn't reflected in his eyes. "When we saw you two lickin' those corncobs it got the blood pumpin' a bit. Kenny and me felt a connection. I ain't never been with an Asian gal before, but I'm open. I hear you know how to please your men." He leaned toward her, and his body odor overpowered the smell of the bus's diesel exhaust, the mix curdling in Li's stomach. His eyes caught hers, and his grin seemed more like the snarl of a rabid animal. It carried the promise of pain and humiliation. "What do ya say, you aim to please me? Us?" His low laugh mocked her.

"Ah, Dan? Danno? You mighta missed somethin' with these two," the guy with the *titties* ballcap said.

The older man kept his eyes on Li. "The fuck you talkin' about?" he growled.

"You missed somethin', big guy." He laughed and pointed to the matching *Linda + Li* heart tattoos. "These two ain't sword swallowers; they're carpet munchers, looks like. I think you're trying to skinny dip with two muff divers!" He laughed even louder.

The older man looked from one tattoo to the other. He cocked his head, and the evil on his face simmered. "Hmmm. Don't that beat all. Lonnie, you ever seen two hotties like this kiss before? I never. Prime women too. I'd like to see that for damn sure."

Kenny's eyes were big. He leaned forward against the back of the women's seat and rested a meaty finger on Linda's shoulder, tracing the heart. Li could almost see Linda's skin crawl, curling away like a fern that's been touched. "Huh," Dan said. "She thinks she's better'n you, Kenny. You kinda repulse her. How's that make you feel?"

Li watched Kenny's face grow splotchy red. He reminded her of a perverted version of Lennie from Steinbeck's *Of Mice and Men*. She had a flashback of two young women being attacked on a London bus a couple of years ago. She needed to do something but wasn't sure what. Her hands were clenched at her sides when Kenny snapped, grabbed Linda's hair, and tried to pull her over the seat. Her partner's scream was the trigger for Li. She exploded out of her seat and brought a left-handed hammerfist strike down across the bridge of big Kenny's nose and his left eye. Her hand was closed into a fist, but she struck him with the heel, protecting her knuckles. She'd been taught to keep driving after contact, and she put everything into it, snapping his nose and blinding him. Stunned, his hands flew to his face, releasing Linda. Li opened her right hand and was already delivering her second blow, hitting Kenny with the fleshy part at the base of her right hand, a palm strike that caught him under his meaty chin. She heard her own tribal scream as she tried to put his head through the roof of the bus with her follow-through. Instead, Kenny's neck snapped back, and he was out, his bulk slumping against his skinny sidekick, pinning him against the window. Dan reached across the aisle and grabbed Li's shoulder. "Fuckin cun…" he started to say as he tried to pull her into him. Li turned her hip and moved into the older man, landing a knife hand strike on the side of his neck with a thud, like a baseball bat hitting a side of beef. The neck has little protection and houses the main arteries that supply blood to the brain. The knife strike threw Dan's vertebrae out of alignment. His grip loosened, and he listed backward. Li saw the guy with the ballcap struggling to push Kenny's dead weight off him at the same time, she heard footsteps pounding up the aisle. The fourth guy who'd been sitting behind the bus driver ran toward her with a fixed blade held at his side. She stepped into the aisle as the guy was almost on her. When the attacker slowed, she flashed her left hand in front of his face, distracting him the way you might a kitten with a ball of yarn. He stabbed at her hand and missed. At the same time, Li put everything she had into a front right kick to his groin. Not exactly like trying to punt a football sixty yards down a football field, but close enough. Her shin caught him in the balls and would've driven his junk up inside his chest cavity if it wasn't attached. He hit the floor, curled up, and writhed in pain. Li noticed the bus had stopped, and she could see the driver talking animatedly into his phone. When she turned back to check on Linda, she saw her slumped down on the floor, out of harm's way for the time being. Her eyes were wide and fixed on Li's. She saw fear reflected in those eyes. *But was it fear of the men or of her?*

Seeing Kenny grab Linda and hearing her friend's scream had caused Li's

CHAPTER TWENTY-FOUR

brain to dump adrenaline into her bloodstream. Her breathing and heart rate jumped, and her muscles came alive. Her years of martial arts training took over, and she reacted before any rational thought crossed her mind. The titties cap guy finally wriggled out from under Kenny's considerable bulk and tried to hit Li with a pathetic right hand. She blocked it with her left forearm and landed a hammer-strike fist on his right temple. His eyes rolled back in his head, and he bounced off the window and splayed across his seatmate. Li heard Linda cry out and felt a hand graze her right shoulder. Dan was reaching out to her across the aisle, wobbly, his eyes glassy. She heard Linda sob again, and she spun once more, sending another knife hand into the same spot on Dan's neck that she'd nailed before. He crumpled to the floor as she heard "Milwaukee Police" shouted from the front of the bus. Li looked down and saw Linda cowering, avoiding her eyes.

Li's heart rate slowed, and she let out a huge sigh. She looked at Kenny, laid out in his seat with his piggish eyes closed, the blood trickling out of his mouth a darker red than his shirt and the shards of his teeth a duller white than the letters that screamed, *MY ASS BLEW YOU A KISS*. Lonnie looked like he was asleep, his long, greasy hair spilled across Kenny's stomach, his prized *titties* cap nowhere to be seen. She looked over and saw the guy who'd come at her with the knife, curled up in the fetal position. He'd vomited, and streams of half-digested food and beer clung to his face, hair, and clothes. *Apparently, we weren't the only ones in the mood for corn,* she thought dully, coming all the way down from the adrenaline rush as her eyes settled on the *BONER DONER*. He was sitting on the floor with his feet under him in an unnatural way, his back against the side of the bus. His head listed toward the side of his neck she'd struck twice with everything she'd had. His flat eyes were open, but vacant, and she noticed the gray of his mustache now matched the pallor of his skin.

Hands throbbing, Li slumped into her seat and closed her eyes to the world.

Chapter Twenty-Five

Cole left the office earlier than usual and called Michele on his way home. Then he swung by Sendik's food market to get provisions. By seven, he stood barefoot on Frau Newhouse's expansive brick paver patio, grilling gourmet burgers, bacon, and cheddar for him and Siracha for Michele. He had on gray deck shorts and a light blue V-neck t-shirt. He worked the burgers over the hot fire with the spatula in his right hand while his left hand caressed a cold glass of Happy Place from the Third Space Brewery just down the street. The balanced, hoppy pale ale had notes of fresh citrus. Cole loved it during the summer, but it was also one of his go-to beers year-round. He brought the honey-colored liquid to his nose, closed his eyes, and breathed in the relaxing smell of tropical fruit.

"Are you making out with your beer again?" Michele asked, setting a plate with sliced onions, jalapenos, and Muenster cheese on one of the grill's attached side tables.

Cole took a big sip and smiled at her. "You know how I like 'em…. Bold. Sassy. Full-bodied."

Michele had just taken a sip of her own beer, and she almost spit it out she laughed so hard. A few minutes later, they sat at a nearby wrought iron table. The lawn and flower garden were large but secluded. They had invited Frau Newhouse to join them for dinner, but it was her night to play canasta with a group of friends. Cole took a bite of burger and nudged a strand of gooey cheese into his mouth with his finger. He stole a glance at Michele attacking her own burger and couldn't think of anyplace he'd rather be, or anyone he'd rather be with.

CHAPTER TWENTY-FIVE

His phone vibrated on the table, and the original ringtone started blaring. He shrugged at Michele and gave her his best, *I'm sorry* look, as he swiped to answer, putting the phone on speaker. "Laney. It's Cole. I've got you on speaker with Michele. We're eating the best burgers ever, so I hope this is good."

"Yeah. About that… I'm still at the office slaving away. Absolutely starving, by the way. I could swing over to your place now while you throw a couple burgers on for me, if that would help."

"That's a negative, Ghost Rider. The pattern is full."

Both Lane and Michele laughed at the Top Gun quip. Michele pulled out her phone and fired off a text while Lane replied, "Fine. Hopefully, you guys have something to write on, 'cause I've got some good stuff here."

"Fire away," Cole said.

"You wanted me to follow the money, and I did. I went back twenty years, and over that time, the pharmaceutical and health products industry spent the most on lobbying our elected officials. More than any other group."

"Really? Big pharma outspent the defense and aerospace industries? More than the energy companies? That's wild," Cole said.

"Yeah," Lane agreed. "Pharma wins the lobbying arms race hands down. They handed out close to five billion dollars over that time. Billions with a 'B.'"

"Wow," Michele said.

"Wow, indeed," Lane agreed. "Under the pharma umbrella, a group called the American Pharmaceutical Advocacy Group, APAG, spent the most, followed by some of the world's biggest drug manufacturers. APAG is their trade association, and they spend twice what any of the individual pharma companies spend on lobbying. I noticed something else. Even though they bill themselves as American, APAG's membership includes companies headquartered in other countries, like Switzerland, Germany, England, France, and others. So, pharma companies from other privileged countries are lining the pockets of our politicians to keep their profits up."

"Sonofabitch! I can't believe this is even legal," Cole said.

"Believe it. And as if big pharma isn't enough, guess who comes in at

111

number two in the race to throw money at our congressmen and other elected officials?"

"This isn't Jeopardy," Cole said, taking a big swallow of his beer.

"What is the insurance industry," Lane answered in his best Alex Trebek imitation. "Led by the health insurance industry, of course. Those guys have historically been the second most aggressive or generous lobbying group, depending on your perspective. And they've been handing out more and bigger bags of cash since the Affordable Care Act came into being. One payer spent the most on lobbying, followed by the American Health Insurance Association, AHIA, and a host of other insurance companies. You bring up the term 'single payer' around those guys, and it's like hitting a hornet's nest with a short stick."

"Big pharma and health insurance, one and two in terms of lobbying spend," Cole said, shaking his head. "Of course, they would be. And those are the two industries Senator Rhodes went after in his speech."

"Here's something else. The CEO of APAG makes more than three million dollars a year, and at least five of the pharma CEOs at individual companies make more than fifteen million dollars a year in compensation. The highest paid makes forty million."

"You can scrape by on that, I suppose," Cole said.

"Right. The president and CEO of AHIA is a piker by comparison, making just under a million. But the CEOs at the biggest health insurance companies are making tens of millions a year like their pharma counterparts. So, we've got plenty of people and companies, not to mention a couple of big trade associations, who all have a hell of a lot to lose if our favorite Wisconsin senator's ideas become law."

"You just have to narrow down your list of suspects now," Michele said. "How hard can that be?"

"Ha. Ha." Cole said. "Lane, did anyone interview the guy who tried to kill Li and me yet? The guy whose brain is still functioning?"

"You aren't gonna believe this. Dan Willis, the director of H.I.G., showed up to talk to him."

"What's H.I.G.?" Michele asked.

CHAPTER TWENTY-FIVE

"It's the High-Value Detainee Interrogation Group. H.I.G. for short," Lane answered. "Their job isn't typically law enforcement. They're supposed to collect intelligence that protects national security. They're the best in the business when it comes to interrogations, and Dan Willis is the best of the best. I'm guessing Gene Olson sent him here because Cole is one of his favorites."

"Whatever," Cole said. "Did Willis get anything out of that asshole hired gun? I would've liked to have a crack at interviewing the scumbag."

"Surprisingly," Lane said, "Our betters thought that might be a bit of a conflict of interest. Him trying to kill you and all. And 'No.' The H.I.G. Meister didn't get anything worthwhile from the guy today. But this was just a first pass. A warmup. I'm sure he'll ratchet the pressure up over the next day or two."

"I'm not sure it'll do any good. I'll bet the thug is being well taken care of by whoever's behind this. It sure as hell isn't a low budget operation."

"We did get a hit on his fingerprints."

"Nice! And?" Cole prodded.

"And both he and the guy you put in intensive care were members of the U.S. Marines until two years ago when they were dishonorably discharged. Terry Hawkins and Roger Jones. Apparently, they liked kicking ass a little too much and weren't all that particular about whose asses they kicked. The D.C. analysts have been digging around, and they can't find any discernable employment for these two since they got booted out of the military. Yet they both live high on the hog. The analysts are digging deeper to trace how they get paid and who's behind the payments. They're making progress."

"So, we got that goin' for us, which is nice," Cole deadpanned.

"Channeling your inner Carl Spackler again," Lane said. There was a brief muffled conversation, and Lane came back on. "Hey! Matt from security just poked his head in my office to tell me that Faklandia Brewing called to tell him they're dropping off a bunch of pizzas for the staff. He said it's on you, Michele. Thanks, from us minions! If they include one of their Thuja Hawaiian pies, I might propose to you!"

"Whoa, Rump. I think you just crossed a line there." Cole said.

"Who's Rump?" Michele asked.

"Nobody. It's nothing," Lane blurted. "He's been drinking, right? That's probably it. Seriously, Michele, thanks for thinking of us grunts stuck here at the office while the boss lives his playboy lifestyle."

"Anything else, Rumparoni?"

"Not at this time, boss."

"Okay. If there's any pizza left over, save me some. I'll see you tomorrow."

"I make no promises I cannot keep," Lane said as he clicked off.

A tub of French onion dip lay between them on the table, and both Michele and Cole hovered over it with a ruffled chip. "You first," Cole said. Made on the other side of the state in the town of Westby, the dip won blue ribbons at the Wisconsin State Fair. "Tell me we're not going to eat the whole tub in one sitting again," Michele groaned, digging in. "I love it, but I'm not sure it's good for my girlish figure."

"Your figure's just fine. And besides," he said, nudging the tub of dip toward her. "It says it's 'farmer owned.' If we can enjoy this while helping our local dairy farmers, it's a win, win. Just be thankful I didn't get the one-pound tub."

A gentle breeze swirled in off the lake, and they enjoyed the quiet for a moment. Normal felt pretty good when you hadn't felt it in a while.

Michele broke the spell. "I've got another angle to look into on Senator Rhodes' shooting."

Cole smiled. "You after my job?"

Michele blushed. "You think I'm silly, right? Like, how can the reporter help?"

Cole turned serious and put a hand on her arm. "You know, I'd never think that. You helped us figure out Deputy Hubbard was the one killing those physicians. Without you on that case, I'm sure more physicians would have been murdered. I don't know of anyone whose ideas I value more."

She saw the truth in his eyes and heard something deeper than respect in his voice. She nodded. "Have you ever heard of brown envelope journalism?"

Cole plopped a salty chip laden with dip into his mouth, and he savored it as he thought about the question. He shook his head.

CHAPTER TWENTY-FIVE

"It's a dirty secret in my industry," Michele said. "It's where a journalist accepts money to slant a story in a certain direction." She waved a chip in the air for emphasis. "Say you're a developer, and you want to fill in some wetlands so you can build a lakefront tower filled with million-dollar condos.

Cole nodded, licking dip off a finger. "I'm liking that. I'm gonna get rich building me some condos. Early retirement, here I come."

"Right. But you're fighting environmental groups, and the city fathers are on the fence. What would your company pay for a big, fat story that touted all the jobs created by your condo project and all the good it would do for the community?"

"That would be worth a lot," Cole conceded.

"Cash for coverage…for stories, for or against. It's called brown envelope journalism because reporters in different countries have been caught accepting brown envelopes with cash to bias their coverage. Some have started to just call it 'brown journalism' now, because the stories are full of shit. It's hard to tell how often it happens. I know a couple bloggers who have deals set up with certain manufacturers, and they're paid three hundred and fifty dollars every time they mention their brands. But even though they're influencers, most bloggers aren't considered journalists."

"Where are you going with this?"

"I'm thinking about that reporter from the New York Times…the only one who wasn't fawning all over our Senator after his speech. The guy's name is James Flood. "When all the other reviews of that speech were overwhelmingly positive, Flood panned it. He said Senator Rhodes has charisma and is a clever orator. But those were backhanded compliments; he basically called Rhodes a charlatan. He went on to describe Rhodes as naïve and said there's no way to pay for the changes he's calling for. I was just wondering, what would it hurt to have a conversation with him to see if anyone paid him to slant that review. Let's say Flood is behind on his rent or car payments. Maybe he likes to gamble a little too much. Is it hard to believe he might quietly take ten or twenty thousand dollars to throw his review?"

Cole mulled it over while slowly chewing on another chip. The sweet, tangy dip, combined with the salt and oil of the chips were simple but guilty pleasures.

"I've been looking into the whole idea of paying reporters," Michele said. "And while I couldn't find many stories where a journalist from a mainstream media outlet was caught taking money from a source, I saw a recent poll that showed sixty percent of the public is convinced it's common practice. When Disney World in Orlando celebrated its fifteenth anniversary years ago, it invited over ten thousand journalists and their families to come down for a free, four-day vacation. Lots of reporters took them up on that. It doesn't seem hard to believe that at least a few reporters for big-time papers or networks would accept bigger money for bigger stories. And, frankly, it would be hard to tell who's doing it and who isn't."

"Kind of like a pitcher taking money to throw a baseball game," Cole agreed, nodding. "A good pitcher can be lights out five games in a row, almost unhittable, and the sixth game, he can't figure out how to get a ball across the plate or keep one in the ballpark. We all just shrug it off as, 'it wasn't his day.' It happens in basketball, too. One game a guy can hit eight of ten shots from three-point range, and the next day he misses every shot he takes. Was it better defense, or did someone slip him money to change the outcome?"

"Exactly. Reporters aren't perfect, either. Every once in a while, we rush a story or get a little lazy and write a clinker. And editors aren't looking for this stuff. Another thing I've learned is that I don't even think it's illegal. It's unethical as hell, and a reporter might lose her job for taking money to write a certain story or review, but she wouldn't be breaking a law that I can see."

Cole hovered over the dip and looked at Michele. She indicated she was done, and he picked up the tub and scraped out the remnants with a sturdy chip. He caught her eyes. "So, you want me to go to New York and have a chat with this reporter, James Flood?"

Either mischief or the day's last rays of sunlight sparkled in Michele's eyes. "No. I'm saying you and I should go to New York and lean on the reporter.

CHAPTER TWENTY-FIVE

Together. I know the industry and the temptations better than you do. I can help you sweat him."

Cole smiled. "Lean on. Sweat. Are we doing this at a fitness center?"

She laughed and threw her napkin at him.

"I like it. But aren't you busy getting your book to print?"

Michele had landed a fat contract from one of the big five publishers to write her account of the case of the reproductive health physician murders. She'd taken a sabbatical from her reporting job with the *Milwaukee Journal Sentinel* in order to finish it while it was still fresh in the public psyche.

"I am," she said. "I turned in my first draft a while ago and already responded to the developmental edits they asked for. My publisher's main office is in New York, and they want to meet with me and my agent to finalize the marketing and publicity plan and to pick out a cover. If you and I go tomorrow, I could kill two birds with one stone."

He nodded. "It's definitely worth the trip. I could have somebody from the New York field office sit down with Flood, but even after everything that's gone down, I don't think there's anybody in D.C. other than Gene Olson that wants me to pursue this." He caught her eye. "I probably won't see you much after your book is released, right? I imagine you'll be on some cross-country book tour."

"Some of it's virtual now, but I will be on the road. I have to admit it sounds kind of glam, but it'll also be a lot of work." Her smile was soft and hopeful. "Are you going to miss me?"

Cole felt his heart fill up, and his eyes misted over. A comfortable darkness covered the patio. He knew Michele still had moments where she was fragile, but he also saw her growing strength. "More than you know," he answered. He leaned toward her, wanting nothing more than a gentle kiss, when his phone's ringtone cleaved the night's stillness.

"For the love of God," he said, shaking his head. He thought about letting it go to voicemail but saw that it was their mutual friend, MPD Lieutenant Ty Igou calling. He showed her the caller ID as he swiped to answer, setting the phone down between them. "Hi, Ty! I'm sitting here with Michele, and I have you on speaker."

"Cole, it's about Li," Ty said. "She and Linda were on their way home from Summerfest on a city bus when they were attacked by four thugs…"

"Is Li okay?" Cole interrupted, panic in his voice.

"Yes. Yes. Physically, she's fine. According to the bus driver, she righteously kicked all four of the bad guys' asses. Three are in the hospital. One of those will never have kids, which is a benefit to society from my perspective. The other two have massive concussions and facial trauma, but I'm told they were both ugly as sin to begin with. They're going to need plastic surgery and maybe dental work. The fourth guy didn't make it; he died at the scene from a broken neck. Remind me the next time I see Li not to piss her off."

Cole tried to take it all in. "So, Li's fine?"

"She was checked out at the scene, and the report I saw said she only had some minor bruising and swelling of her hands. But her friend Linda is in the hospital being treated for shock. She's messed up and refuses to see anyone, including Li."

"You know Li, Ty. Have you had a chance to talk to her yet?"

"No. She came in and gave a statement that was corroborated by the bus driver's story. It turns out these same guys hassled Li and Linda on the SummerFest grounds. We found an officer who backed up that story. We should have video from the bus too. Our guys think Li's a hero, and they didn't push her. She didn't seem to be in shock when she was in the precinct station, but they could tell it hit her pretty hard. They offered to take her home, but she called an Uber. You should know, this will be big news by tomorrow at the latest."

"Jesus," Cole said to both Michele and Ty. "That's two days in a row that someone tried to physically hurt or kill her. I don't care how strong you are, that's got to throw you for a loop." To Ty, he added, "I need to go. Please call me back if you hear anything more. I'll let you know how she's doing after I catch up to her. And thanks for calling, buddy. I really appreciate it."

"No problem, Cole. Talk to you soon."

Cole looked at Michele, and even in the dim light, he saw his concern reflected in her eyes. "I'm sorry, Michele, but I need to leave. I'm going to

CHAPTER TWENTY-FIVE

go find her. I have a bad feeling about this."

Chapter Twenty-Six

Cole changed back into the day's uniform, a navy suit, white button-down shirt, and a burgundy tie. He drove across the Hoan Bridge with the windows down, the cool lake breeze helping clear his mind. Fully dark now, the bridge was lit up in a rainbow of colors that were reflected in the water. Area residents donated five million dollars and counting so they could "Light the Hoan" every night. The lighting changed often, and tonight was a celebration of gay pride. Cole stepped harder on the gas pedal.

Ten minutes later he flipped on the lights in his office and sat at his desk. He heard a crinkle and felt something under him, so he stood up and saw the envelope with *Cole* written on the outside. He traced his name with a finger and wondered, *Who writes in cursive anymore*, but he had a pretty good idea who'd left it for him. He didn't bother with a letter opener, ripping the end in a jagged tear. He unfolded the letter and read…

Dear Cole,

With this letter, I am resigning my position with the Federal Bureau of Investigation. I greatly appreciate all the support you have given me over the past few years, especially the mentorship you provided as I've explored transitioning from analyst to agent. You are an amazing leader and friend. The past two days, I have been tested and failed. In the first instance, my fear led to paralysis, and my inaction could have gotten us both killed. In the second, my anger led me to be overly aggressive. I put three men in the hospital and killed another. My partner saw something

CHAPTER TWENTY-SIX

in me tonight that so repulsed her that I don't think our relationship can be mended. I thought about staying on as an analyst, but believe it is best if I walk away completely. Please tell my colleagues that I care about them and will miss them.

I'm sorry I let you all down.

Li Song

"Dammit!" Cole shouted to the empty room. He ripped the letter into small pieces and threw them in the air. As the confetti fluttered down around him, he picked up his desk phone and punched in a number. "Hey, this is Cole. I need an immediate trace on a cell phone."

Cole pulled up in front of a bar on Milwaukee's near south side a half hour later. A photo of the outside of the tavern probably accompanied the definition of "dive bar" or "hole in the wall" in some online dictionary. It wasn't the kind of place Li would typically hang out, and Cole wondered for a moment if someone might have taken her phone during the day's chaos. But he shook his head as he opened his car door and stepped out into the night; it was exactly the kind of place *he* would pick if he wanted to punish himself. Li would be no different.

He stepped around a wall of Harley bikes and stood in front of the tavern, bracing himself. He looked at the bright sign above him that read, *Jim's Bar*, and heard the angry pop and snarl of old neon. He didn't know exactly what to expect when he pushed through the door, but he figured it wouldn't be good. No warm welcome to be sure. Jim's was the kind of place you might go to get a cold longneck or shot of whiskey on the cheap in the late afternoon. It would be a good place to stop by in the evening if you wanted to test your fist-fighting prowess. After midnight, you'd be smart to carry a knife, or better yet a gun, if you stepped inside.

Cole could hear Jerry Jeff Walker and a chorus of drunks through the door, singing the last refrain of *Up Against the Wall Redneck Mother*. He took a deep breath and pushed into the smoky bar. Apparently, this was sovereign ground and not covered by the state's indoor smoking ban. He stopped just inside and scanned the bar without moving his head. He saw hard men

THE KILLER SPEECH

in jeans and T-shirts and women in shorts and halter tops. Hard men and maybe harder women. *Jim's Bar,* Cole said to himself. *Where the men are men and the women are too.* A smile tugged at the corners of his mouth.

He felt first one pair of eyes on him and then another. Pretty soon it went around the room like the wave at a crowded football stadium until everyone was staring at him. His grin got bigger. He knew he looked like a polar bear at a grizzly convention with his suit and tie. He kept his body relaxed and tilted his head a bit, as he made a show of surveying the crowd. He reached slowly into the inside of his suit coat with his left hand and flipped open his FBI credentials. "My name is Cole Huebsch, and I'm with the FBI," he said in a practiced voice that was even but carried over the jukebox to the back of the bar. "Right now, this is purely a social call. But if I get shit from anybody, I've got plenty of reasons to turn this place and anyone in it upside down." The grin never left his face, and he put his badge back into his jacket and said, "Carry on."

He caught Li's reflection in a mirror toward the back of the bar, sitting in a booth with two big guys crowding her. He walked directly to their table as Jimmy Buffet crooned, "Why Don't We Get Drunk And Screw."

"Gentlemen," he said when he reached the booth. "Thanks for keeping the lady company until I could get here. Now, you can leave quietly and hang on to whatever teeth you still have left. Or you can make trouble. Frankly, it's been a trying couple days, and I'm okay with whatever decision you make." The two men looked at Cole and then at each other, deciding. It could have gone either way, but the bigger of the two men shook his head and pushed back his chair. He headed for the bar, and his friend followed.

Cole blew out a breath and looked at Li. "Nice place. You come here often?" Li was still beautiful, with her long black hair falling over the white sleeveless blouse. But her chestnut and sky-blue eyes were glassy, and she held an icy bottle of Bud against her swollen right hand. Five empty and overturned shot glasses glimmered on the table in front of her. "This place has a certain kind of charm and ambiance," Cole said. "If it were any more of a dive bar, they'd have to cover the walls with wet suits and scuba gear."

Li giggled. "Were you trying to be Harry Callahan with those two guys?"

CHAPTER TWENTY-SIX

Her words weren't slurred, but she took her time saying them, enunciating each one. She reached for the bowl of mini pretzels in front of her and managed to get most of a small handful into her mouth. She giggled again.

"What? Dirty Harry?" Cole asked. He wrinkled his nose and frowned. "Absolutely not. Did you see me pull out my gun and ask the punks if they felt lucky? I was going more for Martin Riggs in Lethal Weapon. I think psycho crazy has a higher intimidation factor." He reached for the pretzels, reflected on all the hands that had pawed through the bowl, and thought better of it. A waitress came to the table and set a napkin in front of him. She wore a wife beater T-shirt and sported cleavage and curled orange hair whose giant waves might have been shaped by industrial-sized tomato cans. She stood with a hand on her ample hip and glared at Cole. "Whadaya want?"

Cole held up a hand, asking for a minute. He didn't know the song blaring from the unseen jukebox, but the words made him do a double take. *Them alligators in the delta, I'm certain that they smelled ya, washin your big ol pussy before you go to town.* "Am I hearing what I think I'm hearing?"

The waitress huffed and rolled her eyes. "The song's called *Washin My Big Ol' Pussy*. It's by Birdcloud." She didn't add, *"I'm surprised you didn't know that,"* but he heard it in her tone. "Now, whadaya want?"

"Tell the barkeep to get me the coldest longneck he's got that's not a Lite beer." She nodded and turned to go. "And Miss?" he said loudly, catching her attention and turning her around. "Tell him that if he spits in my beer bottle, I will rip out his larynx and bring it home to feed my goldfish."

The waitress rolled her eyes and went to place his order. Li leaned into him conspiratorially. "You don't have any goldfish," she whispered.

Cole winked. "You and I know that, but the waitress and the bartender don't." Li laughed, and chunks of pretzel spattered Cole's white shirt. He shook his head again. He could tell that some of the men in the bar were pissed that he'd walked in and done what he pleased, and he felt certain they were pouring liquid courage down their throats and would start trouble at any time. He pulled out his phone and dialed.

"Hey, Lieutenant Igou," he said, loud enough for people around to hear. "It's me. Keep the guys in line. I know the men are spoiling to kick in doors

THE KILLER SPEECH

and knock heads, but the fine citizens in here are playing nicely." He paused, listening, before concluding. "Yeah, I should be out in ten minutes or so. See you then." He disconnected and slipped the phone back into his pocket.

"You called Ty? Why are you bringing MDP into this?" she giggled. "I mean, MPD."

Cole leaned closer and whispered. "That was my voicemail I just called."

Li's face scrunched up in a puzzled expression for a five count before her eyes got big, and she wagged a finger at Cole. "Ohhhhh. I get it. You're being sneak...."

Cole covered her mouth with his hand and nodded. "Yes. I am."

She tried to wink at him, but instead nodded and blinked both eyes. "We need to talk," Cole said, "and this isn't the place for it. I know a spot we can get a bite to eat and a cup of coffee. Come on."

Li wobbled when she got up, and Cole put her arm around his shoulder and started walking her to the exit. They were halfway to the door when the bigger of the two guys who'd been at Li's booth earlier intercepted them with a broken beer bottle for a weapon. Cole was considering pushing Li to safety and putting the guy down when the big guy sneered. "She's not goin' anywhere with you, buddy. She's..." Before he could finish, Li stepped forward with a right front kick, landing it hard in his midsection. He went down, flat on his back, and Li went white. She threw up a syrupy mix of corn, pretzels, whiskey, and beer that splashed the guy on the floor. She retched again, and he got a second coat of puke. She wiped her mouth with the back of her hand. "Sorry," she groaned.

"And that's the way we roll," Cole shouted over his shoulder as he pushed open the door and carried her into the night. The door hung open, and the jukebox kicked up again, and Cole sang along with Big and Rich on "Save a Horse, Ride a Cowboy," as he helped Li to his car.

Cole and Li walked under the large iconic red sign with white letters that read GEORGE WEBB five minutes later. George Webb opened his first diner in Milwaukee more than seventy years ago. When the city fathers created an ordinance that forbade establishments from being open round the clock, he advertised that his restaurant was open twenty-three hours and

CHAPTER TWENTY-SIX

fifty-nine minutes a day, every day of the week, including Sunday. His diner was clean and well-lit and served good food and hot coffee at reasonable prices, which is why Milwaukee now had twenty-eight of the restaurants in the city and surrounding suburbs.

It was still an hour before bar time, and the late crowd wouldn't start trickling in for a while. They had their choice of sitting on the swivel stools at the counter, at a table, or a booth. Cole thought the booth would provide a more stable base for Li; he steered her to the closest one and poured her into it.

He was still settling in when a waitress hustled over and set two colorful paper placemats in front of them, along with their steel eating utensils wrapped in white paper napkins. Then she set down two stout white mugs and filled them to the brim with steaming coffee. The waitress looked to be in her early twenties, and she had a nice smile. Cole read her T-shirt, *I SURVIVED BURGERMANIA*, and her nametag, *Helen*. George Webb himself had promised Milwaukee Brewers fans free burgers if the hometown baseball team ever won twelve games in a row, and his stores made good on that promise twice. It happened during the 1987 season and again just a couple years ago. Webb restaurants served more than a hundred thousand free burgers with all the fixings each time.

"You look like a Helen," Cole said. "And I love the shirt. Which Burgermania did you survive?"

"A wisenheimer, huh? I wasn't even a gleam in mama's eye the first time around!" She nodded at the menu. "Do you two know what you want yet?"

It hadn't been all that long since Cole had put away the burger and chips, but he ordered the Classic Breakfast; two eggs over easy, hash browns, and rye toast. Li tried to get by with just the coffee, but Cole insisted she put something solid in her stomach to soak up whatever alcohol was still in her system.

Li gave in, "Alright. I'll have the California burger with fries."

"Now that's the Li I know and love," Cole said as Helen laughed and finished writing up their order.

Li's head was hanging, and her black hair shielded her face. It had lost some of its luster. Cole unwrapped his silverware and smoothed the paper napkin in his lap. Then he took a big slug of coffee and waited.

After a minute or two, Li lifted her head and tucked her hair behind her ears. She looked directly at Cole, and he was taken again by her eyes, each with its own color and brilliance, but sharing the same sadness and maybe shame. "I'm sorry," she said, tearing up.

Cole smiled. "That's the second time you've said you were sorry in the past half hour, and both times the sentiment was misplaced. First when you puked, twice, on the loser in the bar. If anyone deserved to be barfed on, it was that guy. He was a puke. And there's no need to tell me you're sorry now. If it's about your resignation, I'm not accepting it…not the resignation or the apology. I won't let you make a decision regarding your career within a few hours of being attacked and having to defend yourself and someone you love, and certainly not within a few hours of you killing someone in self-defense. You're an analyst, but you haven't been thinking like one the past couple days. You've reacted emotionally instead of analyzing the situations. What happened today on the bus might not feel good, but if you think it through, you'll realize that you did the right thing."

Li sighed heavily, and her eyes strayed down to her hands. She had subconsciously been massaging her right one. He could tell she was starting to come out of her alcohol-induced fog, but sober and sad were synonyms for a reason. "I don't know what to do," she said.

"Why don't you just sit and listen for a minute, and drink some of that coffee while it's hot. I want to help walk you through what happened on the bus, and maybe what would have happened if you hadn't acted the way you did. Okay?"

Li took a small sip of the coffee and nodded.

"Good," Cole said. "Now, why do you think those guys picked you and Linda?" He waited. "You think it was because the four of them thought, 'This will be a challenge?'" He waited again before answering his own question. "Hell no! They picked you because they're predators and they thought you two were weak. Easy prey. They underestimated you big time. And they each paid a price for it. But if you hadn't handled it the way you did, they

CHAPTER TWENTY-SIX

would have hurt you…both of you. And they would have gone on to do it again and again until someone put a stop to it. So, because you had the courage and the skill to stand up and stop those guys, they won't be on the street anymore to humiliate or maybe murder other women.

"You feel like shit, and I get that. But get over it. Linda may or may not ever look at you the same way she did before you two got on that bus, but you did what you had to do and nothing more. She's in shock now and not thinking straight, but if she can't handle what you did tonight, then maybe she doesn't deserve you. Everyone will tell you that what you did was righteous, but that doesn't feel right to you either, because you killed a man tonight. But I know you didn't mean to kill him. You had to take him off the board and you had to hurt him to do that. In a situation like you were faced with, where you're being attacked and worse, someone you love is being attacked, you can't help but feel anger, fear, or hate. Maybe all three. We're not robots.

"For the record, *I* think what you did on that bus tonight was righteous. I talked to Ty on the way over to the bar you were at, and he told me his guys believe the creeps you beat down on the bus have done this kind of thing before. They have a couple open cases they're checking the DNA against, and they believe they're going to get matches and clear other unsolved rape and battery cases. It will give those women and their families a little peace of mind, and it will make sure those predators are put away where they belong."

"Did those guys really hurt other women?" Li asked, hopefully.

"Yes. We'll know more soon, but what happened tonight wasn't isolated. Four really nice guys didn't just have a couple beers today and go off the rails a little. Four sick, disgusting predators picked on the wrong person, and they were stopped for good."

"Well, I guess that's something," Li said.

"Yeah, if saving people from harm is important to you. But here's the thing, Li. I think you can be as good or better than any agent the Bureau's ever produced. We need more people like you in the FBI and in law enforcement in general…people who look inside when they've had to use force, especially lethal force. But then you have to heal and move on. If you don't develop a little more grit, then you'll prove me wrong about how good an agent you can become. In the end, though, I don't need you to change much at all. Just take a few days and let everything that's happened the last couple days sink in. Sort it out. I'm not going to beg you to stay, and I can't have you quit on me again. If you come back to work, then I'll know you're in for keeps."

Chapter Twenty-Seven

Cole didn't catch more than a cat nap after driving Li home. He and Michele were at Milwaukee Mitchell airport by five a.m. Their commercial flight was airborne by six and landed at LaGuardia in Queens two hours later. Cole dozed the entire flight. They hustled through the terminal without luggage; Cole's head was on a swivel, taking in the airport's new digs, sunlight streaming through expansive windows. This wasn't the hellhole he'd flown into and out of a dozen times before in his career. Even outside as they moved through the queue to get a cab, he noticed the rotten egg smell that used to overwhelm the airport was gone. It was a bright, sunny morning in the Big Apple.

It would be a half-hour drive from LaGuardia to the FBI field office in Manhattan without traffic. But though they'd lost an hour crossing time zones, nine-thirty in the morning was still considered part of the rush *hours* when navigating the city's seven boroughs. Their cabbie said it would take the better part of an hour. They rode in silence, and the bounce and sway of the cab lulled Cole back to a fitful sleep, worrying about Li. When he woke to Michele's gentle tug on his arm, he looked out his window, peering up at the forty-one-story Jacob K. Javits federal building. The New York field office was the largest in the country, housing more than two thousand agents, support staff, and task force members.

The temperature hadn't reached eighty degrees yet, but the high humidity gave the air weight, and they pushed through it and across the street. They entered the pavilion off Broadway and immediately stalled behind a long line of humanity. The skyscraper housed nineteen other federal agencies besides the FBI, including the U. S. Citizenship and Immigration Services, which sees more than one thousand visitors a day. The queue they were caught in waiting to get through security was mostly people in line for green card interviews.

Michele looked at her watch and then to Cole. "We still have a half hour before the interview. Thanks again for letting me tag along. I haven't helped on a case since Deputy Hubbard."

They were resigned to waiting their turn when a strong voice called from the front. "Cole! Cole! Up here!" Cole looked and saw Jack Gokey, the head of the New York field office, waving at them. Cole got a big grin on his face and started moving toward the man. "Come on," he said to Michele.

Each FBI field office is overseen by a special agent in charge, except the offices in L.A., D.C., and New York. Those three offices are headed by an assistant director in charge due to their large size. When Cole and Michele reached the security checkpoint, Gokey waved them through. They put anything that might set off the scanner in a plastic tub, including Cole's Glock, and then collected their phones and other personal items on the other side. The FBI police that kept the building secure ran Cole's credentials, and then Cole introduced Michele to Gokey as he slipped his Glock back into his holster. Gotham's assistant director in charge was a couple inches shorter than Cole and broader. Michele's head cocked when she saw the two men lean into a half-hug. Cole caught the look and explained. "Jack and I go back a ways. He went through Quantico, started his FBI training, a year ahead of me. I got to know him at conferences, because we both share an affinity for craft beers. Whenever we get together for training, we try to discover at least one new beer. I've also called him for advice from time to time, almost from the start."

Gokey led them to an expanse of elevators. "What Cole is failing to mention is that I call *him* for advice far more often than he calls me these days, and that whenever our training is physical, he delights in kicking my ass...which usually takes some doing."

When the elevator doors closed, Cole turned to Gokey. "Thanks for giving us the use of a conference room, and for getting James Flood to the table,

CHAPTER TWENTY-SEVEN

literally. Did he give your guys any trouble?"

"Surprisingly, not much. When my agents caught up with him at his apartment this morning, the first thing he said was he wanted a lawyer. They followed the script you gave me and told him that they would be glad to meet with him and his attorney at the New York Times Building, where they would also feel obliged to have a chat with his editor. Or he could accompany them here alone and have a more private conversation. He opted to come here. Alone."

A bell chimed, and they stepped out onto the twenty-third floor. As Gokey led them down a long, carpeted hallway, Cole thanked him. "You didn't have to watch out for us downstairs. I know how busy you guys are."

"No busier than you've been lately, and a heck of a lot safer, I'd say. Are you going to have time to grab a beer later? I found a new brewpub that's on the way back to the airport that makes an outstanding vanilla porter."

"Rain check. We're heading back tonight, and I'm hoping we can grab an early dinner at Uncle Peter's on our return to the airport."

Gokey looked from Cole to Michele and back to Cole. He nodded, smiling. "I see."

Cole shook his head. "You don't see anything, other than two people who want to get dinner on their way back to the airport."

Gokey shrugged. "He's never turned me down when I've asked him to grab a beer before. You must be special."

"She is that," Cole said, looking at Michele. "Hey," he said to her. "Can I borrow that reporter's notebook you always keep with you?"

She fished it out of her purse and handed it over with a questioning look. Instead of answering, he asked, "You told me Flood has covered politics and entertainment his whole career, right?" She nodded. Cole looked at his watch. "He should have been in there twenty minutes or so already. I don't really believe in icing someone before an interview anyway, so we might as well head in and get this over with."

"I'm going to let you two have all the fun. I need to get back and briefed on the latest terrorist update. No rest for the wicked or the good guys either. Safe travels." They shook hands all around, and Gokey opened the door and then closed it behind them.

Flood was seated at a long conference table but jumped up as soon as the door opened. He reminded Cole of the Scarecrow in Wizard of Oz, if the scarecrow wore a wrinkled brown suit with shiny lapels. "Why did you have me brought here?" Flood demanded in a squeaky voice.

"Sit down," Cole answered. His voice wasn't raised, but it was firm. "I'm asking the questions. My name is Cole Huebsch, FBI. With me today is Michele Fields, who is advising on an investigation. And you are a person of interest in our investigation." The last sentence hung in the air between them as he sat down at the table across from Flood, and Michele sat next to him. Cole looked out the window and noted the view was spectacular from that height. He flipped the notebook open and looked down at it, the book's back to Flood. He looked across the table. "Mr. Flood, I'm going to cut to the chase. We have reason to believe that you wrote a less than stellar review of a speech at the Democratic National Convention in exchange for a cash payment."

"What?" Flood shook his head. "I don't. I have no idea what you're talking about. Who told you that?"

Cole shook his head as if he was disappointed. "I told you I'm the one asking the questions, Flood. And it's irrelevant who shared this information with me. What matters is that you tell us the truth. The longer you lie and dodge, the worse it will get for you."

"I swear I don't know what you're talking about." Flood wiped a hand across his brow and licked his lips. You didn't need Cole's training in micro expressions to tell that the *Times* reporter was full of shit. Cole flipped through the notepad, looking down. "What if I told you we found a rather large deposit in your checking account about the time of the speech in question and that it did not come from the *New York Times*. What if I also told you that through your phone records, we can tell that someone we've been watching related to a key industry has been in contact with you. Would you stick to your story of knowing nothing? The easy thing for me to do here is to make the short drive to the *Times* building and ask your editor if she can clear this up for us. Maybe it's a simple misunderstanding."

CHAPTER TWENTY-SEVEN

Flood shook his head back and forth, and his mouth opened and closed like a fish out of water. Cole was reminded of something the scarecrow says in L. Frank Baum's novel *The Wonderful Wizard of Oz*, "It is such an uncomfortable feeling to know one is a fool." The man's eyes were pleading. "What do you want from me?"

"It's simple, really. I want you to confirm how much you took to throw your review and who paid you. If you lie, I'll know. If you tell the truth, I won't go to your editor with my findings and I won't pursue charges against you. Simple."

Flood put his head in his hands, and a strained sigh escaped his lips. He looked at Michele and then at Cole. "You won't come after me?"

Cole shook his head.

"They paid me forty thousand dollars. Anne Spaith from Dave Frank Communications set it up."

Cole could see Flood was telling the truth. He looked at Michele. "Anything you want to ask him?"

She stood up and leaned across the table, cutting the distance between them in half and multiplying the *Times* reviewer's discomfort. "I don't have any questions for Mr. Flood, but I do have a comment." Her eyes burned into his. "Do you have *any* self-respect?" She straightened, turned, and left the room.

Cole shrugged as he got up to leave. "I guess she thinks you're the kind of person who gives journalism a bad name. I'll have someone come get you in ten minutes or so. Until then, think about what you did and what you might do differently down the road. I don't want to see you again, and I'm pretty sure you aren't looking forward to a repeat of this conversation either. So, keep clean." He walked out and shut the door behind him.

Michele was waiting in the hall, and they walked toward the elevators together. "So, you used my reporter's notebook as a prop?"

"Uh-huh."

"And why did you want to know if he covered anything besides arts and entertainment in his career?"

"Well, if he covered the courts, he might know I was bullshitting him when

I said we had his phone records and bank account statements. We didn't have enough probable cause to get that kind of private information, but I was hoping he didn't know that. His lawyer most certainly would have."

She was smiling at him, nodding, as they passed the reception area, and Cole pushed the down button. "Do you need to tell someone we're done with Flood so they can let him go?"

Cole smiled back as the elevator swallowed them and carried them down toward the ground floor. "They'll figure it out eventually."

When they were outside, Michele caught a taxi to her appointment with her publisher and agent. Cole walked across the street and sat down at a café and ordered an obscenely priced cup of black coffee. He called Lane back in Milwaukee.

"Boss man!" Lane said, "Jetting across the country with a beautiful woman by his side. And before you say anything rude to me, please know that I have you on speakerphone, and that analyst and sometime MMA fighter Li Song is on this call as well. Ouch! I forgot she has a pretty long reach."

Cole was surprised Li made it into the office. Pleased more than surprised. "How's she doing, Lane?"

"She's looked better, boss. Ow! That's twice she's flicked out some kind of left jab that bruised my shoulder. No workplace violence allowed! I know my rights!" But he was laughing.

"When you two are done fiddle farting around, I need you to check the client list of Dave Frank Communications. It's a PR firm based in Manhattan, and they may have offices in other parts of the country. Look especially hard to see if they have any clients from big pharma or health care. We talked to the *New York Times* reviewer, James Flood, and he admitted taking forty thousand dollars from someone named Anne Spaith at Frank Communications to pan Rhodes' speech. We need to find out who gave Spaith the go-ahead and the cash to buy Flood's review.

"Okay, we're on it. What are you going to do now?"

"There's a good chance Dave Frank Communications is on the same island I'm currently on. If that's the case and if Miss Anne Spaith is in said offices right now, I plan to pay her a visit."

CHAPTER TWENTY-SEVEN

"Keep pulling at that thread. I like it."

"Glad you approve, Laney."

"And don't forget, boss, the sun'll come out tomorrow...."

"What?"

"It's from the musical, *Annie*. Make her sing!" Lane was laughing.

"If there's nothing else, I'm going to let you two go."

"Hold on, boss. One more bit of news, and you aren't gonna like it. Remember that guy who attacked you and Li? The one the H.I.G. director himself interviewed?"

"Yes. I recall that gentleman faintly. You tend to remember guys who try to kill you up close and personal."

"Right, well, you said you thought the people who hired him would take care of him, and I think you were right. He died a violent death earlier this morning."

"What? While in custody?"

"Yup. The H.I.G. director thought keeping the guy in with the general population might spook him into being more open to his questions. Apparently, four members of the Raging Disciples caught your attacker alone and jumped him. These were big dudes, and at least two of them had homemade shivs. The story is still coming together, but it sounds like he gave at least as good as he got. He took some hard shots, but he put all four of the Disciples down. He had one good arm, and they say he would have walked away from it, but one guy tried to stab him in the groin and accidentally clipped his femoral artery. He bled out in minutes."

Li chimed in. "The Disciples could have attacked the guy because it went through lockup that he was one of the men behind a Black senator's shooting, but we're betting someone paid them."

"I would agree," Cole said, wondering what this meant.

"On the positive side, this guy was one mean hombre. He took out four toughs with one good arm. And you took *him* out when he was healthy, plus his buddy. The Cole Huebsch legend grows. If I swung the other way, I might crush on you...."

"Ditto!" Li piped in.

"For the love of God," Cole said. "You two are awful." But as he swiped off the phone, he was glad that Li was back at work already and showing some of her old spunk.

Cole's cab pulled to the curb on Madison Avenue thirty minutes later. They'd followed FDR Drive along the East River most of the way, and Cole could see the United Nations Headquarters a block distant as he paid his driver. He turned to the building that housed Dave Frank Communications, and all he saw was another hundred-year-old skyscraper that had undergone one too many facelifts. He hurried inside and up to a suite of offices on the twenty-third floor, where he asked the receptionist for Anne Spaith. He had called ahead to make sure she was in, but he was pointed toward a clutch of overstuffed chairs and told to take a seat. Cole sunk into the cushion and let out a deep breath. He bathed in unfiltered sun and shut his eyes, enjoying the light's warm caress. *The Sun'll Come Out Tomorrow* started playing in his head, and he would have cursed Lane under his breath if he didn't secretly love the song. Eyes still closed, he pictured the cute little urchin with her red hair and matching dress belting out the show tune and its promise of a better morrow.

"Comfy?" It was a woman's voice, and when Cole opened his eyes, he liked the smile that accompanied it.

"Very," he answered, unmoving.

"Were you just humming the song *Tomorrow* from Annie?"

Cole blinked. "I don't believe so. No."

"Well, I hate to spoil your nap, but I'm Anne Spaith, and I'd prefer to have our little chat in my office. I've got a busy schedule this afternoon, so follow me."

Cole groaned as he got up. Anne Spaith was naturally blonde, and her straight hair framed her face well. He had expected her to be flashy, haughty even, but Anne was more like the girl next door who'd grown into the woman next door. He guessed her to be around fifty. When they reached her office, Spaith took a seat behind an older wooden desk, and Cole sat across from her, taking in the surroundings. The desk was the first thing that held his eye. It was simple, but he could tell it had a history. A beautifully stained top

CHAPTER TWENTY-SEVEN

was set off by the black wood of the file drawers. "It was my great-grandpa's desk," she said. "My dad kept it in his basement after grandpa died, saying he was going to restore it someday. After dad died, that's just what I did with it. It means more to me than some anonymous glass and metal monstrosity."

It wasn't a big office, and it was packed with knickknacks and photos...lots and lots of photos of smiling people. She noticed him looking again and said, "Kids and grandkids mostly. I like being reminded of family."

Cole laughed out loud. "I guess I could just sit here, and you can answer my questions without my asking them. That would save me time and energy."

Spaith laughed, too, and then turned serious. "Unfortunately, I have no idea why you're really here. You were a bit cryptic when you called to ask for this meeting. What did you need to ask me that warranted a special trip to Madison Avenue?"

"Would you believe I was in the neighborhood?"

"I don't believe I would."

"Well, that's funny, because I was in the neighborhood. I just left the federal building after meeting with a friend of yours, or at least someone on your payroll."

"Is that so..."

It seemed to Cole the temperature in the room dropped twenty degrees in the last ten seconds. "That's so. James Flood said you've been incredibly generous to him...maybe generous to a fault."

She didn't rise to the bait. "What do you want, Agent Huebsch?"

"I want to know who you were representing when you paid Flood to pan Senator Eric Rhodes' convention speech."

Spaith didn't answer. She just looked at Cole with eyes that constricted and hardened in front of him. His phone vibrated, and he held up a finger to let her know he needed a moment. It was a text from Ty. *We got a hit. No big pharma. But D Frank Comms reps AHIA...health ins trade assoc.*

Cole looked up from his phone. "Care to tell me about you and your firm's relationship with the American Health Insurance Association?"

"Not without an attorney present."

Cole got up and left the office without another word, leaving behind a nervous PR professional and taking with him a promising lead.

Chapter Twenty-Eight

Change of plans, Cole texted Michele from the backseat of another cab. *Please call me when you're out of your meeting.* He was sliding the phone back into the inside pocket of his suitcoat when it vibrated.

"Hey! I'm going to assume by this call that you're done with the big meeting with your publisher and agent. How'd it go?"

"Pretty heady stuff for a Wisconsin girl. They liked my last edits, and the manuscript is ready to go after one final review for stray typos. They showed us five different cover designs. I liked them all, but in the end, we got rid of the ones that were too literal or too gory. The one we settled on has a large shadowy cross and a splash of colors that let your imagination go wherever it will. It should stand out from others on bookshelves, and that's mostly what it's all about."

"Sounds like you had a productive day."

There was a pause, and Cole could tell that Michele was reflecting. These days they both found comfort and not tension during such moments of silence.

"Did I tell you my publisher has final approval on every word? That they have final approval on the cover too and everything else?"

"You did not. Hopefully, they recognize how brilliant your work is and leave it alone."

"That's not how it usually works. But I signed the deal and took the advance. I just want to be proud of the finished product, you know?"

His cab had been idling at a light, and it jumped forward when the light turned green. Cole was thrown back in his seat. "You will be. It sounds like they've respected your opinions on pretty much everything so far. Are they good with the title, *The Killer Sermon?*"

"Yes. And the ARCs are supposed to be ready any day now. I can't wait to get my copies!"

"I'm sure I should know this, but what's an ARC?"

Michele laughed. "Sorry. Those are Advanced Review Copies. They're actual printed books sent out to reviewers a few months in advance of the book's release date. It gives them time to read it before it's available for purchase by the general public. Fingers crossed I get favorable reviews in the *Post*, the *New York* and *L.A. Times* and other papers. There are no guarantees that they'll like or even review my book, but that's how best-sellers are made. It wouldn't hurt if Oprah, Reese, or Jenna Bush plugged it too."

"It'll all work out."

"Thanks. Now, what's this about a change of plans? Does this mean we won't be connecting at Uncle Peter's for a sumptuous Italian dinner before flying back home?"

"You guessed it. I'm headed to the airport now. I'm going to D.C. to get in one more interview before I call it a day."

Michele was interested. "What do you have?"

"Not a lot, but maybe something," Cole admitted. "AHIA, short for the American Health Insurance Association, happens to be a client of Dave Frank Communications. I just left one of Frank's reps, Anne Spaith, and while she didn't admit that she gave Flood the money for AHIA, she didn't have to. It doesn't mean they also hire professional killers, but it's about all we've got to go on right now."

"Do you want me to come with you?"

"I think that would be a bad idea. I'm not sure the FBI or anyone in D.C. wants me to keep poking around in this. In fact, I'm pretty sure they'd just as soon I leave well enough alone. But I can't do that, at least not yet. I'm going to ask for forgiveness here instead of permission, and I don't want anyone else to catch any fallout."

"Okay. I'll see you back home. But I still have time and I might just stop at Uncle Peter's and try to get a table for one. It'll be a lonely little celebration."

CHAPTER TWENTY-EIGHT

"Sorry about that. I'll be home tonight but will likely get in late."

"I'll be there," she said, and they both ended the call.

Cole's wait to get a flight and board it at LaGuardia was longer than the hour and fifteen-minute flight itself. He used the time to catch up on his email. It was nearly five in the late afternoon Eastern Standard Time when Cole deplaned at Reagan National Airport and caught his fourth cab of the day. It was muggy, and Cole didn't feel very fresh when they pulled up in front of another faceless high-rise near the power center of the city. He had called ahead and been assured Megan Baldwin, AHIA's president and CEO, would make herself available when he arrived. He felt sweat beading at his hairline as he trudged into the large cavern-like lobby and to the bank of elevators, hoping all the while to find his second wind. It was only a few hours ago that he had dragged Li to her home, and now he was dragging himself nearly a thousand miles to the east.

Cole was met by an assistant in the AHIA's administrative lobby on the sixteenth floor. She walked with him down a wide hallway and ushered him into the trade association president's modern high-ceilinged office. Megan Baldwin was sixty and slender. Just a few inches shorter than Cole, her blue eyes were set off by her nearly white hair. She looked confident, if not overly friendly, and she was not alone. "Roger Beneker," the man said, stepping forward and shaking Cole's hand. "Megan called and said you wanted to chat. She and I both have other engagements to attend to momentarily. This will be brief, so I suggest we get to it."

Baldwin shook Cole's hand and introduced herself, directing Cole to a seat that faced both her and Beneker.

Cole took a deep breath. This wasn't good. He didn't hobnob with the elite, but even he recognized the name Roger Beneker the fifth, esquire. If there was one top dog among the many power brokers in D.C., it was likely Beneker. He was Cole's age, but he'd left the oldest and wealthiest lobbying firm in the city nearly a decade ago to found his own firm, Capitol Gains, and it was now the biggest lobbying firm in the nation. Beneker was rank with the smell of old money, from his bespoke suit that cost twenty times the one Cole wore, to the round, polished eyeglasses that screamed I'm the smartest guy in the room. His was mostly old-school money made decades before Cole's forefathers ever landed on America's shores. Money that couldn't be spent over a thousand sinfully extravagant lifetimes. Yet he wanted more. He was insatiable. The thousand-dollar hourly fees and hideous retainers his firm charged didn't appreciably add to his wealth. Beneker made his money, not because of his Harvard business or Yale law degrees. He earned it in clubs so exclusive Cole could never name them, much less enter them. He earned his wealth from connections to power honed over the most expensive bourbon in the most exclusive clubs. Connections first made by his grandfather's grandfather and carefully maintained through the years the way an energy company keeps up its power lines…meticulously. Only Beneker's lines of power had withstood every political storm and act of God over the decades.

Cole looked at Beneker, and the cultured man smiled at him, reading Cole like he read his scandalous bank account in detail. His was a smile like the first rattle of a diamondback viper, to let you know you'd best watch where you stepped next, or that next step could be your last.

"Are you going to sit there and gape, Agent Huebsch?" Beneker said. "The clock's running." He may have been Cole's age, but their paths to this point in their lives could hardly have been more divergent. Beneker's was preordained, while Cole's seemed in comparison to be by chance. Beneker was fit. Tennis and handball saw to that. And likely a personal trainer. But though Cole knew he could easily overpower Beneker physically, he also knew that in this arena, he was already beaten. He wanted to get up and leave, but he had to try something. He had read up on Megan Baldwin on the ride from the airport, and he turned to her now. AHIA's president and CEO had a different pedigree than Beneker. She had graduated from the University of Iowa and later earned an MBA from Stanford. She wasn't born with a silver spoon in her mouth, she simply outworked and outthought her way up every rung of the corporate ladder. She'd earned the keys to the C-Suite.

"Listen," Cole fumbled. "Someone tried to kill a United States Senator. And then they tried to kill me and an FBI analyst…a young woman I think

CHAPTER TWENTY-EIGHT

you would admire, Miss Baldwin. The same people then used a rocket-propelled grenade to blow up another man, the first time an RPG has ever been fired with malice on U.S. soil. The people behind this have seemingly unlimited funds and connections."

"And you think my Association is somehow involved in all that?" Baldwin asked. Beneker shook his head at her imperceptibly.

"I frankly don't know what to think right now. What I do know is that someone associated with your firm paid a *New York Times* reporter a large sum of money to bash a speech which was detrimental to your association members. They lost billions of dollars immediately after Senator Eric Rhodes delivered his speech on the high cost of health care. I keep coming back to the question, 'What would AHIA give…what would it do…to keep that message from spreading?'"

"That's quite enough," Beneker said flatly, waving a hand dismissively at Cole. "This is a wild goose chase, and Megan's through playing. We are done here." He stood up.

"Think about it, Miss Baldwin," Cole pleaded, hating the hint of desperation he heard in his own voice. "Give me something. Attempted assassinations. Professional hits. An RPG set off right here in the nation's capital…to silence debate on the cost of health care…."

"Cal Johnson isn't dead," Beneker interrupted.

Cole halted. He turned and faced Beneker. "What?"

"Weezy," he said, smiling smugly. "He's not dead. You keep going on about RPG's blowing people to bits. But the one person involved in that unfortunate incident survived with barely a scratch. You can stop prattling on about that. And you are here in the flesh…not laid out in some claustrophobic morgue. It seems like some amateurs, hardly trained professionals, have been involved in this whole sordid mess."

Cole turned crimson. Beneker shouldn't know about Weezy. It was a power play from the power player of players. He knew that Weezy's life was still in danger. He turned back to Baldwin. "Will you give me anything?"

She looked at Beneker, then stood but remained silent. Cole stood. His shoulders slumped. He turned and was almost out the door when he heard

Megan Baldwin. "Wait just a minute, Agent Huebsch!"

Cole turned back to face them. Beneker put a hand lightly on Baldwin's wrist, but she shook it off. Now it was Beneker's face that darkened. "I'm not admitting to paying a reporter to slant a story," Baldwin said. "But I want you to know that it is a long, long step from tipping a journalist to paying professionals to kill your adversaries. I would never condone or allow the latter. I want you to know that so that you can find out who is behind this."

Cole looked at her an uncomfortably long time before deciding he believed her. He nodded. "Thanks for that. It's something. It almost makes me not want to put Mr. Beneker's head through the wall." His gaze moved to Beneker. "Almost. But not quite." He thought he saw a smile tug at Baldwin's face as he turned and left.

When he walked out of the chilled lobby and into the bright sun and sultry heat, Cole got a phone call from Gene Olson. "Hey, Gene! Did someone tell you I was in town, and you're calling to say you want to take me to dinner? I've had nothing but black coffee all day."

It was silent for a moment. "That's not quite it, Cole. I need you to come in and bring me up to speed on the expansion of your investigation into Eric Rhodes' shooting."

Cole felt stray beads of sweat trickle down his back and didn't think it was caused by the humidity…more the heat behind Olson's call. "You know, I could email you a report on the way to the airport. A long text might even cover it, and you can get home to the wife at a decent time tonight."

"Sorry, Cole. I need you to come in personally and debrief us."

Another pause while Cole digested the fact that it wouldn't just be Gene in the debrief. "Okay, boss. I'll grab an Uber and see you in a bit."

"Not necessary," Gene said. "There should be a Bureau car idling at the curb not far from you. We sent someone to pick you up."

Cole looked around and saw what had to be two FBI agents in black suits lounging against a newer grey Jeep. One of them nodded and waved at Cole, and he nodded back. "Okay. On my way, Gene." He let out a long breath as he disconnected the call.

The two-mile drive took fifteen minutes, the time spent mostly in silence

CHAPTER TWENTY-EIGHT

with Cole staring unseeing out his window alone in the backseat of the Jeep. The younger agents recognized Cole and tried to ask him about cases, but he politely declined.

Cole was dropped off just outside the J. Edgar Hoover Building's main entrance, and as he walked toward its doors, he took in the large, squat, rough, and unpolished concrete structure. When he'd first been dropped off in front of the building two decades earlier as a raw recruit, he'd been less than impressed. It had looked to him like a cross between a federal penitentiary and a parking garage. That view hadn't changed over the past twenty years. He wasn't alone in his negative assessment of the Hoover's aesthetics; the area newspapers commonly referred to it as "Downtown D.C.'s ugliest edifice." It had been built in the mid-nineteen seventies, in an architectural style known as Brutalism. *Feels about right*, Cole thought to himself as he headed into the somber building.

Cole was met inside by another unfamiliar agent, and they went through security, Cole repeating the process he'd gone through not so many hours ago at the New York field office. Their footsteps echoed across the tile floor and over to a bank of elevators. When the large steel doors swallowed them up, the agent inserted his key into the panel and punched the button for the seventh floor. Cole had never been on that particular floor, but all agency personnel knew that the Director's office was on the seventh. His stomach growled, a dark mixture of coffee, acid, and dread.

As they got off the elevator and walked down a long, bleak hallway, Cole couldn't help but feel like he was being called into the principal's office. He didn't feel like he'd done anything wrong, other than take his job a little too seriously. As they walked past the director's assistant, Cole remembered the last time he had been with this FBI director was at the White House, where the man had given him two medals. He'd gotten the FBI Star for sustaining a serious injury in the direct line of duty, and the FBI Medal of Valor for exceptional heroism in the direct line of duty. The agent knocked crisply on a large, dark-stained door, opened it and gestured Cole inside, and then closed it quietly behind him.

Cole stood for a moment in the spacious, high-ceilinged office. Gene was seated at a polished dark wood conference table while the director was on the phone behind his matching desk. A floor-to-ceiling credenza ran from wall to wall behind the director, scores of books and binders showing through its glass doors. Jim Trudell was flanked by two flags, on his right was the U.S. flag, and on his left was the FBI's own, adopted in nineteen forty-one. Draped as it was, Cole couldn't make out the three words on the FBI flag, beyond the Department of Justice—Federal Bureau of Investigation, but he knew them by heart...*Fidelity. Bravery. Integrity.* Director Trudell seemed to be mostly listening to the conversation, nodding and adding the occasional, "Understood."

Cole sat across the table from Gene, and his mentor winked at him. Cole might have smiled for the first time in the past few hours, but just then, the director's call ended. He got up from behind the desk and came around. He had on dark blue dress pants, a white, button-down dress shirt, and a deep red tie. He loosened the tie and unbuttoned the top button on his shirt, spreading it apart a bit with both hands. He took his time unbuttoning his sleeves and rolling them up to his elbows. He sat down abruptly in the chair at the head of the table. "Helluva way to end the day," he said.

The director poured himself a glass of ice water from the sweating metal carafe in front of him. He held it up to Cole in a gesture Cole realized was an offer to pour a glass for him. "That would be great," Cole said, needing the hydration almost as much as he needed another moment to compose himself. Trudell poured a glass of water and slid it over to Cole along with a coaster featuring the FBI seal, and then he drank half the water in his own glass. "Helluva way to end the day," he repeated. He sat back in his chair, then, and took off his glasses, rubbing his eyes and then his temples briefly with his fingers. He looked at Cole for an awkward time without speaking. When he did begin talking, Cole leaned forward, the director's voice was so low.

"Cole, that was the President of the United States of America I was just talking to," Trudell said. "That's twice he's called me in less than an hour, and, coincidentally, both calls involved you. He wanted me to pass along his regards and to tell you that he hasn't forgotten the service and sacrifice

CHAPTER TWENTY-EIGHT

you've made in the past for your country. He's grateful, as am I." He paused and continued to scrutinize Cole as he rubbed the stubble of his early evening beard.

"But the President is also more than a little aggravated," Trudell said. "Those were his words. To me, he just sounded pissed as hell. A coarser man might say he was fucking angry. He told me a story about how he had just gotten off the phone with Roger Beneker the fifth, Esquire. Beneker told the president that you went to the AHIA offices without an appointment and grilled their CEO without grounds. Any truth to that?"

"I called ahead, and the CEO agreed to talk to me."

"And did you even have a basis for questioning Baldwin?"

"I'm pretty sure her association paid a *New York Times* reporter forty thousand dollars to pan Senator Rhodes' Convention speech. I wanted to find out how far they were willing to go to shut up a courageous U.S. Senator who is calling out the health insurance industry for its role in driving up the cost of health care. If it means anything, I only found out when I walked in her office that Beneker would be there."

Trudell shook his head slowly. "Actually, it means nothing to me, other than the fact you know who Beneker is then."

"I've some idea, yes, sir."

"Some idea, huh? I'll flesh that out for you. Roger Beneker, aka the Fifth Estate, is a *really* important guy. If the President of the United States is the most powerful person in the world, then Roger Beneker is the most powerful person in the whole wide universe, because he pretty much uses the office of the presidency as his personal sock puppet, no matter which side of the aisle the president comes from." Cole found himself leaning back into his chair as Trudell's voice picked up in pace and volume. "Beneker golfs and dines with presidents, Supreme Court justices, and the Speaker of the House. Hell, he probably bangs all their spouses with them watching him do it. And then they likely thank him!"

The director gestured around the room. "This is a political office. I was appointed to a ten-year term by the President and confirmed by the U.S. Senate. Any idea what that was like?"

THE KILLER SPEECH

"None whatsoever, sir."

"Good answer," Trudell nodded. "The best way I can put it is that a group of twenty-two ham-handed U.S. Senators zoomed up my rectum with the Hubble Telescope for days on end. When those members of the Senate Judiciary Committee were finally done with me, I wanted them to take the director's job and shove it where the sun don't shine. Instead, I smiled and swallowed that feeling. Now I'm on the inside looking out and I have no interest in being on the outside looking in again. At least not until I'm damn well ready." He paused. "Are you following me?"

"I think I am, sir."

Trudell nodded. "I'll be more explicit. Twice in our nation's history, a president has removed an FBI director. Slick Willy was the first to do it, and then more recently, the Donald did it. Just like that." He snapped his fingers. "It's accepted today that the holder of this director's post that I currently occupy serves at the pleasure of the U.S. President. What apparently isn't as widely known is that the President of the U.S. pretty much serves at the pleasure of Roger Beneker the fifth, Esquire."

Trudell stood up and loomed over Cole. "The president called to tell me in no uncertain terms that *he* has no interest in being on the outside looking in. He asked me if *I* would prefer to be on the outside, and I said I would definitely *not* prefer that. I feel like I'm making a positive difference in the Bureau and for my Country, and I don't plan on getting kicked to the curb because I got stubborn. I don't want that for you either, Cole. You've had a damn fine career. My predecessors and I have handed you the FBI's and our nation's highest medals like a mom hands out Skittles to her kid. You've made a huge difference in Milwaukee, your home State, and beyond. Don't throw that away." He paused again. "Am I clear?"

"Yes, sir."

Trudell looked at Cole and shook his head slowly back and forth. When he spoke, his voice conveyed a mix of weariness and disappointment. "The most troubling thing about your meeting with the AHIA CEO and Beneker is that you knew it would be an issue." He looked at Cole to see if there was any protest and saw none. "Thanks for not denying that. See, Geno

CHAPTER TWENTY-EIGHT

did a little digging and knows that you gave Jack Gokey a courtesy call before heading to New York. I was curious about why you wouldn't give the assistant director in charge here in DC the same courtesy."

It wasn't really a question, and Cole didn't provide an answer. He noticed Gene looking out the window and avoiding eye contact.

"You can head out then. I told my wife I would grill tonight, and the steaks will be going on late as it is."

Cole got up and made it to the door before Trudell called to him. "Cole?"

Cole turned in the threshold. "Yes, sir?"

"Did you really threaten Beneker? Did you tell him you were going to put his head through a wall?" The director was smiling now.

Cole shrugged. "I didn't say I was going to put his head through the wall, only that I wanted to do that."

Trudell laughed, and Gene Olson joined in. "You've still got the biggest set of balls on you of anyone I've ever met," he said. "Take care of yourself."

"The best I can," Cole mumbled to himself, nodding to the director's assistant as he made his way outside the oppressive building and the powers that ran it. As he exited, he noticed the two agents who had brought him there were waiting to take him to the airport. One of them waved to Cole in the day's waning light, and Cole shrugged. It beat another ride in a cab with a long-expired air freshener swinging from its rearview mirror.

Cole was a legend in the FBI, especially among the younger agents. The two with Cole tried to engage him in conversation, but after a while, they could tell he wasn't up to it. "I'm sorry, guys," Cole said. "It's just been a long day with a lot of planes, trains, and automobiles. Well, no trains, actually, but you get the idea." They pulled up in front of his airport terminal fifteen minutes later, and Cole thanked the agents as he got out. He passed through security and, after showing his credentials, kept his Glock. He made his way to his gate and settled into a chair to wait for boarding. He plugged his phone into a charging station and called Michele. "What's up?" she answered.

"I'm not completely sure, but I think I just got my butt chewed out by the director. Did you make it home okay?"

"I just walked in the door and poured myself a glass of merlot. I plan to put my feet up and watch an old movie."

"Sounds amazing. I won't get home until midnight, probably, and all I'm thinking about is crawling under the covers and sleeping in."

"And how about tomorrow?"

"I've been thinking about that," Cole said with the start of a smile on his lips. "I think I'm gonna play hooky."

Chapter Twenty-Nine

The drive from Milwaukee to Cole's hometown of Prairie du Chien, Wisconsin, was just over three hours. Yet this would only be his third visit back since he'd lost both his parents during his senior year in college. The first two trips had been just months ago, as part of his investigation into the murders of the reproductive health physicians. Cole realized he still had a lot of good feelings for his hometown and the people who helped make his childhood a positive one. When he got off the phone with Michele, he called Fwam Vang, a former high school wrestling teammate and the current sheriff of Crawford County, of which Prairie du Chien was the County Seat. Cole told Fwam he was thinking of playing hooky and wondered if he would have any interest in an afternoon of fishing the next day. Fwam said he had a boat, rods, reels, and tackle ready. He told Cole to pick up some crawlers and a little beer and meet at his house whenever he could get there.

Cole was less than twenty minutes out from Prairie on a meandering stretch of two-lane US Highway eighteen. He drove past the Patch Grove turnoff and descended into a deep, wooded valley. At the bottom, a creek loosely paralleled the two-lane road, wandering off like a small pup chasing butterflies but always coming back. Cole had eaten breakfast with Michele and Frau Newhouse, and it was now after eleven in the morning. When he neared the first of two bridges that spanned the Wisconsin River and its backwaters, he smiled broadly, then took a deep breath and held it. He thought of his parents years ago, whenever they would drive this same stretch of highway. His dad had started a contest where all three of them would try to hold their breath from one side of the bridge to the other. He would make a big production out of counting down the last tenth of a mile or so before the bridge started. "Three. Two. One. Hold your breath!"

All three of them would hold their breath then, and when they were almost over the largest and last span that led to the Crawford County side, Cole's father would slow the car. Imperceptibly at first, but then to a crawl. Even if other cars were behind them. When Cole was little, his face would go red, and he thought his eyes might bulge out of his head. But he always made it with a big exhale and his parents' explosive laughter.

Cole drove his Charger through town and down the main street called Blackhawk Avenue, pulling up in front of Stark's Sport Shop. As he pushed through the store's front door, Cole saw Big Bill Hunter leaning over the counter near the cash registers, sharing his opinion on fishing, the weather, and likely his politics with a customer. Cole wore a ripped pair of cargo shorts and a holey, stained tee-shirt that said, "STARKS SPORT SHOP. Boats. Booze. Bullets. The Mecca of all things cool."

Cole smiled to himself as he looked around. *It is pretty cool at that.* He looked at Bill, whose shaggy hair hung down to his eyes like a sheepdog and flared over his ears. He looked sleepy, but Cole remembered him as anything but. Bill had been the freshman heavyweight on the high school wrestling team that Cole captained his senior year. He had shed any baby fat and grown into a strong S.O.B. and a great wrestler by his own senior year. Bill saw Cole approach the counter and stood to his full six-foot-three height. "That's gotta be the rattiest looking shirt I've ever seen anyone wear into this fine establishment. You should spend some time in our apparel section and get something more becoming a man of your stature…which would be short, by the way."

They laughed and shook hands. "By apparel section, do you mean the couple racks of tee-shirts and hoodies that say, 'Wisconsin River Rat?' No thanks. And this," he said, pointing to his tee-shirt, "is an American classic. 'Booze. Boats. Bullets.' You had me at hello!"

"What do you need, little man?"

"Just beer and bait today. I'm playing hooky and left my Glock at home.

CHAPTER TWENTY-NINE

No need for bullets."

"Let me set you up," Bill said. He got him a cheap Styrofoam cooler and filled it with ice. Then he grabbed two four-packs from a chilled beer cooler. "King Sue double IPA and Pseudo Sue IPA, both from Toppling Goliath brewery, just a half hour from here. You'll thank me for turning you on to these IPAs," he said as he separated them and put them on ice.

"I would at that, my little pachyderm, if I hadn't discovered them on my own years ago. I'm the Magellan of IPAs."

"Pachyderm?"

"It's a term of endearment, my friend."

"Whatever." Bill stacked two cartons of night crawlers on the counter and then grabbed a bucket and began to scoop crappie minnows into it.

"You really think we'll need minnows? I kind of just want to soak a line and relax."

"*And* you want to catch fish, right? Who're you fishing with?"

"Fwam's taking me out," Cole said, throwing a pack of jerky on his growing pile on the counter.

"Tiny? That little one hundred eight pounder's gonna tell you that you didn't need minnows, but he'll be wrong."

"I'm pretty sure he's not one oh eight anymore. Closer to one-eighty, I'd guess."

Cole paid and thanked his former teammate. Before he left the store he nodded behind Bill and said, "I think your brother's trying to get your attention."

Bill looked over his shoulder to where Cole was gesturing at a big stuffed white polar bear with one paw raised in the air. The bear had been in the store for two generations of kids growing up in the town to ogle at. Bill laughed out loud. "I haven't heard that lame joke in over twenty years, since the last time you were in the store." He stuck his own big paw across the counter and shook Cole's hand again. "Nice to have you home, buddy."

Cole nodded. "Nice to be home, big guy."

As Cole walked out the door, he could hear Bill yell out. "You're gonna thank me for those minnows!"

THE KILLER SPEECH

As he stowed his purchases in the Dodge, Cole's eyes were drawn to the homey stand across the street. *Pete's*. The same Prairie du Chien family had been selling burgers on this strip of road since 1909, and they always had a line of customers. The delicious burgers were one of his food staples growing up, so Cole joined the line and ordered two burgers with onions. He wolfed them down.

Cole headed to Fwam's house and got a big hug from the sheriff's wife, Mary. "We're glad you came, Cole. Maybe you won't be such a stranger!"

"Highway eighteen goes two ways, Mary. I've told Fwam you guys are welcome in Milwaukee too. We could catch a Brewers or Bucks game."

Fwam had his boat loaded with eight poles and three tackle boxes. "We really need all that gear?" Cole asked. "I'm just looking to wet a line and catch some sun."

Fwam scowled as he stowed Cole's cooler and bait in the boat. "What we didn't need were these minnows," he said, holding up the new bucket Cole had bought. "Let me guess, Billy Hunter told you that you really need these, didn't he? What he didn't tell you is that they'll all be floating on their backs before we even start fishing."

"What can I tell you? He guarantees they'll work, dead or alive."

"Well, if Billy guaranteed it," Fwam laughed. "Then we're good." He put a thick arm around Cole's shoulder and said, "I'm just glad you're here, man."

Ten minutes later, they launched Fwam's flat bottom at a public landing, and Fwam started the newer twenty-five-horse Johnson with one pull of the cord. He pushed the choke in as the motor caught, and Cole caught a whiff of the sweet smell of the gas and oil mix burning. He sat in the middle bench to help balance the load, with Fwam in back manning the tiller. Cole closed his eyes to the sun and listed to the soft burp of the motor as they putt-putted slowly on the narrow slough that led to bigger water. They eased past homes on stilts and others built on higher ground above historic flood levels. They respected the No Wake signs. Fwam opened the engine up when they reached deeper water, and the roar of the motor and rush of wind prevented small talk.

The wind blew through Cole's hair and picked up grains of sand that

CHAPTER TWENTY-NINE

snicked against the shaded lenses of the cheap orange plastic sunglasses he'd bought when he filled up his Charger at a gas station on his way to Prairie. The small flatbottom bounced eagerly over the wakes of bigger boats, and Cole's smile was ear to ear as the would-be fishermen thump, thump, thumped over the waves and out toward the Big Muddy's main channel. Cole pictured himself, happy as a young lab whose owner is taking him hunting. His tongue wasn't lolling, and he wasn't drooling, but if he had a tail, it would've been wagging furiously right about now. *This was exactly what I needed*, he thought.

Fwam motored them over to the Mississippi's main channel on the Iowa side of the river. The water was more than a third of a mile wide here. They floated the edge of the channel in six to eight feet of water off a long, narrow island. Cole squinted into the sun and took in his surroundings. Water lapped against the side of the boat as it bobbed in the waves, thrown off by pontoon boats, cabin cruisers, and smaller craft. Cole could see a large towboat pushing a string of three-abreast barges coming down-river under the Marquette bridge and knew the waves would be much bigger when it passed. Even aided by the river's own two-mile-per-hour current, the tow pushed on at just seven miles per hour. But with a heavy load of likely Minnesota corn, soybeans, and grain stretching three football fields or more, the barge waves would still give their little flatbottom a lift when it finally slid past.

It was eighty-five degrees, and the air was heavy. Both Cole and Fwam had stowed their tee-shirts and let the sun soak in. The breeze ebbing and flowing about them felt good. Ducks surfed the waves near the shoreline, and two bald eagles rode the air currents above.

Fwam handed Cole an ultralight graphite rod and reel combo and picked up one himself. Each was already rigged with a small hook a foot beneath a number three split shot sinker. The sinker was just big enough to take their bait to the bottom, where they expected the fish to be hiding from the early afternoon heat and the overhead sun's intensity. Fwam broke a piece of nightcrawler off and threaded the thick strand of earthworm onto his hook, flipping it over the side of the boat. "You want a piece of crawler? I told Mary we'd have a fish fry tonight, so we need to get serious."

Cole shook his head and smiled at Fwam. "Nah." He reached into the minnow bucket and pulled out a dead minnow, hooked it through the lips, and tossed it over the side. "Let's see what the fish are hungry for."

They didn't wait long. "First fish," Fwam crowed, lifting a tiny panfish into the boat. Cole looked at the little bluegill, which had swallowed the hook and was bleeding from its gills. "Bout the size of my minnow." Fwam tossed the fish into the water, just as Cole felt a tug on his own line. He set the hook, and the light rod bowed as he reeled. Seconds later, Cole pulled a fourteen-inch crappie into the boat. "You got a stringer in any of those tackle boxes?" Fwam looked over, "Whoa! That's a nice slab crappie." He reached into a tackle box and pulled out a rope stringer. "Hand it here, and I'll string it up. Won't take many like that to make a meal."

He had just finished threading the stringer through the crappie's gill and was tying it to the boat when Cole cleared his throat. Fwam looked at his friend and saw two things, his buddy's huge grin and another big crappie that might've been the twin of the one he'd just put on the stringer. "Man, I wanted you to have fun," he said. "But not to *hog* it all!" But his smile was even bigger than Cole's.

When Fwam finished putting the second crappie on the stringer, Cole handed him a minnow. "Go on. Give it a try. I promise I won't tell Bill."

Fwam didn't need to be told twice. He threaded the minnow onto his hook and threw it over the side as the big waves from the barges rocked them like they were in a cradle. They caught fish steadily, keeping the biggest crappies and occasional perch and releasing the rest. Fwam opened two of the icy pale ales and slipped the cans into red, white, and blue *Fwam Vang for Sheriff* koozies.

Cole held up his beer and nodded to the colorful koozie. "Nice touch." Fwam tapped his can against Cole's. "I did get elected," he said. They sipped the beers in silence. A bald eagle swooped down not twenty feet from their boat and snatched up the first fish Fwam had caught. "Nice to see that fish didn't go to waste," Cole said, watching the majestic bird fly away with its prize. His eyes to the sky, Cole pointed to a huge, puffy white cloud and

CHAPTER TWENTY-NINE

said, "Looks like a dragon."

"I'm not seeing it," Fwam said. "Looks more like a swan."

Cole looked over his sunglasses at his buddy. "A swan? Really?"

Fwam shrugged. "You know, swans use the Mississippi flyway these days. Flock after flock migrate through during the spring. Pelicans too. We never saw 'em when we were kids, but you can't miss 'em now."

"Didn't know that," Cole said. He pointed to another cloud. "Now that one looks like a dead body, which probably says a little bit about the mood I came in today. You've pretty much lifted me out of that, Fwam. I appreciate it."

"Thanks, buddy. But you're right about that cloud looking like a dead body. And I'll be damned if there aren't a raft of identical clouds floating right behind it. What the hell does that mean?"

Cole felt a tug on his line and set the hook. His ultralight rod bent double, and he could hear and see his line peeling away. He tightened the drag to slow down whatever brute had inhaled his minnow.

"That ain't no panfish," Fwam said, grabbing a net. Cole kept reeling, and the fish turned. It had been headed for the island, but now made a beeline for the deeper water in the channel. Cole turned with it and fought to keep the fish from getting under the boat. He kept his line tight, and the big fish began to tire. It stayed on the bottom, and they hadn't caught sight of it. "What do you think it is, maybe a huge sheepshead?"

Cole glanced at his buddy. "You're asking me? I haven't fished these waters in more than two decades. But that's what I love about fishing with live bait on the Mighty Miss, you never know what you're going to catch. It could be a monster bass, walleye or northern. Or it could be a carp, sheepshead, buffalo or other rough fish. No matter, we have enough fish to eat, and this is fun."

"It's a walleye," Fwam shouted, catching a flash of gold. "And a damn big one. Don't lose him!"

Cole brought the fish close to the boat twice, but Fwam couldn't quite reach to slide the net under it. Cole grinned at his friend. "If you didn't have those little alligator arms, that walleye would be in the boat already." They laughed like two kids without a care.

They netted the fish on the third pass, and as Fwam lifted it into the boat, he mumbled, "Happens every time. You start catching nice fish, and other people crowd you."

Cole looked at the vee-bottom boat closing in on them, and grabbed Fwam's bicep. "They're not friendly," he whispered. "Get in the water now."

Fwam heard the urgency in his friend's voice, but still plunged his hand into the bottom of his biggest tackle box. Cole kept his death grip on Fwam's arm and threw himself backward out of the boat, pulling his buddy into the water with him just as gunfire erupted. He heard the slugs impacting the aluminum boat at the same time he heard Fwam's muffled yelp, and he feared the worst. Fwam pulled free as they sunk to the bottom, where the sediment was so heavy you couldn't see your hand if you held it in front of your face. Cole stayed on the bottom and listened to the other boat's motor idling nearby. Adrenaline pumping and trying to calm himself to preserve oxygen, he weighed his options. He could make a break for shore, but he'd be the proverbial dead duck going that route because he'd have to walk through a foot or more of mud and muck near the bank. There'd be no sprinting through that. He could swim underwater with the current for a while, but the boats would be drifting that way too. He considered swimming under the surface against the current, but instead, he swam along the bottom, under his boat and their attackers' boat, staying beneath and ahead of the motor.

His lungs cried for air, but he waited beneath the surface and noted the gunfire had stopped. He rewound the scene that had just played out in his head and saw two gunmen, one in the back by the motor and one in the front. Their boat wasn't much longer than Fwam's, but it was higher in the bow than the stern. In his mind's eye, he saw them both looking away from him, waiting for him and Fwam to surface, either dead or soon to be if they had their way. People who drowned on the river sometimes didn't reappear for days and miles downriver. Cole pictured these two gunmen growing impatient. If they really were facing away from him and he moved quickly, then he had a chance. He quietly surfaced and took a lungful of

CHAPTER TWENTY-NINE

air, grabbing the edge of the boat near the back and heaving himself over the side. The boat rocked violently, and the men tried to keep their balance as they turned to see what was causing the commotion. Cole grabbed the closest guy by the collar of his shirt and pulled him backwards and into the river with him. He dragged him down to the bottom as the man struggled. Cole had breathed deeply before plunging back into the water with his prize, but his reluctant companion had been too startled. Cole was going to hold him under until he passed out, but he could feel his opponent reaching for a gun or a blade. Instead of holding him down, he changed his momentum and pushed him upward. He felt more than heard the thump of the man's head ramming the boat's steel rib. The man stopped struggling, but Cole banged his head against the boat's bottom once more for good measure. He felt the river tugging at his opponent and released his hold, letting old man river take him where it wanted. Cole had used up air in the fight and needed to replenish his supply. He was deciding his next course of action when he heard two muffled shots and then a loud clunk in the boat above him. He swam away from the boat underwater twenty feet or so. Fighting against the panic caused by a lack of oxygen, Cole cautiously lifted his head above the waves, grabbing another lungful of air and looked toward the boats. He treaded water and saw...nothing. Just two empty boats bobbing together, their aluminum sides clanking together from time to time. Readying himself to drop back into the water, he yelled out, "Fwam! Are you okay?"

Fwam heaved himself over the side of his boat and stood up shakily, soaking wet, and yelled. "Right as rain. You?"

"Mostly good, I think. What the hell happened to the guy in the front of their boat?" Cole said, swimming slowly back toward the boats.

Fwam held up a black pistol. "He took two in the chest from my Glock twenty-two. You might say he'll be sleeping with the fishes tonight."

Cole made his way back to Fwam's boat. He pulled himself in and leaned forward on the middle bench, head down and arms resting on his knees, water running off him in streams. "You've got a way with words. You maybe stole them from Mario Puzo, but still, not bad."

"What happened to the guy in the back of the boat?"

"He went overboard and hit his head under the boat. The river's got him."

Fwam looked at his friend and shook his head. "So, this is what it feels like when someone tries to kill you."

Cole met his friend's eyes. "Pretty much. Yeah. Wet or dry, this is what it's like."

"Kind of a rush," Fwam said.

"Only if you live through it," Cole answered, just as a loud clamor started by his feet, causing Cole to scramble backward over the bench seat.

"Looks like we still got the walleye," Fwam said as the big pike thrashed about the boat's bottom, entangled in the net. Maybe you can slide him on the stringer while I take care of something else."

Cole reached down and pulled the heavy walleye out of the net. As he slid the fish on the stringer, he asked, "Did you get winged or something? I could've sworn I heard you yelp as we went into the water."

"Not winged. Stung," Fwam said, wagging his hand at his friend. A big red and white spoon with a large, barbed treble hook was impaled through the thumb of his right hand. "I was reaching into the tackle box for my gun when you pulled me overboard. I got this and the Glock. The hook and the waves increased the degree of difficulty on my shots." He grabbed a needle nose plyer from another tackle box and snipped off the barb, then slid the hook back out of his thumb. "Damn. That was a fine spoon. Shame to have ruined it."

"Agreed," Cole said, putting the heavy stringer of fish back in the water. "You could've cut off the thumb and saved the lure."

Chapter Thirty

Fwam tied the boats together, and Cole threw an anchor in the water to hold them in place as close to the crime scene as possible. There would be no plastic yellow tape with repeated black lettering *Police. Do not cross.* Their beers had survived upright and were still plenty cold inside the koozies. Fwam called for help on his cell phone, and they sipped the IPAs while they waited. Within minutes a custom-built plate boat arrived on the scene, piloted by two law enforcement officers from the Iowa Department of Natural Resources. The low-profile boat with its big open bow was a multi-use vessel that served them well as they went about their typical job of checking fishermen and hunters and for rescue and body recovery assignments. But this scene was anything but typical. Both officers had been on the job more than three decades and, while they had investigated a couple of suspicious deaths on the river, neither had proven to be a homicide. They came in close and tied up with the other two boats. The officers wore starched tan short-sleeve uniform shirts with bright red Iowa DNR Conservation Officer patches on each shoulder. The bottom yellow lettering read, *Since 1891*. The officers looked at the two shirtless, muscular men in one boat and the dead man in the other and kept their hands close to their sidearms. One of them nodded to the dead man whose blood was splashed across the inside of his boat. "Now, that's not something we see every day."

A Clayton County, Iowa, patrol boat came alongside next, and Sheriff Red Wacouta nodded his recognition to Fwam as he threw him their bow line. "A fine kettle of fish this is, Sheriff Vang. Couldn't just keep the trouble on your side of this big ol' river, huh?"

Fwam raised his beer can in a salute to Wacouta. "Think of it as just another joint exercise, Red. You'd be pissed at me if I didn't do my best to share the excitement."

They talked a while about jurisdictional issues. Wisconsin and Iowa had concurrent jurisdiction on the boundary river under their articles of statehood. When a crime such as attempted homicide occurred on the Iowa side of the Mississippi, their law enforcement would respectfully take jurisdiction. But Cole knew that this stretch of river was part of the Upper Mississippi River Wildlife Refuge under the U.S. Fish and Wildlife Service. A homicide or attempted homicide on these waters would fall squarely under the jurisdiction of the FBI. Cole shared this with the Iowa officers, and they agreed. He then called his lead agent in La Crosse and told him to get down to Marquette, Iowa, immediately to head up the investigation.

Cole asked Wacouta if he could expedite collecting fingerprints and DNA from the dead attacker, and his deputy followed up while the DNR officers went downriver to see if they could find the second body. Then the sheriff invited Cole to join him in the patrol boat, and his deputy sat down with Fwam in his. They were almost finished taking their statements, when they heard a short blast from the DNR boat's siren. The four men looked to the south, where they watched the DNR officers struggle to pull a body out from under a fallen tree at the river's edge. Dead weight.

Two hours later, Cole sat atop a sturdy picnic table on Fwam's patio as the last tender rays of the day's sun warmed him through the filtered light of a honey locust tree. His friend was nearby, absorbed in the task of frying their fish filets over a large propane-fed skillet. Cole felt a sense of urgency to get back to Milwaukee to better work the case, but he also wanted to keep a watch on his buddy for a while longer, to make sure he was okay after having to kill someone. Li was a recent reminder to him that it could hit a person hard. Cole nursed his second beer of the day, cocooned in another of Fwam's campaign koozies, and called Lane on his cell. The analyst had left several voicemails and text messages over the past two hours, but this was the first chance Cole had to return them.

CHAPTER THIRTY

"Holy shit!" Lane said, answering on the second ring. "Do you walk around wearing a bullseye shirt? All anyone is talking about is you being attacked again. Are you okay?"

Cole looked past his friend at the wooden sign that hung over the sliding door that led to his kitchen. *Bless this home.* "Yeah. I'm fine," he said, mostly believing the words himself.

"I'm glad to hear that, but everything's not so fine around here. The word's gone through the office, hell, the entire bureau, that nobody is supposed to help you try to track down who paid for the hit on Senator Rhodes or who's behind the attacks on you and Li and now you and Fwam. People are saying this is coming straight from the Director. It would look bad to can you six months after he and the President of the United States pinned a fistful of medals on your chest, but anyone else is fair game. Everyone knows that if they lift a finger to help Cole Huebsch on this, that they'll be fired. Again, this is above Gene. It's coming straight from Trudell!"

Cole enjoyed the bugless early evening, knowing that the mosquitos could easily be swarming soon after sundown. "So, all we have is jack shit. Is that about it?"

"No. We don't have jackshit. What we have, well, it could be gold. You've made a lot more friends than enemies in the Bureau, Cole. The people that actually get stuff done in the FBI don't like it much that one of their best and bravest has almost been killed twice now, and the politicians in charge want to pretend there's nothing to see. They may be doing it covertly to protect their jobs, but they're working harder than ever to get you what you need to solve this and put an end to it…regardless of Trudell's threats."

Cole thought about the network of agents and analysts working behind the scenes, putting their livelihoods on the line for him, and he choked up a little. "So, tell me about this gold your network of covert analysts has mined."

"Right," Lane said. "The first nugget is solid. We found checking accounts for both Roger Jones and Terry Hawkins, they're the guys that tried to kill you and Li. Jones has six hundred thousand dollars in his account, and Hawkins just over a million. Each month like clockwork twenty thousand dollars is deposited into each man's account. Additional, larger sums are deposited randomly, but at least every three months. My counterparts in DC say it looks like these two clowns have been getting paid a monthly retainer, and then bonuses based on project work completed."

"Bonuses for killing people and God knows what else," Cole said, gripping the edge of the table. "Which leads to the question, 'Who the hell was paying them?'"

"Yes. And here's where I tip my hat to my sisters and brothers at J. Edgar. The money has been wired through an elaborate network of shady banks in countries whose laws allow a lot of secrecy. Switzerland, the Caymans, Hong Kong, Monaco, Singapore, etc. But the best news is, they've located the source, the bank where the payments originate."

"Okay. My heart is racing here, Laney. Don't disappoint."

"Wouldn't dream of it. The bank is in Ireland, and they're willing to roll over on their depositor."

"Why would they do that?"

"Because when our guys got into their system, they looked around and "found quite a bit of other shady international stuff. The Irish bank was told to either give up all relevant information about this one account, or all the other stuff will be made public shortly."

"So, when will we have something?"

"How about now, boss? I have it here in my hot little hands." Cole could almost see the proud look on Lane's face. "The money came into that account from a private security contractor that goes by the name of DC Security Professionals, Inc. The DC either stands for the city it operates out of or its founder and sole proprietor, Dexter Carter. Jones and Hawkins served in the Marines, and their unit teamed up with Carter's Seal Team more than once. DC Security Professionals is flush with cash and counts APAG, the American Pharmaceutical Advocacy Group, among its rather elite client roster."

"Tell me APAG is Carter's only client," Cole said.

"The one and only."

"That is absolute gold. I'm going to owe a whole lot of analysts a night out

CHAPTER THIRTY

when we can make this right."

"The least you can do," Lane agreed as they ended the call. Cole enjoyed the quiet and began to consider the next options they could take to catch whoever sent the killers. He didn't notice Fwam approaching until his friend was at his side.

"How did you know?" Fwam asked, setting a heaping plate of golden brown panfish and walleye fillets with a generous dollop of potato salad in front of Cole.

"Hmm?"

"When the boat came up to us while you were battling that walleye, all I saw was a couple of fishermen who wanted to drop a line where they knew fish were being caught. Happens all the time. But you knew before they brought their guns up that they had bad intent. How was that?"

Cole looked at his friend in the waning light and thought he saw self-doubt. He picked up the plate and a fork and took a big bite of walleye. He chewed, savoring the crisp batter and clean white meat while considering his answer. "It happened fast, but when you pointed them out, the first thing I noticed was that they were both wearing Gatorz tactical sunglasses. That seemed out of place. Unlike the orange plastic model I sported today, those sunglasses are military grade and cost two hundred or more a pair. I haven't seen many outside the Navy Seal and special ops communities. I'm not sure there's another pair in Prairie du Chien or Marquette. And then, when I saw their spotless tee-shirts that screamed *River Rats*, I figured they had just picked them up at Starks in a failed attempt to fit in on the river. Besides, can you blame me for being a little jumpy? If we took a dunk for no other reason, it was a hot day, and the little swim would've cooled us down. Of course," Cole said, hiding a smirk behind another sip of ale, "I didn't realize in the moment that you might impale your thumb or another appendage on a treble hook."

Fwam laughed. "I forgot how hilarious you think you are." He got serious again. "This is heavy stuff. You ended up saving both our lives."

"Funny, I didn't see it that way. I remember you knocking down would-be-killer number two so that I could come up and breathe. Gotta tell you,"

Cole said, finishing the last of his beer. "That lung full of air tasted as sweet as anything I ever drank in before."

"Okay. Try another piece of fish. I fried it in my secret-recipe batter."

"Don't worry," Cole said, shoveling a tender piece of panfish in his mouth and nodding at his plate. "I'll empty this before you can say, 'God bless Billy Hunter,' and then I've gotta get back to Milwaukee, where I've got bigger fish to fry. Pun intended!"

Chapter Thirty-One

Cole tanned easily, but today his face was pink, and his shoulders and chest were tender under his dress shirt. *A little sunscreen wouldn't have been a bad idea yesterday*, he thought, but he enjoyed his time on the river with Fwam before the bad guys showed up and ended it way too soon. He stood at a window in his office, squinting out at the huge expanse of Lake Michigan, watching the waves throw themselves against the shore, one after another. The early morning sun danced off the spray, millions of sparkling jewels tossed in the air. He was pulled into the rhythm of the waves and thought again about the saying, *like lemmings to the sea*. He remembered sitting here and having that phrase run through his head on the chaotic first day of this case, not long after Senator Rhodes was shot, and he met Karri Rhodes in the ICU. He'd looked into the saying since and knew lemmings didn't just follow a leader or a herd thoughtlessly to their death. It was a myth that made for a great metaphor. And he knew that Hawkins and Jones, his and Li's would-be killers, hadn't mindlessly targeted them. They'd been sent by someone who didn't want Senator Rhodes' attempted assassination investigated further. He had two more names now, Mike Duffy and John Jage, the men who'd died the day before trying to kill him. He not only had their names, but he also knew that they served in the same unit as Hawkins and Jones and that they were getting regular checks from the same Irish bank. In the baseless metaphor, they became two more lemmings to the sea. *Were there more on the way?* DC Security Professionals was funneling a lot of cash to hard men to do hard jobs. Deadly jobs. He would go after Dexter Carter, no matter what Director Trudell said, but he needed a plan first, and it had to be tight.

A steady *hick, hick, hick* sound caught his attention, and he looked at the wall clock, second hand trembling as it jerked its way round and round. He wondered if anything in life ever really ran smooth, and if all we ever did was go in circles, if we looked at things long or closely enough. It was a sad thought. "Timer, old boy," Cole said with a forced smile. "Trusted friend and ally. There's no quit in us, right?"

Li coughed from the door, with Lane looming behind. They were both shaking their heads. "Can we come in, boss, or do you need more private time with the clock?"

He waved them in, and they sat at the table. Lane set a fresh cup of coffee in front of Cole as he joined them. "You okay? Seems like a question I'm asking you more and more. Shows my compassion, I guess."

Cole took a long sip of the coffee, followed by a deep breath. The coffee's taste, steaming aroma, and caffeine lifted him. He raised his mug to his analyst. "Thanks, Lane. And yes, I feel pretty good this morning, all things considered. As much as some people don't want us to get to the bottom of this, it seems like the puzzle pieces are finally coming together." He looked from one to the other, holding eye contact with each for a beat. "I appreciate the fact that both of you are still with me, chasing this down."

They were silent for a moment, and then Li started singing in a passable Dionne Warwick imitation, "That's what friends are for!"

They broke out laughing, and Lane took over, "For the good times. And the bad times. We'll be on your side forever more…." It was a truly cringeworthy Elton John cover, which made them laugh louder.

When they caught their breath, Cole asked, "Any chance we'll get anything from the bomb that blew up Weezy's place?"

"ATF has taken the lead on that. They're pissing their pants because that was the first time anyone used an RPG on U.S. soil with hostile intent." Li said. "They'll go through every grain of dust on the site before they're through."

"Alright. Hopefully, they pull a lead or two."

"Don't count on it," Lane answered. "I have a friend inside ATF, and she

CHAPTER THIRTY-ONE

thinks they'll find enough fragments and scraps to piece together what type of grenade it was and who made it. Beyond that, not much. It would be nice if they could come up with a lot number and follow the trail to who signed for it last. But there won't be a serial number. And when you manufacture tens of thousands of these things, somehow some get, well, misplaced. Someone at the manufacturer notes they shipped five thousand, but they really made ten more. Someone else on a testing range says they fired twenty, when they only fired seventeen. And another guy in supplies signs for ninety, when there's really one hundred. You want more?"

"Crap. Sounds like the chances of ATF finding something useful is about the odds of you sweeping Mila Kunis off her feet."

"No!" Lane said. "I just told you there is almost zero chance that ATF will be able to help our case. As for me and Mila, that's maybe fifty-fifty. The beautiful actress falling for the handsome, ex-lacrosse-playing FBI guy...that could be the cover story of *People* magazine any week now!"

"Remind me not to have you fill out my bracket for the NCAA Tourney next year," Cole said. "I'm not completely sold on your skills as a prognosticator. But getting back to the case, what else do we have to go on outside of the fact that DC Security Professionals likely paid hitmen to kill Senator Rhodes, me, Li, Fwam, and the Harris brothers?"

Li shook her head. "Nothing, really. Although I'm pretty sure me and your friend Fwam weren't primary targets. We would've simply been collateral damage."

Cole nodded, thinking. "Well, then we need to figure out how we take what we have and get to the people who've been paying Dexter Carter. If APAG is his only client, then it seems like there's only one answer to that question. But we need to be damn sure we're right, because APAG has friends in the highest places...including the White House and our Director's office. Do we have anything on Carter yet?"

Lane slid a manila folder across the table to Cole while he talked. "Grew up in Biloxi, Mississippi, the son of a Navy SEAL legend who lost his life in combat when little Dex was six. He grew up idolizing the SEALs, and his mom took him to see a Navy recruiter on his eleventh birthday. I kid you not. His mom signed him up for something called the Navy League Cadet Corps, which I guess is like the Boy Scouts for Navy geeks. He graduated to the Naval Sea Cadet Corps when he turned fourteen, and whatever training or education the kids received took place at Keesler Air Force Base in Biloxi. His mom pushed him every step of the way. It seems like she wanted Dex to be a surrogate for her lost husband. And little Dex did what mommy wanted. He started going to the Navy recruiter's office a couple times a month when he turned fifteen, just to show the recruiters he could pass the Navy SEAL fitness test. And he wouldn't just scrape by, he would blow it away. When the recruiter told him SEALS also had to be good teammates and that he should demonstrate that, he joined his school's baseball and soccer teams and made all-conference in both.

He earned his SCUBA qualification before he was sixteen. His mom took him to a local rifle range and bought him lessons, and the kid became good with both rifles and handguns. He was one of twenty-five teens from across the country accepted into a two-week training course led by real Navy SEALs called baby BUDS. It gives the students a pretty good idea of the training the SEALs go through, and Dexter excelled at it.

He was smart in the classroom, too, earning mostly A's. Maybe not Ivy League smart, but good enough where he could've gotten into most colleges without a problem. Instead, he graduated early from high school, and his mom signed his enlistment papers into the Navy when he was seventeen. Only a handful of nineteen-year-olds graduate SEAL training in any given year; Dexter Carter did it at age eighteen."

Cole had been skimming through the file while Lane talked, but he set the file down and rubbed his eyes, before looking at him. "So, Dexter loses his larger-than-life Navy SEAL dad when he's six, and he becomes obsessed with following in the old man's footsteps. And he makes it. So why don't I see a happy ending for this story?"

"I don't know," Lane said. "He served honorably for the next thirty years after enlisting, fighting in several hostile areas, and earning a number of commendations and promotions along the way. Five years ago, he was honorably discharged with the rank of master chief petty officer, close to

CHAPTER THIRTY-ONE

the highest rank he could attain without a college degree. Maybe he had his fill and decided to take the pension. He'd get seventy-five percent of his full salary at that point."

"You said he was smart," Li offered. "Maybe he got tired of seeing younger SEALs jumping him in rank just because they earned a college degree. I read where two-thirds of Navy SEALs have degrees."

"Maybe," Cole said, taking another sip of coffee and cradling the warm mug in his hands. "He joined the Navy, put in his thirty, and he's been out five years...which means he's only fifty-two."

"Only?" Li and Lane said in unison.

"Ha! Yes, only. Says the old man in the room. I'm pointing out that Dexter is still almost a decade away from being able to draw his social security, even a reduced amount." He skimmed through the file again. "At his rank, he would've been making a little over a hundred thousand a year with drill and hazard pay thrown in. That's good money, but he wasn't getting rich by any means, and we already know he didn't come from money.

Cole held up the manila folder, "There's nothing in Carter's official files that indicate he went rogue, and guys who do go to the dark side and get caught aren't typically given an honorable discharge. But if he put in thirty solid years, all but the first in the SEALs, he could've saved someone's bacon who ended up in a position of power, where he or she could intervene on his behalf. Do we know anybody in the Navy who could see if there's more here?"

"Not without setting off alarm bells in Director Trudell's office," Li said.

Cole's cell phone went off, and he turned it so the others could see the caller ID, *Gene Olson*. "Speak of the devil."

"More like *guardian angel*," Li said as the analysts got up and left the room.

"Morning, Gene. How're you?" Cole asked, getting up and going to the window.

"If I was any better, they'd call me Cole Huebsch!"

"That's old, Gene, but still good."

"Like me, you mean."

Cole chuckled, but he knew Olson had a way of bringing his guard down

171

before getting to the hard stuff. "What's on your mind?"

"No time for small talk?"

"Not when they're trying to kill me from one side while the other side is trying to tie my hands behind my back." Cole surprised himself with his bluntness.

Gene sighed. "That's why I called. You and I need to make sure we understand each other. Now more than ever, we need to be on the same page."

Cole felt the tension in his shoulders and tried to roll it out. "Not much to understand, is there? I heard you and the Director loud and clear in his office the other day. *Stand down.* If Trudell had tattooed it on my forehead where I can see it every time I shave, it wouldn't have been clearer. You two saw to that. And now they came after me again, and almost killed a friend of mine in the bargain. What am I missing?"

"What did I tell you in the Director's office?"

Cole thought back to the meeting, watching his reflection in the window scowl and shake its head. "I guess it's not *what* you said, it's what you didn't say. You sat there mute while our fearless leader told me he didn't give a shit if me or people I care about are killed. He just wants to make sure the Washington elite aren't inconvenienced by my questions. And he wants to keep his fucking job!" He could feel his voice rising more than hear it. Blood rushed to his face as he walked a tightrope with the person who had been his best ally, friend, and mentor since he'd joined the bureau.

"Maybe I own some of that. I could have stood up to my boss like you're doing right now. I could've defended you. But it doesn't really work like that here in the swamp. You don't win a fight here by lining up against the opposition like the British did against us when we fought for our independence. It's more guerilla warfare. Strike and retreat. If I stood up and supported you in his office, the Director would have pushed me to the side. He would have a hard time firing me without cause. But he could neuter me.

"Trudell sees you like a champion show dog. Think of a beautiful black and white springer spaniel. The deepest glossiest black fur broken up with

CHAPTER THIRTY-ONE

the most brilliant white patches. It's got the long feathery tail, and people ooh and ahh when they see it. And he sees me as your handler. He expects you to trot around beside me when I want you to and to sit on command. Right now, he expects you to heel at my lead. But that's not how it works. Trudell isn't the best Director we've had, but he's far from the worst either. I think he cares about the bureau and the country in his own way, but people do strange things when they have a gun pointed at their head…and that's what he feels like right now. What he doesn't know is that I'm not your handler; I'm more like the guy who follows behind you and hands you a treat and an 'atta boy' from time to time. You do what you do as well as you do precisely because you're *not* on a leash.

"Trudell's right though, that when it comes to FBI agents, you are a fucking show dog. An amazing one at that. And the training helps for sure, but it's mostly just your damn bloodline and how you're wired somehow.

"'You can't control him, you can only hope to contain him,' as Dan Patrick would say." Gene wasn't long-winded, and that was the most he'd said to Cole without pause in a long time. While he was listening, he heard through to the deeper meaning behind the older agent's words. "You're the guy who rallied the troops behind me. It didn't just happen organically. You reached out to your closest agents and analysts, men and women you think are most likely to be loyal to you, me, or both of us. And you asked them to put their careers on the line to help me out."

"Help *us* out," Gene corrected. "You aren't alone in this, and you never have been. Li and Lane, and the rest of your team in Milwaukee would run through walls for you. They'd throw their jobs or even their lives away in order to help you. I would too."

Cole felt ashamed for doubting his friend. "It could come down to that, Gene. I'm sure you've brought the people you think are the most loyal to you in on the case, but it only takes one of them to see exposing you as their big chance at a promotion. Then you're done. And worse, whoever's behind all this doesn't seem to think twice about killing anyone they see as a threat. If they think you are on the wrong side of this, they could come after you."

"You forget it sometimes, that I'm a big boy, and not just in size either. I'm still first and foremost a special agent, and I can take care of myself…or go down fighting."

Chapter Thirty-Two

Cole spent the rest of the morning and afternoon catching up on email, digging out after being gone from the office a couple days. He left the building early and pulled up unannounced behind the familiar gray sedan in front of Senator Rhodes' house at four in the afternoon. The two agents recognized Cole's old Dodge, and the driver gave Cole a thumb's up out his window. Cole gave a quick wave and then looked across the street at the pretty yellow house. He smiled when he saw the Senator in an animated conversation with their mutual friend, Alan Anderson.

As Cole climbed the steps onto the porch, Alan's deep voice boomed. "Here comes the human target." He made his big hand into the shape of a gun, his index finger the barrel, and pointed it at Cole. "Bang!"

"Ouch! That hits a little too close to home. You guys have a pretty good source of information, because not too many people know about the attack on me yesterday. Not yet, anyway."

The men stood up and shook Cole's hand, and Cole noticed that there was no cane in sight. "What brings you here, Cole?" the Senator asked.

"We've made some progress in the case, and I thought maybe sitting down for a while and walking through it with you might help me. I didn't know Alan would be here, but I'd appreciate his perspective too."

Eric pointed to the dregs of two ice teas sweating in tall glasses on a table between him and Alan. "Can I get you a drink?"

Cole thought about it. "It's after five o'clock in Washington, DC. You wouldn't happen to have a beer in the fridge, would you?"

"A kindred spirit," Eric said. "Be right back."

Cole pulled a chair over and placed it so that its back was to the street, and he faced Alan and Eric's empty chair. Alan moved the table so that it was in front of all three of their chairs, and Eric returned with three beers on a tray and made a show of setting one each in front of his guests. He had poured their beers into frosted glass mugs. "This is called Mosaic Theory. It's an American IPA from Component Brewing, made by three cousins right here in Milwaukee."

"God bless America!" Cole said as he reached for his glass.

"So, we're too good to drink out of cans now?" Alan asked as he palmed a mug and took a big swallow.

"Damn straight," his host answered. "I want to enjoy the beer's color and the texture of the head almost as much as the taste."

"A man after my own heart," Cole said, and Alan harumphed.

"Give me a chance, and I'll make a gentleman of you yet," Eric said to Alan.

"God help us," his old friend said, and the three of them laughed.

They sipped their beers in a comfortable semi-silence for a while. Birds called back and forth from the trees, and Cole could hear the Senator's children playing inside the house. Cole sat back in his chair and felt a cool breeze ruffle his hair.

"You said you wanted to talk about the case," Eric said. "We've got time, but when Karri calls us in to dinner, then we gotta up and go. Karri likes her cold food cold and her hot food hot. You can join us, if you'd like. I'm sure Karri would be okay with it."

"She'd insist!" Karri said, sticking her head outside the screen door, brightening the porch even more with her smile. "If I didn't have dinner on the stove, I'd join this little powwow." She nodded toward Eric with a grin, "This guy's milking his injury for all it's worth. He'll wear out that porch chair before he's back to work full-time!" She ducked back into the house, and the screen gently banged shut behind her.

"Sorry. I should have gotten right into the case. I guess I got carried away with how peaceful it is here," Cole said.

"From what we hear, peace and Cole Huebsch haven't gotten together much since this whole thing began," Alan said. "You're either lucky or good.

CHAPTER THIRTY-TWO

Either way, we're glad you're still upright."

"You and me both," Cole said, raising his glass. "Let's toast to that. And I hope I'm lucky *and* good, because it looks like I'll need both of those attributes to see this through."

Cole took a full hour to bring Eric and Alan up to speed on the case. They were called in to supper before he could get to his questions, but Cole enjoyed the warm interaction with Alan and the Senator's family every bit as much as he enjoyed Karri's amazing lasagna with sides, including warm buttered rolls that melted in his mouth. The three men cleaned the dishes and the kitchen, while Karri helped the kids, and then they moved back to their chairs on the porch. The waning light was softer now, and the temperature was perfect. They each nursed their second beer for a few minutes, enjoying the sights and sounds of a beautiful Milwaukee neighborhood summer's eve, before Cole cleared his throat.

"What are you gentlemen thinking?" Cole asked.

Alan set his beer on the table and steepled his fingers in front of him, shaking his head. "Early on in this case, you asked me if I thought it was plausible that the health insurance industry or big pharma would kill to stop Eric or others from derailing their gravy train. And I said it was certainly plausible. I might have even gotten a touch huffy when I said it. But sitting here now, with you saying it's not only a possibility, but a likelihood, it's still hard to believe. The stuff of fiction writers."

"But what else can it be?" Eric asked. "You tracked the money paid to the goons that attacked you right back to APAG and big pharma." He looked at Cole. "Have you sat down with their CEO yet? I know Nichole Sebastian. Think Cleopatra with greater power, wealth, and spooky allure. And more poisonous asps. I don't get queasy easy, but she scares the shit out of me. And that's the damn truth!"

"Watch your language, Senator," came Karri's voice from inside the house. "You've got precious little ears in here."

"Sorry!" Eric called back.

Cole shook his head. "No. I haven't met with the APAG CEO yet. When I learned that the health insurance industry paid the *Times* reporter to pan your convention speech, I flew to DC and talked to their association CEO. Roger Beneker the fifth, Esquire, was at her side. He took me to task. Megan Baldwin never admitted bribing the reporter, but she did tell me they would never pay to have someone shot. It's easy to say, but I'm pretty good at picking up tells or lies, and I believe she was telling the truth. The problem is that Beneker went directly to the president, who went directly to the Director of the FBI, who called me on the carpet and told me to march this investigation into the swamp."

"But that's not you," Eric said with a scowl. "Well, it wasn't me either, but the whole system grinds you down. Early in my term as Senator, I saw that the U.S. was paying three times the cost of prescription drugs as any other country. My first thought was, 'What the hell? We need to do something about this.' On a national scale, it's bankrupting our country. And on a personal level a lot of people aren't taking the meds they're prescribed because they simply can't afford them. When they have to choose between buying groceries, paying rent, or paying for their prescriptions, their meds come in last. I started out by going to my own party leaders, but they changed the subject whenever I brought it up. I was ready to go rogue, and I stepped across the aisle to talk to my Republican colleagues. Again, nothing. Nobody would talk about it, even though it's the elephant in the room. I finally came back to Wisconsin and sat down with the former legislator who talked me into running for office in the first place. She apologized to me and told me that big pharma was the one industry that owned both sides of the aisle nationally, lock, stock, and barrel." He paused to take a big sip of his beer.

It wasn't dark yet, but the big shade trees and the dying sun cast a dimness to the scene, muffling the light and sounds. Bats had begun flitting about high above them, keeping the humans mosquito free and their own bellies full.

Lock, stock, and barrel," Cole mused, with a slight smile. "You know that's a gun reference, right? I think the phrase started being used in England not all that many years before the American Revolution started. It describes the three elements of a firearm at the time, the lock or firing mechanism, the stock, or handle, and the barrel of the gun. Lock. Stock. And barrel."

CHAPTER THIRTY-TWO

"Well now, Cole, that's quite, um, enlightening," Alan said, trying but failing to hide a big smile behind his mug of beer.

Cole laughed. "Sorry. I didn't mean to take that down a rabbit hole. It's just a fitting choice of words, given big pharma seems to have a gun pointed right at the heart of our country now. And nobody's been in their sights or crosshairs more lately than yours truly."

"You know, I tried to buck the system," Eric said, looking away, down the quiet street. "I gave an interview with the Washington Post, where I asked some of the tough questions of the pharmaceutical and health insurance industries. Less than twelve hours later, I was called into a private meeting with the Senate Chair, President Pro Tempore, the Majority Whip, and a handful of other leaders. I was told in no uncertain terms to back off. It was made clear that the monies that came in from big pharma and health insurance were critical to the success of the party and its agenda. When I tried to argue and ask the question, 'At what cost?' I was shut down. A couple of the leaders couldn't look me in the eye. I sensed they agreed with me, had maybe been in my position a few years before. But everyone eventually goes along, or you lose all your campaign dollars. If you tried to take on those two industries and their lobbies, then you'd be shunned when it came to campaign cash…and not just by the two with the fattest wallets. I believe the party would make sure that none of their other cronies, industries or individuals, supported you. You'd have no meaningful committee assignments and no cash to fight your next election. Completely neutered. I'm sorry to say that I left those high-level meetings with my tail between my legs, and I heeded the establishment's advice. I was selfish, thinking about Karri and the kids and this house. I didn't want to lose everything we've worked for. That was a powerful motivator for me."

"But something happened at the Convention. No more Mister Nice Guy," Cole said.

Eric smiled again and nodded. "That's right. The party leaders invited me up on that stage because they thought they'd brought me in line. They'd instructed me to talk about equity and civil rights. They wanted me to point out the differences between the two parties when it came to those issues. I was willing to do that. My plan going in was to be their good soldier and do just that. But when I heard Ray Charles sing *God Bless America*, I decided 'to hell with it.' Instead, I spoke from the heart about what I believed were the issues of the day. Of our time. Maybe part of me knew all along that I was going to give the speech I gave. Otherwise, why would I have had that prescription bottle in my pocket? The perfect prop. But I didn't know in my own head and heart that I was going to give *my* speech and not someone else's until Ray sang about patriots who 'more than self, their country loved.' Those words and Ray's emotion galvanized me."

"And a helluva speech it was," Alan agreed.

"I did kill that speech," Eric agreed, laughing. "That's for damn sure!"

"Word choice!" Karri yelled out, and all three of the men laughed.

"Sorry!" Eric called back. He looked directly at Cole. "The day after the speech, when I woke up after surgery, I felt like I'd been run over by a fully loaded city bus. And in those fogged moments of pain and confusion, my first thought was that maybe it was the leaders of my own party who had driven the bus that hit me."

"What else can you guys tell me about big pharma?" Cole asked.

Eric answered first. "I've met a lot of people in the industry, and they include some of the brightest and most compassionate people on the planet. Scientists, for example, who devote their lives to beating cancer and pretty much every disease you can imagine. However, I've also seen levels of greed and inhumanity from the C-suite, the CEOs, COOs, and CFOs, that you rarely see anywhere else. Unless maybe in organized crime. But the mafia and cartels are pikers compared to the worst of the big pharma parasites. Occasionally people will scream when the cost of common meds skyrocket. When the manufacturers of insulin and epi-pens raised prices exponentially over a short period of time there was a big outcry. But it died down. It always does."

"And while a brave or stupid reporter will spotlight the price gouging from time to time, they always fade to black pretty quickly," Alan added. "Because the pharmaceutical industry spends more on advertising than almost any other industry. You try to watch your favorite show on television, and it

CHAPTER THIRTY-TWO

seems like every other ad is from a pharmaceutical company. And most of what they're promoting directly to consumers, the public can't buy without a prescription from their doctor. They're drug pushers like the worst guy on the street corner, but with a much, much bigger budget."

"And when a reporter writes a story damaging to the drug companies, you can bet their editors, producers, and others higher up the food chain hear from those companies. At a time when even big daily newspapers are asking their readers for donations to help pay for reporting, it's hard for them to attack maybe their biggest advertisers and turn off one of the few decent spigots of money they still have," Eric added.

"Another thing to consider is this," Alan said. "With one or two exceptions, every major media outlet shares at least one board member with a pharmaceutical company. There is a huge connection between big pharma and the mainstream media that people don't realize, because the press sure as hell isn't gonna tell em."

"So big pharma has the money, the means, and the motivation to do whatever it takes to keep its profits soaring," Cole said. "And we've got plenty of examples of pharma CEOs who lack a moral compass."

"You mean like addicting a whole generation!" Alan said.

"Exactly like that," Cole said.

It was dark outside. Some time ago, Karri had turned on their soft exterior lights. She had put the children to bed and came out to join the conversation, with her own beer in hand. She rested against the porch railing. "Did you solve the world's problems?"

"Nah," Eric said. "I'm not sure we've even helped Cole much tonight. Mostly been a lot of bitchin' and moanin' going on."

"That's not quite right," Cole said, finishing his beer. "I had a good idea who was behind this before I stopped over. But you guys have helped me with motive and more." He got ready to hoist himself out of his chair when his cell vibrated. He looked at the screen and the text from Michele. *I think I've found something you should see.*

Chapter Thirty-Three

It was almost ten when Cole climbed the steps to his home on the second floor of the castle mansion. He tried to be quiet, because he knew Frau Newhouse typically went to bed around nine-thirty. Michele heard the creak of the ancient wooden stairs, and she met Cole as he opened the door. He could tell she was excited.

"I brought you a late-night snack," Cole said, holding out a large foil-covered plate to her. "Lasagna, homemade rolls, and greens, courtesy of Karri Rhodes."

"Sounds delicious," Michele said, ushering him into the foyer and closing the door behind him. "But right now, we've got work to do." He followed her to the kitchen and watched as she put the plate in the refrigerator and then sat down at the big wooden table. Her laptop was on, and she patted the seat next to her. "Have a seat. I promise I won't bite."

While Michele worked at the keyboard, Cole grabbed a glass from a cupboard and went to the fridge. He pushed the lever for ice first and then filled the glass with water. He took a sip and held it up to Michele. "Want one?"

She was engrossed in pecking at the keys and didn't look his way. "Uh uh."

He sat in the chair and scooched a little closer to Michele, trying to see the screen better. She turned it in his direction and looked at him, excitement lighting her face along with the glow of the monitor. She was like a bloodhound who had caught the scent.

"You think you're on to something big here, correct?"

"Think? You'll be the judge, but this feels like something ginormous." She

CHAPTER THIRTY-THREE

bounced her eyebrows up and down for effect.

"Show me."

"I started thinking about how someone had tried to kill Senator Rhodes because he gave a speech, and that led to another thought. If they'd try to kill someone because he gave a critical speech, what would they do to someone who wrote a scathing article or delivered a damning television report? I googled *big pharma scandal* and other similar phrases, and then I noted who wrote the article or gave the television report. Then I searched online to see if I could find out anything about the reporters. She pointed to the screen. Read this."

Cole did. It was a brief obituary from the *L.A. Times*, about one of their reporters who'd been killed in a mugging a couple of years ago. Cole turned to Michele. "It's a sad story. Michael Kasun, the reporter, was only thirty-six when he was murdered. That's too young to die. But what am I missing?"

Michele held up a finger. *Wait for it.* She pulled up a second article. It was another *Times* story dated two weeks before the obituary, an investigative piece on the unchecked cost of pharmaceuticals in the U.S. and how the country's existing anti-trust laws were useless when it came to big pharma. The article described in detail a pay-for-delay strategy used by the industry where one company would pay another to hold off on bringing a generic version of their drug to market, artificially keeping the price of their medication high, as well as their profits.

Cole looked at Michele and shrugged. "That's another great example of the industry's greed and corruption. Am I missing something else?"

"Look at the by-line. Look at who wrote the story."

Cole scrolled back up to the top of the article. Under the headline, BIG PHARMA PROFITS UNCHECKED, he read, *by Michael Kasun*.

"You think it's a coincidence?" Michele asked. "Less than two weeks after the *L.A. Times* ran the story about big pharma greed, Mike Kasun is killed in a mugging gone bad. This was supposed to be the first in a series, but there were no follow-ups. The exposes died with Mike."

"Jesus," Cole said. "It's a big coincidence, for sure. But it seems like a stretch to link the death to big pharma. Accidents happen."

"That they do," Michele agreed, "And when you cross big pharma, those accidents happen all too frequently." She turned the laptop back to her and hammered the keyboard again. When she turned the screen back, Cole saw a *Washington Post* story about the high cost of medicine and the role big pharma plays in that cost. The feature was driven primarily by a lengthy interview with Wisconsin Senator Eric Rhodes. He scrolled back up and read the by-line, *by G. A. Donaldson*.

Cole looked at Michele, but she was already typing, bringing up another story. He could tell she was upset. Tears welled in her eyes, and she quickly wiped them away. "I'm guessing Donaldson didn't enjoy a long life after he wrote that article."

"That would be an accurate prediction," Michele said, turning the screen back to Cole. This wasn't a small obit; it was a half-page story honoring Donaldson, who had experienced a sudden and fatal heart attack just a week after his interview with Eric ran in the paper.

"My God," Cole said. "This is incredible."

"There's more," Michele said. "I spent the past three hours looking for reporters who covered stories at a national level that were critical of big pharma and who died within a month of those stories running. I came up with six. Five were big city daily newspaper investigative reporters, and one was a television correspondent with CNN. The journalists covered big pharma's price gouging, paying physicians to prescribe their drugs, and addicting whole nations. All but Donaldson were in their thirties and forties, and the causes of death were attributed to car accident, overdose, suicide, and mugging gone bad. Never the same twice. Donaldson was in his mid-sixties, and he apparently had a heart attack. I'm not buying it." She teared up again, and now those tears ran down her cheeks and patterned her t-shirt.

Cole put his hand on her slender forearm. "I don't buy it either."

She shook her head. "You must think I'm soft."

"No. I don't. But I can tell this has touched you deeply somehow."

She nodded and leaned back in her chair. "Do you have time for a story?"

Cole's smile was tender. "For you, any time."

"I remember walking into my first journalism class. I was a freshman and

CHAPTER THIRTY-THREE

just excited to be in college. We were in a medium-sized classroom with tiered seating, and pretty soon, it was maybe seven minutes after the hour, and no professor. A buzz grew, because we'd heard there was an unwritten rule that we could leave if the prof still wasn't there ten minutes after the hour. It was a warm early fall afternoon, and the prospect of an extra hour in the sun was attractive to everyone in that room.

But just as a few bold students stood up and started for the doors, Professor Gerald Nivens walked in. As he walked up to the podium to begin his lecture, the bold scurried back to their seats. Nivens eyed the students, looking every bit the professor in his dark glasses and brown tweed sports jacket. The podium was an older but sturdy two-piece model made of walnut. The base came up to the bottom of Nivens' ribcage. It could be used alone or with the second piece, which was made of matching stout wood, and nested atop the base. It added height and offered more space for notes. Nivens continued to look out over the students, seemingly trying to read something in them. He leaned forward, gripping the top piece of the podium, before jerking it up to shoulder height and slamming it back down on the base. The bang was deafening in the hushed room and reverberated off the walls. Some students jumped in their seats while others froze in terror and confusion.

The bang was gone immediately, followed by an even more disturbing silence that was complete, like the room had been sealed off from the outside world. The one collective question that rose like a dense fog in the room was, *Is he mad?* Not angry. But the next level after bat shit crazy. Now the question hung in the air louder than the slamming of the podium. *Is he mad?*

Then Professor Nivens gave a simple directive. "If any of you are here today because you like to write… Please. Leave. Now."

Eyes darted between the students, most with a *guilty as charged* look on their faces. Pretty much every student in the room had chosen to study journalism because they liked to write, and maybe because people had told them they were good at it. You could take that talent and try to pen bestselling novels, but most knew that was a long shot. For every Lee Child and John Grisham, there were thousands of writers who didn't make enough to pay rent or put food on the table. So here they were, first class in journalism one oh one, because they liked to write. And their professor had just told them to leave.

Nivens looked out over them again and sighed. He shook his head and laid his papers out in front of him. "Let's get started then."

Cole watched Michele, lost in the story, and realized he was holding her hand. He gave a little squeeze, and she returned it, continuing. "Professor Gerald Nivens spent the rest of that lecture and the whole semester teaching us about journalism and what it meant to be a journalist. We learned about the price that journalists have paid throughout the years in order to bring the important truths of the day to their fellow citizens. So many journalists have died pursuing a story both here and in godforsaken lands rife with war. Others spent years in jail because they had integrity and honor, men and women who wouldn't give up their sources when bullied and even beaten.

"That class ended up being the one you never wanted to miss. It came during a time when entertainment news had already caught on, and Professor Nivens taught us that facts matter more than opinions. He taught us to see journalism as a noble profession and to honor those who went before us. That's why I get so pissed off when reporters like James Flood smear the profession. That's why I hurt when a young man like Mike Kasun is killed for doing his job. I met him at a national conference a couple of years ago. I went right up to him and introduced myself, because he was writing the big, important stories I was hoping to write. He took the time to encourage me. And G. A. Donaldson was an icon in our field. He was one of those Nivens held up as an example when I was in school, who'd been hurt covering a war and imprisoned for not divulging a source. Donaldson called out presidents on both sides of the aisle when they abused their power, and he was attacked for it every time. But he never backed down. The only thing they could do to silence him was to murder him." She gripped Cole's hand harder and looked directly at him, "You can't let them get away with this. You need to catch these people and put a stop to what they're doing."

Chapter Thirty-Four

Cole was seated at the table in his office at seven the next morning. He nursed his second cup of strong black coffee while Li and Lane read through printed copies of the notes Michele had made the night before. They were detailed, including footnotes and facts to back up all her points and assumptions. Timer's labored counting off of the seconds soothed Cole somehow. He hummed the theme from the *Jeopardy* game show.

Lane looked up at Cole, halfway through the pages. "Really?"

After a while, Cole said, "It's still a long way off, but here I was, wracking my brain, trying to figure out the perfect Christmas gift for you two. And now I have it…matching online Evelyn Wood speed reading courses. You're welcome!"

Li rolled her eyes. "Unlike you, this is brilliant. We had a smoking gun before, but now we might be on top of the entire smoking freaking arsenal."

"And know this, chief," Lane said. "Michele is to Karl Rove what you are to George W. Bush. She's your brain. No denying it."

Cole got a sour look on his face like someone had spiked his coffee with vinegar. "Come on…"

"Nope. This is genius. And she's Huebsch's brain."

"Whatever. My brilliant analysts can't come up with this stuff, so my, uh, roommate has to."

"Roommate?" Li asked.

"Housemate?"

"Mate?" Lane asked.

"Not like that, Rump! Jesus! Anyway, I have something I'd like you two to follow up on. I need you to check the bank records of the hit men hired by APAG. See if you can match the list of murdered journalists that Michele found to the timing of when those seemingly random payments came into their accounts. If the payments were consistently just before or after the deaths, it would cement our case even more. Also, dig deeper. You've got a lot more resources at your disposal than a laptop and Google. Michele dug for three hours and came up with the six dead journalists you just read about. See if you can find any other journalist deaths that seem to coincide with payments to the hitmen. Can you do that for me?"

"Easy peasy, as a sage old mentor of mine would say," Li said.

"Actually, not so old if we're thinking of the same handsome guy."

"Right. Well, we'll try to have that information for you by mid-morning. That work?" Lane said.

"It does, indeed." The analysts gathered their notes and were almost out the door. "Li!" Cole called. "Could you stay for a moment?"

Lane walked out and shut the door behind him. Li walked back over to the table and sat next to Cole. "What do you need?" she said.

"Nothing else right now, other than to hear how you're doing."

She paused before answering, "I'm okay." But she did a poor job of hiding the sadness in her voice.

"What if I remind you that I've been trained by our government to pick up on even the smallest of tells and white lies. That means that if one of my people is walking around with the weight of the world on her shoulders, I can pick up on that."

"I get it," Li said. "Put on a happy face, right?"

"No. That's not what I'm saying at all. Let's try a different approach. Have you heard anything from Linda?"

Li's mouth tightened. "No. She hasn't responded to my texts or my calls."

"Have you tried to reach out to her parents?"

Linda lowered her eyes. "Her mom and dad have never really accepted her for who she is. They stopped pushing her to find a man and get married a couple years ago. But since then, they actively avoid the subject of who

CHAPTER THIRTY-FOUR

she's dating. It's taboo in their house." She looked up and met Cole's gaze with watery eyes. "I don't exist to them."

"I'm sorry," Cole said. It was the best he could think of to say.

Now Li wore her pain and sorrow like a cloak, the fabric of which enveloped her. "Linda's brother called me last week. He told me she's not doing well, that she hasn't worked since the attack on us, and that she's withdrawn into a shell. They have a close relationship, and he told me he can't really get through to her either. He said she stopped taking *his* calls and texts almost a week ago. I'm worried."

"I don't blame you. What do you want to do about it?"

"I'm not sure there's much I can do if she won't take my calls or respond to my texts."

"Okay. Just promise to let me know if you think of something I can do to help."

Li left the door open behind her when she went back to her own office, and Cole looked at the empty doorway for a moment before moving on to other active cases. His team had run down a tip provided by a major U.S. apparel manufacturer earlier in the week. With the cooperation of the Milwaukee Port Authority, they uncovered a stream of knock-off Nike, Gucci, Ray Ban, Levi, and other brands flowing into the port. They documented everything they found and put tracking devices on a wide array of items in an effort to corral the eventual buyers. They were also working with agents from other countries in moving upstream, tracking the offending ships' origins and ports of call they'd stopped at along their journey to Milwaukee. Cole wasn't interested in a small one-time bust; he wanted to disrupt the overall flow of fake goods that were hurting the American economy.

Next, he caught up on the case they had pulled together on a smaller local suburban police department where the chief and a few of his officers had decided to worry more about their own wealth and less about the welfare of the people they had sworn to protect. His team had turned one of the officers, and now had video and audio of the chief himself taking money from drug dealers and threatening to hurt anyone who tried to get in his way. They had shared their evidence with federal prosecutors, and Cole expected indictments to be handed down within days. There were few things he detested more than cops gone bad, local or federal, and he planned to be there in person when the chief was taken into custody.

It was eleven thirty when Cole poked his head in Li's office. Li was at her desk with multiple monitors, and Lane sat in a chair facing her with his laptop in his lap. *So that's how it got its name*, Cole thought. He rapped on the door frame, and they both looked up. "Give me something new," he said.

"We're not done yet," Lane said.

"You told me 'easy peasy' by mid-morning. It's closing in on noon."

"We *can* tell you that payments were made into the accounts of the APAG hitters within twenty-four hours of five of the six reporters' deaths that Michele tagged as suspicious. That's a win for us good guys and gals," Li said. "No payment for the sixth, which likely means there's either another hitter we haven't found yet, or the car accident really was just an accident."

"That doesn't account for all the 'random' payments the hitters received. Does it?" Cole asked, making air quotes with his fingers around the word random.

"No. It does not," Li said. "But we've also found supposedly natural cause deaths of two bloggers critical of big pharma, where payments were made to our hitters within a day of those deaths. There could still be more out there."

"Have you shared this with anyone else yet?" Cole asked

Li shook her head. "We didn't need anyone in DC to help with this part of the investigation…."

"The investigation that wasn't," Cole interrupted.

"Right," Li said. "We didn't want to hit any tripwires that might alert the director or anyone else that we're still working this. But this is huge. Staggering, really."

"That's for sure," Cole agreed. "Now we just need to come up with a way to finish it that doesn't result in me being fired or killed."

Chapter Thirty-Five

Cole was sitting at his desk the next morning when Lane stepped into his office. "Good morning."

"Morning, right back at you," Cole said, looking up from his computer screen. "You and Li come up with anything else?"

"Not yet. But I'm not sure how much more there is to find. Seems like we have enough to go after Dexter Carter and his security firm, at least."

"I think we have more than enough to nail Carter, but I want the leadership at APAG or whoever else is behind this. Carter's just a tool to that person or persons. If we want to stop this, then we need to cut off the head of the snake, and not just the tail that will simply grow back."

"Ick. I don't like that analogy. Not at all," Lane said. "And I'm pretty sure snakes don't grow their tails back, so it's either a myth or just plain stupid."

"Switching subjects, what's your opinion on how Li is doing since she and Linda were attacked?"

Lane cocked his head. "I don't want to say anything that might hurt her."

"Hurt her? I'm not asking for a fitness assessment. I'm asking as someone who gives a shit about her as a human being and a friend, and not as her boss."

"I know," Lane said. "Thing is, she's still on top of everything work-wise, and she's just so damn smart. If she weren't gay, I would've asked her out a long time ago. She feels like a sister to me now. But half the time when I barge into her office lately, I catch her staring off at nothing. Twice I walked in, and she was just sitting in front of her computer with tears running down her face. I'm worried about her."

"Okay. Thanks for sharing that. I want to help her get through this like you do. How is she this morning?"

"That's why I stopped by to see you. She called in sick today."

Cole grabbed his jacket off the back of his chair and headed out the door. Lane stepped aside and Cole called over his shoulder, "Thanks, Lane. I'll check it out and let you know what I find."

Cole knew Li lived in Wauwatosa, but he'd never been to her house before. He got her address from personnel as he drove and pulled up in front of a cute two-bedroom bungalow on north seventieth street twenty minutes later. A cold front had clashed with the summer heat and resulted in a thunderstorm. Cole didn't have a raincoat, and he got soaked as he followed the curving walkway to Li's door and rang the bell. When nobody answered, his own alarm bells started going off in his head. He was getting ready to break in when he heard soft footfalls from inside. Then he heard a lock disengage, and the big wooden front door was pulled open. Li stood looking out through the screen door. She had on pajama bottoms and a white sleeveless tank top. Her face was puffy, and her hair was all over the place.

After an awkward silence, Cole said, "Good to see you too! Are you going to invite me in?"

He could see the gears turning slowly in her head as she contemplated her options. Finally, she reached forward and pushed the screen door open an inch. "That's the kind of warm reception I'm accustomed to," Cole said, opening the screen all the way and easing past Li and into her living room. All the shades were pulled, but Cole could still feel the warmth of the cozy room. The refinished hardwood floor was covered with a large beige area rug, and all the furniture looked overstuffed and comfortable. A large photograph of the Milwaukee skyline at night caught and held a person's eye when they entered the home. The cityscape and a huge moon were mirrored in a shimmering pond. Cole pointed to it, "One of Linda's photographs?"

Li smiled as she nodded. "The girl froze her cute little butt off taking that shot. She was by the lake on a fall evening and shot back toward the city over a lagoon. It was a crisp evening, and she took shot after shot to get it just right. She was a bit of a perfectionist in that way."

CHAPTER THIRTY-FIVE

Cole pointed to another large print that dominated the room. It showed what looked like the aurora borealis or northern lights shining through distorted ice formations. "Is that Iceland? I know a guy who flies to Reykjavik every other year just to get a chance at a photo like that. It's beautiful."

She shook her head. "That's sunrise over Lake Michigan, taken one morning when the temps were ten below without the wind chill. We get world-class ice formations here too. I guess it's just a fact of life that too often we feel the need to go halfway round the world, when life's treasures are in our own backyard."

"She really is an amazing artist," Cole said.

"She was better known for her portraits, the way she captured the essence of people with her lens. But she could do nature and architecture too. She just had a gift."

"Had?"

"Yup. She died three days ago."

"God, Li. I'm so sorry."

She stepped into him and hugged him, clinging to him. He was cold and wet, but she didn't let go. When she finally spoke, she said, "Her brother called me last night. He'd been drinking. He told me that Linda took her own life, swallowed a cocktail of prescription medicines, and never woke up. This happened three nights ago. Her parents had her cremated and are acting as if she never lived. Her brother told me they didn't want me contacted, but he felt I should know. I guess the liquor gave him the courage to go against their wishes. God knows Linda and her brother rarely did."

Cole felt both her warmth and her sadness leach into him as he held her, but he also felt anger and resentment. "I didn't know how bad she was hurting. Maybe I could have helped if I just knew," she said.

"But you couldn't have known. Nobody would talk to you, including Linda." He just held her for a while, before adding, "It sucks when you realize that no matter how much of a badass you are, that you can't always protect the people you love. And you loved her very much, didn't you?"

Li went rigid and then stepped away from him. "You know about love, do you?" She scowled, and her eyes turned dark and mean. "You were married once and let that go without a fight. And now you have an amazing woman who obviously wants to be with you, and you keep her at arm's length. You push her away without realizing it. Or maybe you know exactly what you're doing to her, and you're just that callous!"

He swallowed and looked down. Her words wrapped themselves around his heart like strong, slender fingers. Squeezing. Constricting. He couldn't breathe, let alone speak. A crack formed between them, and with each moment of silence, it grew until it felt like the next minute, they might be on opposite sides of the room, and the next on opposite sides of the world. He couldn't let that happen, so he swallowed his pain and pride and reached out and pulled her back into his arms. They hugged, Li clinging to him even more desperately, and Cole felt her body convulse with sobs as her tears ran down the side of his neck. After a minute, she stood back, awkwardly wiping her eyes and sniffling. "I'm sorry. I've never hurt this bad, and I'm taking it out on the one person who's been here for me the whole time." She took his hands, her beautifully mismatched eyes boring into his. "I'm so sorry."

Cole smiled his own sad smile. "It's okay. And I'm pretty sure you answered my stupid question."

Li smiled weakly. "Well, if it wasn't love I felt for Linda, I think it's the closest I'll ever get to it in my lifetime."

A more comfortable silence ensued before Cole broke it with a question, "What now?"

She thought about it, before nodding more to herself than to Cole. "Now we keep working. We finish this case, and you finish the job of making me the finest federal agent ever." She arched her eyebrows at him in challenge.

"I think I can make that happen," he said before leaving her. As he slid into the Charger and drove away, he thought about how Li had described his relationships, and the truth of her blunt words rode with him.

Chapter Thirty-Six

Cole went back to the office, but he sleepwalked through the rest of his day. All the active cases his men and women were working on competed with fragments of thoughts on his personal life. His crew had filled in most of the puzzle in the Senator Rhodes' case, but they were no nearer to closing it in a way that would be meaningful to Cole. He wasn't after the owner of a security firm; he wanted the person or people behind the killings so they couldn't simply hire a new group of hitters when things cooled down in a few months.

Cole left the office before six p.m. and headed for the sanctuary of the castle mansion. He wanted nothing more than to curl up in the fetal position on the couch and watch an old movie or maybe read Jack London's *Call of the Wild* for the umpteenth time. But as he trudged up the weathered steps he heard Frau Newhouse through her thick door, "Cole? Cole?"

He hesitated. He wanted to keep going and pretend he hadn't heard, but he had grown to love her like his own grandmother, and he needed to see what she wanted. His shoulders slumped a little more. She didn't ask him for much, and it made him feel like this was another person from whom he took more than he gave. He knocked. "*Guten abend*, Frau!"

"Good evening to you also," came her muffled reply. She opened the door to her kitchen and stepped aside. "Come! Come!" She beckoned him in with a sweep of her arm. He walked in and noticed a stack of papers on the oak table, which she moved off to the side. She patted a chair, looking at him intently through large pale blue eyes that matched the color of her simple housedress, eyes that had seen eighty-seven years of wonder, sorrow, and all things in between. "Sit with me, Cole. Let's have a beer and talk. I worry about you."

He settled into the chair while she went to the refrigerator. She came back with a cold twelve-ounce bottle, a sixteen-ounce can, and an opener Cole thought might be antique. He opened the bottle in deference to her frail hands; her lager was the now inexpensive national brand that still carried her surname. The beer she'd selected for him was a local hazy IPA. She set two tall pilsner glasses on the table, while Cole cracked open his can and studied the label. Frau Newhouse saw this and smiled, saying, "I like the name."

Cole laughed out loud, since the beer was *Naked Threesome*, brewed in nearby Waukesha by Raised Grain. He looked directly into her eyes, grinning, "I've never had a *Naked Threesome* before."

Frau blushed and clucked her tongue.

"You started it!" Cole laughed.

"Ya. I did." She sat by him. Cole poured half of the can into his glass, admiring the ale's thick, full head. He took a deep swallow and licked the foam from his upper lip.

Frau poured the entire bottle into her glass and then sprinkled some salt from a shaker into her beer. It foamed over the side of the glass, and she dabbed at it with her always handy kitchen towel. She took a sip and smacked her lips. "*Das schmeckt gut!*"

"Mine tastes good as well! You are too kind to me," he said, touching his glass to hers. "Thank you!"

They sat in a comfortable silence for a while, each savoring their beer. Cole thought back to the first time he'd ever sat and had a beer like this with Frau Newhouse, twelve years before. She had seen the quizzical look on his face when she added salt to her beer, and she told him it made it less bitter and more flavorful. She told him it went back generations, and she thought the habit had been brought over from the Old Country along with her family's original beer recipes. She'd never gotten him to add salt to his beer, and he'd never converted her to the hoppy IPAs.

Frau broke the spell. "I am thinking," she began. "I am an old woman, and

CHAPTER THIRTY-SIX

it is time I should get my affairs in order."

She seemed to be waiting for something from him, so Cole nodded that he understood and for her to go on.

She reached out and put her hand on his. "I would like for you to do something for me, Cole."

He nodded again. "Of course. Whatever it is, you know I will if I possibly can."

"Ya. I know," she said. She pointed to the pile of papers she had pushed aside. "I wonder if you will care for my house when I am gone."

Cole sighed. He had been wrestling with his thoughts since he'd stopped to see Li earlier, and he didn't want to think ahead to a time without Frau Newhouse. He'd moved in not long after his divorce, and she felt like the only family he had. "Do we need to talk about this right now? I have a lot going on, and I don't want to think about the day when you won't be here. Besides, the way things have been trending lately, it's likely I'll leave this earth before you do."

She made her peculiar clucking sound again and squeezed his hand. "You are a survivor, Cole. I don't want to hear you talk like that. I am getting old, and it is right for me to do this. I would have done it before, but I haven't had anyone close in my life for many, many years."

Her words softened him, and he squeezed her hand gently in response. "I will help you in any way I can. That's my promise to you."

She nodded, glowing, then smiled gently again. "And what of you, Cole, are your affairs in order?"

Cole tilted his head. "Hmmm? What do you mean?"

"What are your intentions with Michele?"

Cole had taken another big sip of his IPA, and he coughed. "My intentions? My affairs?" When he caught his breath, he answered, "I can assure you my intentions are pure."

"Maybe too much so."

Cole shook his head. "I don't understand. Michele told me that she shared her story with you, that she was raped by a coworker who drugged her. I think you can tell I care for her, which is why I asked your permission to let her live here with us in the first place. But I won't rush her."

It was pleasantly warm in the little kitchen, but a coolness settled between them. "That was almost a year ago when that horrible man took advantage of her. She needs more than a wooden man who stands guard over her."

"A wooden man? You think I don't have feelings?"

"I know you have feelings, Cole, but you don't listen to them. You push them down inside and don't let them come out. You need more in your life, too."

He looked at her even more closely, and felt she was right. He shook his head, though, finishing the beer in his glass and standing up. He took the half-full can with him and went to the door. He opened it but turned back to Frau before leaving. "I need to go, and please know that I respect you and know that you care for me as I do for you. But my life is complicated right now, and dangerous. Very dangerous. I don't want to bring Michele deeper into my world than I already have. If something happened to her, I'm not sure I could handle it. Good night," he said, closing the door behind him and trudging up to his place, slamming the rest of his beer on the way.

Cole made himself a ham and cheese sandwich and poured himself another cold beer. He wolfed down the sandwich and went to what Frau called the den. It was a two-story library full of dark wood paneling and featured rolling ladders, a mammoth fireplace, and his favorite reading chair…a big overstuffed dark caramel leather one with a matching ottoman. The library was a shared space and could be accessed from either floor of the house. Cole took his beer and a tattered copy of *The Call of the Wild* with him down a winding staircase and over to his chair by the fireplace. He knew there was a hardcover first edition copy of his book in the library, along with others by London, Hemingway, Steinbeck, Twain, and other masters, some signed. But he never took them off the shelves other than to admire them from time to time. He liked his stained and dog-eared copies that he could re-read without needing to be delicate. He could see well enough to navigate by the evening light seeping through the room's big windows, but he turned on the reading lamp that seemed to lean over his shoulder to read along with him. Settling into the chair was like a comforting embrace from an old

CHAPTER THIRTY-SIX

friend. All he wanted to do was to shut out the world and escape into the crazy world of the Klondike gold rush of the late 1800s, and the story of a dog named Buck who is ripped from his genteel home and forced to make his way under harsh conditions. *The story of my life,* Cole muttered as he opened the book and read. He was engrossed from the opening paragraph and deep into the second chapter when his phone began vibrating on the side table. Buck had been bludgeoned with a club and torn open by the fangs of other dogs, and Cole had never felt such an affinity for the big St. Bernard, shepherd dog mix.

"Shit," he said, bending the top of the page to save his place in the book and closing it. He set it beside the phone and looked at the screen. *Janet Wifey.* He had never edited her name in his phone contacts, and it looked a bit odd. He was in a good place with his ex, but he hadn't heard from her in months. Michele had appeared on her news show twice over that time, enjoying it much more than their first interview, which had ended in a catfight on national television.

It had grown dark outside while he'd been transported with Buck to the frigid north by Mr. London, and the soft glow of the lamp spotlighted him alone in the large, quiet room. "Hey," he said, keeping his voice low.

"Hey yourself," Janet said. "I know it's been a while since we connected, but I wanted to check in and see how you're doing. For old times' sake and all that."

"Friends don't need a reason to call each other," he said. "And it feels like we've reached that point."

She was quiet. "Yeah. That's how I feel too."

"What made you pick up the phone and call?"

"I finished reading Michele's ARC of *The Killer Sermon*, and since you were one of the main characters, I couldn't help but think of you."

"Okay, wait. She sent you an ARC?"

"Yes. Authors and publishers typically send them out to reviewers and other authors a few months before a book releases. They've always been paperbacks, but more and more these days, we're getting ARCs in an e-book format. I got one I could download to my Kindle and read it in one sitting.

Anyway, I promised Michele I'd write a blurb for her if I liked the book, and I absolutely loved it. It was a big case, and she nailed it from every angle. I felt like I was with the two of you every step of the way as you solved it. What did you think of it?"

"Um, I haven't read it yet."

"Really?"

"Yeah. She hasn't asked me to read it, and I haven't asked her to show me a draft manuscript. The last thing I want to do is have her think I'm reviewing it for the Bureau."

"Did you ever consider the fact that her story could torpedo your career if she painted you or the Bureau in a bad light?"

"For about a second. I've come to trust her, pretty much completely."

It was quiet for a moment before Cole added, "I know she'll tell the truth, and I'm not ashamed of anything we did to catch that killer."

"Are you at least a little curious about how she portrayed you?" She was teasing him now in a way that took him back to a time years before when there was nobody else in the world for him but her.

He smiled. "Of course. I'm human."

"Sometimes I wonder."

"What?"

"Nothing," she laughed. "But your instincts are still solid, because Michele painted you in a good light."

"Yeah?" he asked softly.

"Yeah. Put a modern-day Sir Galahad in a blender with Mel Gibson from Lethal Weapon, and that's pretty much how you come across in the book...without Riggs' suicidal tendencies, of course."

"Well, that's nice," he said, grinning. He couldn't help remembering how he'd made a similar Lethal Weapon comparison to himself not that long ago in a bar with Li.

"You're smiling right now, aren't you?" Janet laughed.

Cole sat up in the chair a little straighter. "What?"

"You're feeling a little full of yourself. Admit it!" She laughed even harder.

He laughed with her and felt better than he had since leaving Li's home

CHAPTER THIRTY-SIX

earlier in the day.

"Do you love her?" Janet asked.

"What?" Her quick lane change caught him off guard. He forgot sometimes that she interviewed presidents, heads of state, and A-list celebrities for a living.

"Come on," she prodded. "It's just two old friends who've been through a lot together. I hope you know by now that I still care about you. I want you to be happy."

He didn't answer immediately. When he did, he said, "Thanks, Janet. I want you to be happy too. I guess it took us a while to get to this point, but I'm glad we're here. Let's not lose that." They said goodbye shortly after, with Janet's question about Michele still hanging between them.

Cole went to bed before the ten o'clock news, but his swirling mind wouldn't let him sleep soundly. Between Li, Frau Newhouse, and Janet, he felt like the main character in a twisted Dickens novel…who'd been visited by the ghosts of his relationships past, present, and future, except maybe in the wrong order. He finally gave up and got out of bed around midnight. He went to the kitchen and filled a glass with ice water and carried it back to his room. French doors led out to a small, covered balcony and he pushed open one of the doors and stepped into the cool night air. The storm had long since passed as he settled into one of two wooden Adirondack chairs and took in the scene. He heard a few cars on nearby streets, their engines shifting through gears while their tires made a steady *shhhhhh* sound as they rolled over the wet pavement.

A mist of rain had settled onto the edge of the chair, and the dampness and a gentle breeze combined to raise goosebumps on Cole's legs and arms. His boxers and tee-shirt didn't provide much warmth, and the ice water he sipped didn't help the situation. A thousand hidden city lights bleached the night sky, scouring it of its stars. There were still a handful scattered about, weak and dim, like small flashlights whose batteries were in their death throes. He remembered evenings growing up in his small hometown, where the sky was encrusted with countless blazing stars. And if he walked even a few blocks toward the bluffs and away from the small houses, how the night sky was awash with layer upon layer of stars…the galaxies opened above him.

He'd been raised to equate light with goodness and truth, and heaven's light surely shown brighter the farther one moved from the city and its hordes of people. But it was man's own light that drove away the starlight. He pondered that sleepily until he felt a warm hand on his shoulder. He looked up to see Michele. She was wearing shorts and a tee-shirt that looked gray in the dim light. She moved the table and pulled the second chair so that it nestled against Cole's. As she settled into her chair, she spread a large comforter over both of them. "I stole this off your bed," she told him.

"It feels good."

"You aren't the quietest roommate I've ever had. That icemaker on the fridge makes a racket. I wondered if you'd just go back to sleep or if you were up." She looked out at the sky. "Looks like you're trying to figure out what makes the universe tick."

"I kinda am," Cole admitted. "But I'd settle for understanding just my little place in it."

There was a pause, and then Michele asked, "So, is there a place for me in Cole Huebsch's universe?"

Cole wasn't prepared for the question. He turned and saw Michele staring at him, waiting for an answer. "And I thought I was thinking deep thoughts," he said.

"I'm not looking for glib," she said.

"Okay. I guess I just wasn't ready for this conversation right now. It must be one o clock in the morning. You think this is a good time for this?"

She shook her head. "You think there will ever be a time when you'll want to talk about it?"

He could feel his heart racing, and he took a calming breath. "I think now is as good a time as any." He reached for her hand over the blanket and held it. "And the short answer to your question is 'Absolutely.' I can't imagine my life without you right now."

"Right now?"

"Whenever. You've become an important part of my life."

CHAPTER THIRTY-SIX

"How? In what way?"

Cole sat up a little straighter. "I thought we were finding that out, together." He could tell she wasn't satisfied with his answer. "What do you think? Something made you ask the question, so maybe you should just tell me what's on your mind. I've got a million things on mine, and I'm not sure I'm thinking straight right now."

"You want it honest?"

Cole worried that she might tell him she was moving on, but he didn't hesitate to answer. "I do."

She looked away from him at the void in the sky. "I think you see me more like a puppy you rescued than the woman you can't live without. It's time you stop trying to save me, Li, the Senator, and everyone else and take care of yourself for once. I wonder all the time how you feel about me. I might ask if there's someone else, but you don't ask questions you already know the answer to. You're in love with your job and always will be. It's easier to deal with complex cases, puzzles, than people close to you. It's easier to put clues under the magnifying glass than to look into your own heart. You've lost people you loved before, and I get that. You loved your parents, and you lost them too young. You loved Janet, and you lost her. And maybe you're afraid it will happen again."

He sat there, as wooden as the chair beneath him, her words a weight stacking on top of those of Li's, Frau Newhouse's, and his ex-wife's, causing his shoulders to slump. Wooden. Everyone thought they knew him better than he did, and they might be right.

Michele sighed when Cole didn't answer. She slid the comforter off and stood up. Looking down at Cole, she said. "The thing that hurts me the most is that you don't think I'm strong. You might think I'm smart and you might think I'm pretty. But you see me as a person who's weak and vulnerable. Well, I'm not," she added, her voice firmer. "I can take care of myself. I always have. I need you to stop protecting me and start loving me, if you want to, that is...."

She turned to go back inside, and for the second time in the last twenty-four hours, he felt a fissure growing quickly and widely between himself and someone he cared about. Before Michele took a step, Cole reached out a hand and caught hers again. "Please don't leave," he said softly. She turned to face him, and his eyes shimmered in the pale moonglow. She saw a hunger and a longing in them and something more. Something more honest than words. She leaned down and hugged him, and they kissed deeply. She helped him to his feet. "Bring the comforter," she said, leading him into the bedroom and shutting the door behind them. She looked at him with complete trust, slid down her shorts, and stepped out of them. Then she slipped her tee-shirt over her head. She looked at him with a nervous smile.

Cole stood mesmerized, in awe of her beauty.

"Am I going to do this alone?" Michele asked nervously.

"No," Cole said, slipping quickly out of his own clothes and pulling her against him. "You don't ever have to be alone again."

Chapter Thirty-Seven

Cole woke up. Michele was gone from his bed, but the spot beside him was still warm where she had slept the night before. He rolled onto her side of the bed and inhaled her smell from her pillow. He got out of bed, pulled on his underwear and tee-shirt, and walked down the hall. The high-pitch whir of the coffee grinder kicked in, masking the sound of his footfalls as he stepped into the kitchen. Michele was facing away from him, gazing out the window and into the gardens. He reached around her and pulled her to his chest, kissing the top of her head. "Good morning," he whispered in her ear.

She turned and hugged him, looking up into his eyes. "Good morning." She blushed a little. "It's not going to get weird between us, is it?"

He kissed her lips, letting it linger. "If this is weird, then I'll take all the weirdness I can get."

They separated, and Michele made coffee while Cole got a glass of ice water. "What does your day look like?" Michele said.

"I guess I'll get to the office, and we'll continue to try to pull the case against Dexter Carter tighter. If we move now, he's all we'll get. I think APAG and someone higher than Carter is behind all the murder and mayhem. How about you?"

"I'll be reviewing the itinerary for my book tour and the promotional plan for my book. They want me involved, and I'd have it no other way."

"Janet called out of the blue last night to tell me she finished your book, and she loved it. Sounds like you've got your first fan."

"Aren't you my number one fan?"

"You know I am. But you haven't let me read the book yet."

"I guess I've just been nervous that you won't think it's good, that I didn't get it right."

"Well, Janet said it's amazing, and I'm sure I'll think the same." He changed the subject. "You want to grab dinner somewhere together later?"

She pulled him to her and cupped his backside, purring. "Let's just meet back here and grab something quick so that we can continue getting to know each other a little better. She turned him around then and patted his butt playfully. "Now go take a shower and get to work so you can get back here and take care of me in the manner I'm accustomed to!"

"Yes, ma'am!" Cold said, and he did just that.

Cole was in a great mood when he walked into his office. It seemed like the sun was shining a little brighter and clearer this morning, and his office felt warm and inviting. The first thing he noticed was a large, flat banker's box used to ship mirrors and artwork that was leaning against one wall. "Huh," he said out loud as he pulled out the key to his Dodge. He used the key to rip open an end of the box and slid out a framed painting that looked to be two feet by three feet. He turned it so that it was right side up, and the colors, textures, bold letters, and brush strokes jumped out at him. A big smile lit up his entire face when he saw Weezy's B.M. mark in the painting's lower righthand corner. He looked at the back of the painting and noticed a note taped there. He pulled it off and read,

Agent Cole,

Nobody ever really did anything for me before, and I never saw many people who could tell the difference between right or wrong or who gave a shit which was which. You and Li remind me of Batman and Robin...or maybe Batman and Batgirl. Anyway, keep fighting the good fight and don't let ol' Weezy down! If ever you need a hand, just give me a ring. BM

Cole turned the painting around again and leaned it against the wall. He stood back and looked at it, illuminated by the shaded sunlight. Letters forming Cole, Li, and MKE for Milwaukee were woven into the piece. He loved the colors and shapes. He sensed something more, something deeper in the painting, but couldn't describe it.

CHAPTER THIRTY-SEVEN

"It's beautiful, isn't it?" Li said.

He turned to see Li step through his doorway, and he nodded. "It's amazing. I don't think I've ever gotten a gift from one of the...." He hesitated. He was about to say, "bad guys," but he didn't see Weezy that way. Not at all, and especially not now. "Anyway, I love it."

"He sent me one, too," Li said. "It's as beautiful a piece of art as I've ever seen." She pointed to Cole's painting. "He captured you perfectly."

"Hmm?" Cole turned to her. "Not sure what you mean by, 'he captured me.'"

She pointed again. "It's a portrait of you."

"What?"

"Step back a little more," she instructed him. "You're locked into the first thing you saw. You need to look deeper. The O here is your ear, and the K is part of your nose. Your mouth is...."

Cole stopped her. "Wait! I see it. It jumps out at me now that you've pointed it out."

"Like most of my insightful comments."

"Hmmm?"

"Nothing."

"It's crazy good."

"I agree. He captures the essence of you. Maya Angelou said, '...People will forget what you said. People will forget what you did. But people will never forget how you made them feel.' This painting makes me feel your honor and integrity, your courage."

"I don't know about all that," Cole said, blushing slightly. "But it's beautiful and I'm going to mount it on the wall. We can't accept anything from crooks, but I think Weezy is one of the good guys."

After catching up on his email, Cole reached out to Lieutenant Williams in Baltimore and set up a video conference with Weezy. Later, he and Li logged into the meeting from the conference room. When Weezy came on the screen, it looked like he was sitting in the great room of a lodge somewhere. There was a two-story high floor-to-ceiling stone fireplace in the background, with massive shoulder-mounted elk heads on either side of it.

"Hey, Weezy," Cole said. "Did you go country on us since we last talked?"

"Hell no. Lieutenant Ron got me stashed out in the boonies 'til ain't nobody tryin' to blow my muthafuckin head off my shoulders." He turned in profile and grinned. "It's a head worth savin' for damn sure!"

Cole and Li heard a clicking noise coming through the laptop's speakers. *Click. Click. Click.* It sounded almost like static. "Do you hear a clicking sound?" Li asked. "Maybe we should log in again."

"That ain't static," Weezy said. "What you all're hearin' is Scootch, prancin' around on the wood floor here. Lieutenant Williams let me get a damn fine dog to bring out here in the sticks with me. Scootch keeps me company while the Lieutenant is out fightin' crime and shit. Scootch! Come here, boy! Come!"

The clicking sounds picked up in pace and frenzy, and suddenly, the dog was in Weezy's lap, its face inches from the camera, nearly filling the laptop screen back in Milwaukee.

Li screamed, and Cole jumped back and yelled, *Holy mother of God!* The dog licked its nose and stared at the camera with beady black eyes. Cole caught his breath. "It looks like something you might get if a nurse shark mated with a chihuahua."

"A chihuahua with horrible orthodonture having the worst hair day ever on the planet," Li added. "And it's got more ear hair than my great uncle!"

Weezy was laughing. "Hey! You're gonna hurt Scootch's feelings."

"Sorry," Cole said. "At least you rescued him. I can't see anyone else taking that little guy home with them. I think I'd bring home a Chucky doll before I'd bring a little guy like Scootch into the house."

"At least you didn't pay thousands of dollars for him," Li said. "Probably just paid to get his shots up to date."

Weezy stopped laughing. "Are you fuckin kidding me? Scootch is a muthafuckin' Chinese crested dog! They win the damn world's ugliest dog contest like every other year. He was a steal at two thousand!" He set the dog on his lap. "Remember that old Jimmy Soul song, *If you wanna be happy*? It goes, 'If you wanna be happy for the rest of your life, never make a

CHAPTER THIRTY-SEVEN

pretty woman your wife?'"

Li shook her head, but Cole said, "Oh, yeah. I remember that tune. My dad would sing it sometimes just to tease my mom. It had a nice beat, though."

"Damn right, it did. And the sentiment is the same with canines. You wanna be happy? Get an ugly mutt!"

"Okay, then! No offense, man." Cole said. "We just wanted to see how you're doing and tell you how much we love the paintings you sent. I know it's been a crazy few weeks for you, and it's been insane here too. That was a nice surprise to walk into the office this morning and see your paintings. They're just beautiful."

Weezy was thoughtful. "It was fun painting them. Something a little different. Lieutenant Ron brought me some canvas, paint, and brushes so I don't go stir crazy out here. I'll be back in the city before too long, but this has been a nice change of scenery."

"Thank you for the paintings," Cole said, Li echoing him. "We're having them hung in our offices."

Weezy seemed a little emotional. "Thank you both, too. I don't complain, since it wouldn't do no damn good anyhow. But I ain't had many breaks in my life. When you tracked me down, you could've tried to put me behind bars, or at least come after the money we made. But now I've got some bank, some friends on the force, and maybe a shot at a better life. I'm already rehabbing a building in a nicer part of the neighborhood. Weezy's on Ghoul gonna be open before you know it!"

"That's awesome," Cole said. "We're happy for you."

"You all got my notes? From the back of the paintings?"

"We did," Li and Cole said, nodding in unison.

"Everybody says to call them if you need anything. But they don't mean it. This is for real. You need some help in DC, BM, hell...anywhere. You just let me know. I'll be fuckin' Robin to you all's Batman and Batgirl! Those notes are redeemable any time you need something. I deliver. You feel me?"

"Yes," Li said.

"I do," Cole agreed. "So, before we let you go, how'd you come up with the name Scootch?

Weezy smiled. "Whenever that damn dog walks on that big white throw rug behind me, he scootches his fuckin ass along it, leaves a little damn scootch mark behind. Drives Lieutenant Ron berserker! That's his damn mark. The name fits!"

Cole and Li were laughing as they said goodbye.

Chapter Thirty-Eight

Nichole Sebastian didn't live in DC. Her eight-point-five-million-dollar home sat perched on the Potomac River in Old Town Alexandria, Virginia. The house was twenty minutes from her office without traffic. And, while DC's traffic congestion was considered the third worst in the United States, with the long and strange hours she kept, the traffic to and from her home was somewhere between non-existent or manageable for her driver and her. She had torn down the stately Colonial that used to sit on the lot and built a sprawling concrete and glass structure, much to the dismay of her staid neighbors. But Sebastian liked causing dismay. Reveled in it even. If there was a drug more potent than making people feel powerless and inconsequential, she hadn't tried it.

The back of the house featured walls of high-ceilinged glass that afforded amazing views of the water and the sparkling white sailing yacht tied to her personal dock. She'd had the boat two months now and had yet to take it out on its maiden voyage. But it looked damn good from her point of view. It was leased through APAG, a prop that told everyone that mattered that she mattered. She had no idea what it cost or how to sail it. Soft, dappled morning light poured into Sebastian's living room, and Frank Sinatra sang about *The Tender Trap* from discrete speakers. The door chime rang at precisely nine, and Sebastian rolled her eyes. When she heard footsteps coming down the hallway, she called out, "I told you I gave the inside staff the day off and left the door unlocked. Didn't I say you should just show yourself in?"

Dexter Carter stepped into the room then. He caught Frank's crooning,

You're hooked. You're cooked. You're caught in the tender trap. It felt like an omen. His brain encouraged him to turn around and run, but the rest of him insisted he stay. He wore a lighter weight gray suit, a white cutaway collar dress shirt, and a blue silk tie. "I'm sorry. I rang the bell as a courtesy, to let you know I was here." As he entered the room, his eyes didn't go right to the view of sparkling water, nor to the robin's egg blue sky, or the pristine yacht. They went to Nichole Sebastian, who stood looking at him from the windows, which backlit her long, silk nightgown, and highlighted her ample cleavage and a slit that went all the way up her thigh. Blood rushed to his brain, his heart, and one other organ. He groaned involuntarily.

"Consider this your annual review," Sebastian said to Carter, waving him over to her. "I called you here this morning to tell you that your *performance* lately has been unsatisfactory. And I don't like being un*satisfied*. She chose each word and its delivery with nuanced care, delighting in Carter's growing discomfort. He walked over and stood next to her in front of the windows.

"Take off your jacket and throw it on the couch," she said. He did so wordlessly. "And your shirt." It followed the jacket. "Next, your t-shirt." He took off his white undershirt and tossed it atop his jacket. "And now your belt." Carter maintained eye contact with her as he followed her directions, laying his belt with his other garments. He stood straight and hoped that his flat stomach and chiseled upper body would somehow move her. But he saw no emotion in her gray eyes, except maybe smoldering anger and revulsion. She stepped forward and put her hands on his shoulders, turning him so that he faced out toward the water. Then she slithered behind him.

He stood in front of the windows, acutely aware all at once that those same panes of glass that gave him an expansive view also allowed a person to see in. More precisely, it allowed many people to see in. Carter's face reddened as he stood bare-chested, noticing for the first time the obscene number of gardeners and landscapers at work in Sebastian's backyard. One man was mowing the lawn, though it seemed it had already been cut. Another was pruning a tree that looked well-manicured. Others were pulling imaginary weeds, and still more were moving handfuls of mulch to and fro. Carter didn't remember seeing a single landscaper in the front yard when he'd

CHAPTER THIRTY-EIGHT

strolled up the walk. And then he knew why. The woman who owned the house had drawn them all to the backyard for a view of her in the sheer silk nightgown. And now Carter was in the fishbowl, standing front and center on the stage Sebastian had created for them.

"I'm lowering one of my spaghetti straps," she whispered in Dexter's ear. She pressed herself against his back, and he felt the warm, extended bud of her nipple nudge him. She reached around and undid the button on the front of his slacks. She moved lower to unzip them. Carter was losing his mind, but he still noticed that Sinatra had moved on to another hit. *I've got you under my skin.* "We need to talk business," Sebastian said, her breath hot against his neck. Then she pushed his pants down, so they fell around his ankles. "It's about the FBI agent, Cole Huebsch, and it's a dirty, sordid business," she hissed, slipping her fingers inside his briefs and sliding those down too. He stood on display, painfully erect, and felt his whole body flush crimson. She leaned against him from behind, and he felt warm, silky flesh. His lust was hot and painful and insistent.

Her left hand slipped around to his navel and then lower, its heat searing his abdomen. "I'm sure, like you, Agent Huebsch is well *equipped* to do his job," she said, moving her right hand around and lower to cup him. "But also, like you, I'm not sure he has the *balls* for it." She squeezed softly, and Carter felt a wave of euphoric pleasure. She squeezed harder, and he felt crippling pain. She relaxed her grip, but still held him. "When Agent Huebsch's director told him to back off, he did exactly that. He went back to Milwaukee with his, um, *tail* tucked between his legs. "That's good, right Dex?"

"That's very good," Carter cooed.

"Alas, it's just not a very satisfying outcome to me, Dexter. I'm not the least bit satisfied right now. Do you know what would satisfy me?"

Carter was under her spell now and couldn't think. "Wha, What?"

She stuck her warm tongue in his ear. "You know what I want, Dexter? You know what I need? I need you to kill Agent Huebsch. He's humiliated you. Emasculated you. And now he needs to pay."

"Needs to pay," Carter repeated.

He waited expectantly for the feather-like touch of her fingers to pleasure him. Instead, she took his left hand in hers and placed it on his own manhood. "This is all up to you now, Dexter. It's what you'd call a one-man job," she whispered. "I need you to do this for me. To see to it personally. *Stop. Fucking. Around.* And just kill him. DIY!" Against his will, his hand began to move, picking up speed as she scourged him with her words. Outside, the workers tried unsuccessfully not to watch the fishbowl as the man pleasured himself, and the woman of the house sneered at them. Sinatra's "Witchcraft" floated to them from the patio speakers.

Chapter Thirty-Nine

Two evenings later, Cole stepped outside of the Castle Mansion just after nine. He had checked the weather app on his phone, and it showed a fifty-fifty chance the city would see rain and maybe a thunderstorm over the next three hours. Cole didn't mind those odds or the thought of getting wet. He bounced lightly on his toes as he witnessed the edge of a full moon begin its rise above the waters of Lake Michigan. Michele was reading in the den, and Cole felt the need for a workout. It was comfortable between them, and Cole was grateful for that, especially since the rest of his life felt damned uncomfortable right now. He and his team were no closer to arresting anyone higher than Dexter Carter, and it was beginning to look more and more like the people behind the long string of murders and attempted murders would go free. That frustrated the hell out of Cole, and there was nothing he liked to do more when he was frustrated than to get in a grueling workout.

It was still close to eighty degrees, even this close to the lake, and he wore just his running shoes and a pair of nylon running shorts with a small inner pouch that perfectly fit his house key. He bent from the waist and raised his arms behind his back, the extent of his stretch. And then he ran.

He started out at a jog and picked up the pace as he warmed up. He ran east and south a mile through the city streets until he reached the Summerfest grounds. The sight of the colorful sky gliders usually made him smile, but tonight as he passed them, they seemed gray and lifeless in the dark, and made him think of the attack on Linda and Li and the sorrow that followed. He was sweating freely when he turned to follow the lakeshore north; the occasional cooling zephyr washing over him felt exquisite.

He ran past Discovery World, the city's sleek science and technology museum, and saw the Dennis Sullivan Schooner docked behind it. Inspired by the tall ships that carried cargo across the Great Lakes in the eighteen hundreds, the Dennis Sullivan stood nearly one hundred feet tall and stretched one hundred thirty feet long. Its ten sails could spread four thousand six hundred square feet of canvas. Cole wouldn't have minded being under sail right now, heading out of the harbor for parts unknown. Instead, he ran.

He picked up his speed as he continued north, finding his rhythm inside a six-minute mile pace. He passed the Milwaukee Art Museum. Since Calatrava had built it twenty years ago, it had become an icon on the city's lakefront. Huge, white moveable wings soared over it, and the building was considered by the locals to be as great a work of art as any of the superb pieces it showcased. Cole was proud of the city he called home.

He ran on past the yacht club, and the rows of beautiful boats secure in their slips. He'd passed a few other runners and walkers early in his run, and the odd bicyclists, their blinking lights mirroring the twinkling lights of boats on the water. But he had the sidewalk to himself now. He could hear the waves slapping against the sea wall and the shore, and he heard the hungry cries of gulls searching for food.

He thought about Senator Rhodes out for a similar run on the morning he was shot. It seemed so long ago. Cole felt his presence with him now, running stride for stride with him. He enjoyed getting to know the Senator and his wife, and wondered if he and Michele could ever have what Eric and Karri shared. He thought about their fierce, yet steady love and the laughter of their children.

He kept his pace, breathing in and out, hard and steady, all the way to Bradford Beach and up to the beach's end in North Point. The beach would've been crowded with families and sun worshippers earlier in the day, but the park closed at nine. Cole ran in place a moment. He hadn't really planned out his run beforehand. He had just wanted to get in a workout and be alone with his thoughts. Four miles into it now, he could head home

CHAPTER THIRTY-NINE

on city streets and make it a seven-mile run and call it a night. Or... He looked around. When he turned away from the lake, he saw the North Point Water Tower looming above in the distance. The spindly tower, with its Victorian Gothic styling, had sat atop the hill above the bluffs for one hundred and fifty years. And Cole had an idea. He remembered a story about a Marquette basketball coach who brought his teams here to this very spot at the beginning of training. The players would run killers or gassers up the bluff and then jog back down until they could barely walk. It helped set the tone of toughness for the season and brought the team closer together. He wondered if Eric had faced this test.

What the hell, he thought, and raced up the face of the hill. He attacked it with aggression, taking out his frustration from the case on the bluff. Cole liked to push himself during workouts, but five times up and back, and his hips and hamstrings were talking back to him. The breeze picked up, and it began to spit rain on and off, but Cole was still overheated. He knew why they called them gassers now, because he was gassed. He decided to ignore his aching joints and muscles and fatigue and to fire up the bluff one more time. He was slick with sweat as he swung his arms and leaned into the hill, his breath more ragged now than controlled. His chest burned, and sweat ran into his eyes, nearly blinding him as he approached the top. He stumbled over it and right into a fist.

Cole had felt more than seen it coming, and he ducked so that the punch missed his chin and landed instead on the crest of his forehead. He still saw stars, and not those in the sky. Only his forward momentum kept Cole from tumbling comically backward down the hill. "Damnit!" his adversary yelled. Cole bent down and put his hands on his knees, sucking in air. The moon peaked through the clouds over his shoulder and spotlighted the attacker in front of him, the man furiously rubbing his right hand.

"Dexter Carter," Cole croaked. "I've been meaning to look you up."

"I thought you might be," Carter said, shaking out his bruised hand.

"I gotta admit, though," Cole said, wanting nothing more than to stall and catch his breath, "I'm kinda surprised you're fighting your own battle for once. Your MO has been more to send others out to do your evil deeds."

Carter took up a fighting stance. "Sounds like you're calling me a coward."

Cole straightened up. "If the shoe fits...." Before he could finish the thought, one of Carter's Converse Chuck Taylors was headed for Cole's face. Cole blocked the kick but couldn't get out of the way of Carter's fist that banged like an anvil into his ribs. Most of the breath he'd worked so hard to catch rushed out of Cole's lungs again. He staggered away from the bluff to gain distance and time and to figure out a way to defeat the former Navy Seal.

Carter kept stepping into Cole, pressing his advantage. He had watched Cole working out and knew he was exhausted. He fired brutal combinations of fists and feet. And Cole was taking a beating. He could sense in advance and block Carter's first blow, but he was having a hard time avoiding the second and third punches and kicks that followed. Besides the knot on his forehead, Cole now had bruised ribs and forearms and a busted lip. He had a bloody cut on top of his right eye that blurred his vision.

Carter was an expert at hand-to-hand fighting and martial arts, and he threw everything he had at Cole. It didn't take long for Cole to realize that he had one chance and one chance only, and that was to get in close, tie Carter up, and get him to the ground.

Cole kept trying to circle away from Carter, but his opponent knew what he was doing and constantly cut him off and attacked. Cole felt a chill wind blow over him, and it began to drizzle, light sprinkles at first, then harder. He glanced over his shoulder and the moon had been blotted out by angry dark clouds. The grass and dirt on top of the bluff grew wet and slippery. The wind picked up, and the rain came down in sheets, big cold drops that stung Cole's back. Lightning flashed, followed by ear-splitting claps of thunder, and Cole felt like a gladiator fighting to the death.

"How'd you know I'd be out here?" Cole asked, straining to catch his breath and stalling again. "This run wasn't planned out beforehand. I purposely vary my runs both to avoid monotony and to avoid being predictable."

Carter bounced on the balls of his feet, and a bolt of lightning spotlighted the cocky smile on his face. "Serendipity, my friend. I was just going to watch you tonight. See if I picked up a pattern that I could exploit later. But

CHAPTER THIRTY-NINE

when you started running up this hill over and over, I couldn't resist. It's almost too easy." He stepped in again and fired a straight left jab that Cole blocked, followed by a hard right hand that grazed the right side of his jaw. "Shit!" Dexter cursed. "The hand's not broken, but it's bruised as hell. I'll have to ice it down back at my hotel after I kill you."

This must be why they call these bluff runs killers, Cole thought idiotically. "It's nice to know I hurt you a bit," he said. "Even if it was taking one of your punches. So, tell me, what caused a decorated Navy Seal to go bad in the first place? Was it money?"

No reply.

"Was it the fact that everyone with a degree passed you up in the Seals?"

"Fuck you and every college boy like you. I didn't give a shit about that. I just liked taking names and kicking ass. Right about now, you're starting to see that I'm still not half bad at it."

"Was it a woman?" Cole asked. Carter laughed, but it was more of a nervous titter, and Cole could tell he'd struck a nerve.

"A woman. Hmmm. Someone like Nichole Sebastian, maybe?"

"Fuck you," Carter said. Though he was drenched, he still looked fresh and confident.

"Nichole Sebastian," Cole said again. He was taunting Carter, trying to make him lose his cool. "I can't wait to meet her."

Another bolt of lightning lit up the night, and Cole saw Carter's face turn from focused to ugly mean. "Too bad you'll never get the chance." He planted his back foot and launched a front kick at Cole's midsection. Cole anticipated it and caught it. Before Carter could follow with another strike, Cole lifted his opponent's leg high in the air and then swept his back foot out from under him. Carter crashed to the wet ground with a splat, and Cole was all over him. Carter was face down in the mud and grass, and Cole lay on top of him, wrenching the other man's arm behind his back and twisting it. Carter grunted, but said through gritted teeth, "You killed some good men of mine."

"How good could they have been if I defeated them?" Cole said, breathing deeply, trying to regain his strength. Carter snapped his head back in a reverse head butt, but Cole anticipated it and kept his head out of range. Carter tried pushing up from the ground, but Cole kept all his weight on him, pinning him there. "Easy big fella. One of three things is gonna happen next, and it's your choice which it'll be," Cole wheezed. "The first option is you keep struggling, and I'm going to push your arm so high up behind your back that it'll blow the rotator cuff and everything that holds your shoulder together. It'll all be shredded and unusable, no matter how many surgeries you undergo." Carter tried to buck Cole off him again, but Cole held him tight to the cold, wet earth.

"Second option. I tap you on the back of your head. Well, tap might be a misnomer. I'll hammer the back of your head with the meaty part of my fist. Think of swinging the mallet at a carnival and trying to ring the bell. When I tap the back of your head, it will drive your face into the ground, snapping your nose and concussing you. Depending upon how hardheaded you are, you'll take a nap ranging from a few minutes to eternity." Carter continued to struggle helplessly.

"The third and final option is that you cooperate with me. You let me take you in, and you share everything you can about what Sebastian and APAG have been up to. The murders of journalists, the payments to offshore accounts, the attempts on the life of U.S. Senator Rhodes, and certain FBI agents. Everything. You'll still likely spend the rest of your days in prison. Not ideal, but I recommend option number three for sure."

Cole heard the wail of sirens in the distance and saw the lights of police cruisers coming from two blocks away. Carter continued to squirm without effect beneath him. He thought about Carter's men attacking not only him, but Li, Fwam, and the Senator. "Option two it is," he said, bringing his right hand crashing down as hard as he could on the back of Carter's head. Even with the mud to soften the blow, he heard the bones in Carter's nose, and cheeks snap when his face bounced off the ground. Cole hung on grimly and didn't collapse until the local police were at his side and pried him off the man.

Chapter Forty

It was chaos when the police arrived on the scene. They'd received a call from a neighbor out walking her dog, and she said two men were trying to kill each other out by the old water tower. Two squads rolled, and it took two officers to pry Cole off Carter's still body. Cole had no identification and was too spent to speak coherently. When he didn't answer the responding officers' questions, they cuffed his hands behind his bare back. Paramedics arrived about the time the officers determined that Carter was still breathing, and his heart rate was more or less normal.

Cole sat in the mud and watched as the paramedics put Carter on a stretcher and loaded him into the back of their rig. "Danger…. Dangerous…. Dangerous man!" Cole stammered. His words were slow and slurred.

An officer came and stood over Cole. "You got something to say, studly?"

"Yeah. That man they just…the man they just put in the rig. He's a…he's a killer."

"That's a little harsh, I'd say. It looks like he kicked your ass, but you're still breathing."

That reminded Cole he should breathe, and he took in two sweet lungfuls of air. He hurt all over, but it seemed like his brain was thawing out. "I'm with the FBI. That man is a killer. You need to cuff him immediately before he comes to."

At that moment, Cole didn't look like FBI to the cop, but he sure sounded like an agent. "Come again?"

Cole saw the paramedics get into their ambulance, and he raised his voice. "The man the EMS just loaded into their rig… His name is Dexter Carter.

He is a stone-cold murderer. If you don't stop them from driving off, there's a good chance he'll come to and kill them. And if he gets away now, we likely won't find him for a long time, if ever. Stop them now and cuff Carter securely. Then call Captain Ty Igou of the Milwaukee Police Department. He'll vouch for me. I'm Cole Huebsch, Special Agent in Charge of the FBI's Milwaukee Field Office." Cole found his voice as he spoke, and he almost shouted the last words.

The officer looked at Cole and saw an alertness and steel he hadn't seen earlier. He ran over to the ambulance as it was pulling away, and he talked to the driver. He opened the back of the rig and secured Carter smartly to the rail of the stretcher, and he called his partner over to watch him get safely to the hospital. Then he called someone over his radio and got into an animated discussion. Finally, he walked back over to Cole and freed his wrists, helping him to his feet.

"Sorry about that," the officer said. "I had no way of knowing who you were when we found you. I apologize that I was wrong."

"No problem. But you were wrong about something else, too."

"What's that?"

"He didn't kick my ass. He might've gotten in a few lucky shots, but I was on top of him when you found us, right?"

The officer laughed. "Right. I guess it only *looks* like he kicked your ass!"

Another ambulance arrived on the scene, and the EMTs tried to convince Cole to go to the hospital with them. But Cole was having none of it. Instead, he half stumbled, half walked north. It took him an hour to cover the two-mile trek to Atwater Park in the neighboring suburb of Shorewood. Atwater Park was five acres of open space and featured its own sandy beach. But Cole was here to see an old friend.

The warm and cold fronts had fought it out at the same time Cole and Carter had. The cold front won the round, if not the fight, and it was twenty degrees cooler than when Cole had started his ill-fated run. He walked across the grass and sat at the base of the Spillover II sculpture. The eight-and-a-half-foot tall piece by Jaume Plesna was a favorite of Cole's. It was an open work steel structure, made of metal letters of the English alphabet

CHAPTER FORTY

spot welded together. A faceless man, sitting with his legs pulled up to his chest, gazing out on the vast lake. But Cole sat with his head down, his back turned to the lake and its stark and awesome beauty. He groaned as he shifted his weight, trying to get comfortable on the concrete base. He looked at the statue, staring out into the distance, seemingly searching for answers and meaning like he was. "Penny for your thoughts, Dave." He called the piece David Letterman, which usually cracked him up. "What? No words of wisdom for me tonight? Cause wisdom is something I could really use right about now."

A cool breeze blew intermittently, and Cole noticed the moon playing peek-a-boo through the statue with the help of some low, fast-moving wisps of clouds. He couldn't tell if the weather would turn angry again or clear up. If it was a metaphor for his life, Cole thought he should opt for an umbrella or, better yet, the nearest storm cellar. He touched the welt on his forehead and licked his split, swollen lower lip. The EMTs had cleaned up the cut above his right eye and secured it with a butterfly bandage. He had bruises and abrasions above and below the eye, which was already half swollen shut. Moonlight streamed through the letters that were Dave and spilled onto Cole. But it offered no warmth or comfort. He felt as hollow as the statue he sat beside. He rubbed a bruise on his cheek and was surprised when his hand came away wet. It had stopped raining, and he hadn't realized he was crying. Getting hit in the face was never easy for him to take. When he wrestled in high school and college, there was always a practice or two a year where the coaches would pull out padded gloves and headgear and encourage the young men to punch each other's lights out. It was supposed to help them take a blow, to keep their focus, and to fight through it. It was supposed to toughen them up.

And Cole supposed it had, but at a price. Getting hit in the face was personal, degrading somehow. Carter hadn't just landed a few punches and kicks, he really had kicked Cole's butt. Cole could more easily point out places on his battered body that felt okay than to identify the myriad of places that were in agony. His ability to get Carter to the ground and keep him there was the only thing that had kept Cole alive. Of all the attempts on his life, tonight was the closest he'd ever come to dying. He felt it literally in his aching bones. And just after he'd found something, someone, to live for. Michele. He shivered, overwhelmed with self-pity.

With his head down, he didn't see the lights, but he heard the *clump, clump* sound of four distinct car doors opening and closing. He could feel more than hear people coming across the grass toward him. Coming *for* him. He didn't look up; he just sat next to Dave Letterman, who looked out over the endless water unseeing. It could be the EMS squad, trying again to convince him to let them take him to the nearby hospital to get checked out. If it was, he would just tell them no again. It could be the police, called by neighbors, to tell him the park closed hours ago, and he'd have to leave. Or it could be more goons, backing up Carter, coming to finish the job he'd set out to do himself. Right now, he didn't give a damn if they killed him.

He felt a warm, familiar touch on his shoulder, the same shoulder that had taken a bullet not so many months ago. Cole looked up to see Michele, and her eyes teared up as soon as they met Cole's and saw the tears in his. She handed him a heavy, old Marquette University Wrestling sweatshirt. "You look like you could use this." She nodded to Li, Lane, and Ty. "And I think you could probably use your friends right now even more." Cole thanked her and moaned as he pulled the sweatshirt on. She sat next to him and leaned her head on his shoulder. He felt her warmth in more ways than one.

"One of my officers called and said some stubborn son of a bitch was fighting by the water tower. He asked if I'd vouch for you," Ty said. "He told me what you looked like and what you told him, and I said it could be none other than the FBI's top gun in Milwaukee. When he called me back to say you refused help from the paramedics and started wandering off north on your own, I called Michele, Li, and Laney, and we came looking for you."

Lane sat down on the other side of the statue. "Stubborn son of a bitch was a pretty good description. Almost like an artist's sketch in words!" He patted the statue. "I think David Letterman here would approve!"

Cole felt even warmer, more from having his friends close than from the bulky sweatshirt. "Thanks for finding me." He winced when he wiped at his eyes, forgetting the beating his right one had taken. He shifted his gaze from

CHAPTER FORTY

the lake and looked down. "I'm ashamed to say this, but I'd pretty much given up. I'm not sure I've got much left to give."

"And here we all thought you were Superman!" Li said. "You're human after all, just like the rest of us."

"You've been here for each of us when we've needed you," Michele said. "Maybe you can lean on us once in a while. Like now, for instance."

They all sat around the statue, feeling the connection with each other and their surroundings. It was cool, but the sky had cleared, and the full moon and the company filled Cole with a feeling of hope that he couldn't have imagined just a few minutes before.

"Ahem," Lane coughed into his hand. "Aren't you holding something back, Li?"

"Oh, right! I forgot all about this," she laughed, pulling a six-pack of *Zombie Dust* IPA from behind her back. She pulled them apart and handed a can of the hoppy beer to each of them. She set the last one down by the statue. "And the last one is for David Letterman."

They all laughed as they popped open their beers and took a drink. "Still cold," Cole said. "But I thought you were a Lite beer drinker?"

"I am. I bought this for you as a gift after you stopped by my house to give me the pep talk. I felt like such a heel for how I acted and what I said. I really was sorry. And I know a good IPA is the way to your heart."

"I'm taking notes here," Michele said, and they laughed again.

Cole looked at Li and held Michele's hands in his. "All you did was tell me the truth. That's what friends do. Thanks." He looked around and made eye contact with each of them, nodding. "Thank you all."

Michele stood up and tried to help Cole to his feet. He had stiffened up and struggled to stand. Li and Ty lent a hand, and Cole got up with a loud groan. Michele looked him up and down and smiled. "We need to get you home. To say you need your beauty sleep is the understatement of the year." Cole groaned again as everyone laughed, and they helped him up the hill to the car.

Cole didn't crawl into bed until after two in the morning, and when he awoke, he was alone. He reached over to where Michele had lay beside him, and the sheets were cool. He looked at the alarm clock and wasn't surprised to see it was after nine. He slowly got out of bed and pulled on a pair of shorts and a tee shirt, grabbed his workout bag, and headed to the YMCA with a change of clothes in a garment bag. He started out with slow laps in the cool water of the indoor Olympic-sized pool and finished the last half of his mile swim in a fast, steady crawl. He worked out the stiffness and some of the soreness from his body and was somewhat surprised that everything was working the way it should. He eased into the warm Jacuzzi for ten glorious minutes before showering, changing into his suit and tie, and heading over to the office. He checked his battered reflection in the locker room mirror before he left, and realized he now felt a lot better than he looked.

Cole was surprised to see Gene Olson's big frame sitting at his desk when he walked into his office a little after eleven. It was rare when the deputy director made his way to Milwaukee, pulled more often to New York, Los Angeles, and other larger cities. Gene pushed out of the chair and shook his hand. He had a smile on his face. "Good morning," he said. "But just barely." He made a show of looking at his watch. "Hell, it's almost noon, for Christ's sakes. What kind of office hours do you keep anyway?"

"Really?"

"I suppose you're going to tell me you worked late, huh?"

"Something like that," Cole said.

"I heard all about it, which is why I'm here." Gene pointed to the hole in the wall that Cole had framed. "Nice decorating touch, by the way."

"Glad you like it. It was a gift from a mutual friend of ours, Agent Jeffers. He threw my chair against the wall while demonstrating the finer points of leadership. How's Collin doin' these days? Didn't you send him up to Anchorage for some growth and development?"

"Yes. I did. I would've sent him to Nome or Barrow if we had field offices in those more remote places. He got too full of himself. He keeps trying to get me to bring him back to the lower forty-eight, but he hasn't been through a winter up there yet. I'm hoping that makes him a changed man."

Cole shrugged doubtfully. "We'll see."

CHAPTER FORTY

"Yeah, well, you should watch your back when he returns. He didn't like you before this and this is just going to drop you lower on his best friends' list." He paused. "Has anyone told you lately that you look like hell?"

Cole rubbed the knot on his forehead. It had already receded a bit. But he also knew his face and especially his right eye sported the colors of a nice sunset. "Not quite that eloquently. But everyone's a critic," he said. "And you should see the other guy."

"Matter of fact, I did just that this morning. And other than his beak, I'm not sure he has a scratch on him."

"So, I definitely won't be charged with using unnecessary force then."

"You most definitely will not." Gene's laugh mingled with the sunlight to brighten up the office. "I rousted Dan Willis after I got the call about your little skirmish last night, and we flew up here. He wants a crack at Dexter Carter, to see if he can get him to talk, and I wanted to have a chat with my favorite SAC. Seriously, how are you doing?"

"I'm one big bruise covered by a few lacerations," Cole answered. "But I swam some laps before coming in this morning, and everything seems to be moving the way it should." His words became choppy. "I got lucky, Gene. Carter pretty much had me. It was a little too close for comfort. I kind of lost it afterward, and only a little help from my friends allowed me to keep my shit together. It didn't feel good. That's for damn sure."

"I still don't understand why you don't just shoot the bad guys, like the rest of us agents."

"Yeah, well, I'll try to remember that in the future. But carrying the Glock in my running shorts would've been a problem. Not a lot of room in there."

Gene's laugh echoed in the office. "You think there's much chance that Willis will get anything out of Carter?"

"No. He's loyal, even if it's to people who are twisted. And I got the feeling last night that Nichole Sebastian has him wrapped around her little finger. Or maybe some other body part."

"What else you got?"

"You've seen everything. We can convincingly tie the murders and attempted murders to Carter and his outfit. But even though it screams of the American Pharmaceutical Advocacy Group's involvement, it's really all circumstantial. And the way they've got our nation's capital rigged, we'll never get any kind of warrant to search their offices or their CEO's house."

"So?"

"So, during my swim today, I decided I'm going to fly to Washington and confront APAG's CEO directly. If the director wants to fire me for it, so be it. If I have to pay for my flight, that's fine too. I doubt Sebastian will tell me anything, but I need to try. I've got nothing else and if we let more time slip by the evidence we have will just degrade with every passing week and month."

Gene nodded. "Do it. With this latest attack, *everyone* at the home office is looking to help you and openly defy the director. If he continues to try to isolate you now, he'll have an open mutiny on his hands."

Cole let out a breath. "Whew! I was a little afraid you'd fight me on this."

"No. The rich and powerful might get away with things the rest of us wouldn't, but there are always limits. And Sebastian and APAG have pushed their limits too far." He paused a beat, thinking. "You should take Li with you when you try to sit down with Sebastian."

"You think?"

"Yeah. Having a woman's perspective will help, and you definitely want a witness when you talk to that woman."

Cole nodded. "You're right about that. I want to keep Li close right now anyway."

"Perfect. As soon as Willis gets done interviewing Carter, we'll be flying back to DC. You and Li can catch a ride with us." Gene looked around the office, and his eyes landed on Weezy's painting. "That's amazing. The artist really captured you."

Chapter Forty-One

By late afternoon it was still sunny in the private administration lobby of the American Pharmaceutical Advocacy Group. APAG's C-Suite alone took up an entire floor of the modern D.C. building. Cole sat with Li, waiting for an audience with the CEO, knowing violent storms were due to hit the mid-Atlantic region at any time. They'd been waiting nearly an hour when Nichole Sebastian's assistant approached them. Without introduction or making direct eye contact, he said, "Agent, Huebsch. Agent Song. Follow me." Cole gestured for Li to follow the assistant, and he brought up the rear. Out of the corner of his eye, he saw the wispy gray tendrils of a low-hanging cloud cross the windows before he turned down a hall.

The assistant led them to a tall door and held it open, gesturing them inside. They walked into an office with a wall of tall opaque glass and saw a woman sitting at the end of a glass and marble table. She stood as they entered, introducing herself as Nichole Sebastian, shaking hands with Li and Cole in turn. She looked down at Li with a smirk and held Cole's hand an extra beat. He felt her heat and power and tried not to blush as her gray eyes bore into his. When she released his hand and moved back to reclaim the head of the table, Cole shook his head to clear it. *Get your shit together*, he told himself. He and Li sat down at the table next to each other. Sebastian hit a button on a remote, and when nothing outward happened, he wondered if she was recording their conversation. She hit another button, and the white exterior walls faded to clear; the sudden expanse of sunlight and clouds took their breath away.

Cole looked back to his host and noticed her blouse was unbuttoned to provide a view of silky-smooth cleavage. She returned his look knowingly and smiled. She used her striking looks, wielded them like a weapon of mass destruction. "You asked for this meeting, Agent Huebsch. What can I do for you?"

"Yes, well, before we start, I want to thank you for seeing us on such short notice. We know you're incredibly busy. We wanted to talk to you about the security firm that you use here, DC Security Professionals."

"I'll try to answer your questions, but as you can imagine, I'm not all that close to that side of the business. I've got others who work under me who attend to such things."

"Of course. I understand." Cole pulled out a reporter's notebook he had borrowed from Michele before leaving for DC. He and Li had hitched a ride back to Washington with Olson, and he had scribbled some questions for the interview during the flight. He started out with general questions which could easily be fact-checked. *When did you first employ DC Security Professionals? Who signed the contract with them on behalf of APAG?* He then moved on to more open-ended questions. He told Li that this was the transition where they both needed to watch Sebastian closely.

"In what capacity do you use Dexter Carter and his firm?"

She smiled, "For security, naturally."

"Could you be more specific? Do they provide physical security for your offices? Do they provide cybersecurity for your operations? What about your personal protection?"

"All of the above, I believe."

He switched gears, trying to throw her. "Tell me about your relationship with DC Security Professionals' founder and owner, Dexter Carter."

"Relationship?" She raised an eyebrow and pursed her lips. "Nonexistent would be the word for it. I have no more relationship with Mr. Carter than with the owner of the firm that cleans our building."

"That's odd. I spoke with Mr. Carter last night, and it was clear that he felt close to you. Can you explain that?"

"I can't, I'm afraid. Some women are attractive to the opposite sex. Men

CHAPTER FORTY-ONE

want to be with them. They fantasize that a relationship is there when none exists." She let the words settle on them, then glanced dismissively at Li. "I suppose it could even happen with a woman like your fellow agent here."

Li felt a slow burn as Sebastian continued. "I also think when you reach a certain level of success as I have, people want to see themselves as being close to you. Perhaps it makes them feel more important. Or they believe it will help their own career. Whatever. I can't speak for Mr. Carter."

Cole hated the smug look on her face. He snuck a glance at Li and could tell she was frustrated as well. He looked back at Sebastian and realized he hadn't seen her blink once so far. Who doesn't blink? Snakes and lizards are who, but only because they don't have eyelids. His own eyelids started to blink rapidly, unnaturally, and he forced himself to control it. *Damn it! She really was a pit viper.*

Sebastian took advantage of the gap in questioning. She smiled as she asked Cole a question of her own, "Did you have an accident, Agent Huebsch? I apologize, but I can't help but notice the bruising and discoloration of your face. It must be painful."

"I'm actually fine." He was getting nowhere, so he decided to push her harder. He looked back down at his notes. "Listen, I'm going to get to the point here. Dexter Carter and the people he employed were killers. They tried to kill U.S. Senator Eric Rhodes. They tried to kill me. And they tried to kill Li. Further, they…"

Sebastian interrupted with a smirk, "Sounds like they're not very good at killing. Although they seem to try very hard."

"This isn't funny. We've traced payments made by DC Security Professionals to the hitmen who were paid to make the shooting of Senator Rhodes look like something else. And keep in mind he was shot the morning after he gave a very compelling speech laying partial blame for the high cost of health care directly at the feet of the companies that support APAG."

"That seems like a big leap."

"Not so big, really. We also tracked payments that were made to the same group of hitmen soon after they murdered journalists who wrote critical stories about the pharmaceutical industry."

"That's curious. I consider myself fairly well-read, and I haven't heard anything about journalists being targeted for murder for any reason, let alone for writing about the industry I work in."

"The murders were made to look like accidents. Car crashes. Heart attacks."

"Seems awfully far-fetched."

Cole knew she was lying, but he didn't have much left in the notebook to cover. "Do you know how many clients DC Security Professionals has?"

"Not a clue."

"Just one. And you're it."

It wasn't a question, and Sebastian just sat there with her annoying smirk, eyes locked on Cole's and ignoring Li altogether. Cole went off script. "Are you sure you weren't close to Dexter Carter? He intimated to me that you were. We can get a warrant to review your security camera archives. I wouldn't be surprised if it showed Dexter Carter coming in and out of this very office. We can interview your staff, including every member of your C-Suite and all of their personal assistants…including yours." He let that hang in the air.

Sebastian leaned toward Cole, exposing even more cleavage. Her eyes mocked him. "You could *try* to get a warrant. Not to be crass, but you have about as much chance of getting a warrant as you have of getting into my panties."

Cole was frustrated. He tried not to blush crimson and failed miserably. He wasn't interviewing James Flood. He knew that going in. He had expected Sebastian to keep her cool. She'd graduated tops in her law school class at Columbia and followed that up with an MBA from Harvard. Her undergrad from Stanford wasn't bad either. But she wasn't just cool, she was ice. She smiled a dead smile, and Cole was out of tricks. He sighed and shook his head slowly. He was getting ready to stand when Li cut in. "You changed your name right after your senior year in high school. Changed it from Jane Smith to Nichole Sebastian."

Sebastian turned her cold stare on Li. "What is the relevance?"

"I saw your high school yearbook. I imagine you were called 'Plain Jane' a

CHAPTER FORTY-ONE

lot, and you wanted something with more gravitas."

Sebastian kept her composure, but Cole thought her complexion darkened, and the fake smile left her face. "What point are you making?"

"Does wearing a half million dollars in jewelry make you feel more beautiful or more powerful?"

Now Sebastian gave Li her full attention. Before she could respond, however, Li gestured around the room, "Does sitting in this office make you feel more successful? Do you wear those heels of yours so that you can look down on others?"

Sebastian's face was now a scowl. And the murderous dark cloud that slid slowly past the windows was reflected in her eyes. "What in the hell are you getting at?"

Li's smile reflected the fake one Sebastian had flashed earlier. "May I call you Nicky?"

"No, you may not," Sebastian hissed.

Li nodded to the window. "You think you're above it all. Don't you? You believe you can do whatever you want, and there will never be any repercussions. No payback. But that's not the way things work in the real world."

Sebastian smiled again, and this time it was genuine. But it was twisted and malevolent. She stared at Cole, and he wanted nothing more than to turn away, the urge ten times stronger than when he faced the carnage in the barn at the beginning of the case in what seemed a lifetime ago. He gritted his teeth and held her gaze. He could sense Li doing the same.

"Oh, but I don't live in your world," Sebastian said. "I don't live in your small prison cell of a world where you buy your clothes off the rack, look for discounts, and stand in long lines for a sale. And I take what I want because I'm simply better than you in every way imaginable." She pushed a button on her remote, and Cole felt intuitively she had stopped recording the conversation. She stood and walked slowly to the windows. She turned to them again and swept her manicured hand out and down. Her perfect brows arched, and a slight smile played at her lips. "It's a long drop. Careers... Lives... All can be ruined so quickly. So effortlessly."

"Are you threatening us?" Cole said.

The smile grew larger, a crooked Cheshire cat smile, playing at the corners of her full mouth. "Heavens, no." She said, walking to the door. "Don't be absurd. But face the facts. You have nothing beyond the flimsiest of circumstantial evidence. You could try to get warrants and subpoenas, but, well, I doubt you'll have much luck with that. If you try to take this further, your own government will not only support me and the industry I lead, but they'll also turn on you." She opened the door. "So please leave. Now."

Cole and Li got up and moved to the door in defeat. They knew she was right. Sebastian put a hand on Cole's arm as he walked past, and he stopped, catching her hard look. "I'm not inclined to theater, Agent Huebsch. I'm known more as a doer...." And she threw back her thick black hair and laughed. Cole shook off her hand and escaped from the room, Li close behind.

They stood outside under the APAG building's wide awning while a blustery wind misted them with cool air. Suddenly, heavy sheets of rain pounded the pavement and the cars that lined the street, sending shoppers and businesspeople alike scurrying to find cover.

"What next?" Li said.

"Well, I have a little time to kill before I pick up Michele. She has an appointment in an hour with the owners of East City Bookshop, trying to line up an event with them for late fall. That's just a good stretch of the legs down Pennsylvania Avenue from here, but I'll Uber it if this rain doesn't let up." He looked across the street. In the window of what could only be a tavern, Cole saw a neon sign touting *Imperial Double IPA*. He turned to Li and said, "I've got a plan," and then raced into the downpour and across the street. She scampered after him, shocked by the cold of the rain that soaked her immediately. He held the door for her, and they hustled into the bar. The place was maybe half-full but would pick up when the rain slowed, and the buildings around them emptied for the day. They chose a booth and sat down.

A waiter was at their side immediately. "Is the Imperial IPA brewed locally?"

CHAPTER FORTY-ONE

"Not more than three miles from where you're sitting, as a matter of fact."

Cole broke into a grin. "I'll have a pint of that. And whatever my friend here would like." Li decided on a glass of Chardonnay while Cole glanced at the beer menu. "Eight percent alcohol by volume. I may have to pick something a little less potent for beer number two."

They sat in silence and collected their thoughts. When the waiter returned with their order, Cole took a sip of the IPA that gave him a foamy mustache. "A right smart ale," he said to the waiter, and Li shook her head.

When the waiter was gone again, Li asked the obvious question. "Where do we go with this investigation now?"

Cole took another sip of his beer and savored the hoppy goodness. "This is where it ends." He looked at Li with a smile as sad as her frown. "It sucks, but it is what it is." He paused, thinking. "It reminds me of deer hunting. I used to pride myself on the fact that every deer I ever shot at ended up in the freezer. Each year I hunted, someone in our hunting party would wound a deer that we couldn't find. But not me. For the longest time, every deer I shot at went down and ended up on our table. I took pride in that. But then that came to an end. It was late in the day, and I had an awkward shot where I had to lean out around a tree. I thought I could still pull off the shot. When I pulled the trigger, the deer stumbled and staggered off. I waited a bit and then went to tag the deer. Instead, I ended up following a spotty blood trail in the dark for over an hour. When snow started coming down and covered any trace of that deer, I had to give up and head home. It left a bitter taste in my mouth for a while, but you get over it. You rationalize and tell yourself that the deer ended up providing food for other animals, and you shove the thought from your mind that it suffered before dying. You have to realize that in life, there's only so much you can do. You need to know when to give up. We disrupted their operation. She might not be able to rebuild it. We have to believe in karma and the idea that Nichole Sebastian and her ilk will ultimately get what they have coming to them."

"I know you, though," Li said. "Giving up isn't in your DNA. There are a lot of cases we've eventually solved where the trail was cold."

"Thanks, I guess," Cole said, taking another large sip of his beer. "But this case is over for us. The director will have a fit if he finds out we questioned Sebastian. He would have had to fire me to keep me from interviewing her, and even then, I would've talked to her as a private citizen. We took our shot, and she didn't crack...even though you found a way to push some of her buttons and knock her off her game a bit." He raised his glass. "I salute your effort."

"But you think she was behind the attempt on Senator Rhodes' life? She was Dexter Carter's puppeteer, right?"

"Absolutely. I'm also certain she put out the hit on you, me, and the dead reporters. But thinking she's the mastermind and proving it are two very different things. In my book, she's no different than those thugs you took care of on the Summerfest bus. Well," he paused again, "except that she's a lot easier on the eyes and nose."

Li looked at him. "I'm not so sure about her being easier on the eyes. You had a hard time facing her, just like I did. It was scary. And she's worse than those scum on the bus. Way worse. Because despite the evil that surrounds her like a cloud when she lets her guard down, God gave her a lot of talent that she's perverted."

"Someone gave her talent," Cole agreed. "But maybe it wasn't God. Maybe it was that other guy, the one with the horns, tail, and pitchfork."

"I'm just saying that she could have used her brains and her looks and that incredible body of hers and changed the world for the better."

"So, I wasn't the only one to notice that incredible body of hers?"

"Do I look blind?"

Cole smiled. "No. But now you have me confused. I'm not sure if you want to hammer her in the face or ask her on a date."

Li didn't react to his attempt at humor. "I'm serious. Sebastian is way worse than those guys on the bus, and not just because she had other opportunities in life. I don't know, maybe she had it bad growing up, but at some point, things broke her way. You told me the guys I fought on the bus would have kept hurting women if I hadn't stopped them." She pointed to the building across the street. "Do you think Sebastian stops now?"

Cole shook his head, draining the last of his beer. "No. I think this will

CHAPTER FORTY-ONE

embolden her. The FBI was onto her, right in her face, and then slunk away. That's how she'll see it."

Li's eyes narrowed. "So, we just slink away? That's how it's going to be?"

Cole shrugged.

"Fuck!" Li said, loud enough to turn the heads of other nearby patrons.

Cole signaled for another round as Li slammed the rest of her wine. "That's my word, by the way. I copyrighted it."

Li wiped her mouth with a napkin. "When it came to power, those guys on the bus had nothing outside of the momentary power when they terrorized women. But their power is nothing compared to Nichole Effing Sebastian. She's got the juice of this whole city behind her!"

"Calm down," Cole said softly. "You're right, but just take a couple deep breaths, in and out. And stop using the F-bomb. I own that word." He reached across the table and took one of her hands in his. "Fate can be a bitch. We just have to hope it catches up with Miss Nicky sooner rather than later."

Chapter Forty-Two

Cole stepped into the East City Bookshop about the time Michele's meeting with the owner was starting. The indie storefront was the size of a larger house, and he felt a homey vibe as he browsed. Bright colors and shelf upon shelf of books took his mind off Nichole Sebastian. He felt a quiet electricity in the air as people discovered new authors, worlds, and ideas. He was greeted by a staff member drinking from a *Lit Happens* mug, and he smiled.

Cole had decided he was going to do his best to put the APAG case behind him. Michele was flying from DC to San Francisco later that night, and he planned to be on the plane with her. He was going to try to convince her to extend the trip and spend a few quiet days in Sonoma wine country. He called the office on his walk to the bookstore, and his schedule was clear for the next week. He had a ton of vacation time saved up, and it was high time he started burning through some of it. He was lost in thoughts of sipping a hearty cab with Michele on a sun-dappled terrace when he felt something cold and wet bump the palm of his hand. He looked down in time to see a smiling golden retriever nudge his hand affectionately again.

"Hey buddy," Cole said, scratching the dog behind his ears. "Do you have something on your mind?"

The dog stepped to a table next to Cole. "Woof woof! Woof woof! Woof!" The dog's owner shushed him.

Cole looked at the table and saw stacks of Stephen King's *Fairy Tale* displayed. "What are you, Steve's best friend or his publicist? Either way, I'm looking for a paperback. I'm going to be traveling, and it'll be easier to

CHAPTER FORTY-TWO

carry."

The retriever cocked his head at Cole and then looked at the table stacked high with King's books again.

"Okay," he relented, picking up a copy. "Who am I to ignore a five-woof review."

At the same time, in Baltimore, a slender, tattooed man wearing jeans, a white muscle shirt, a ballcap, and sunglasses snatched a set of keys when the valet stand at a restaurant was unattended. He drove out of the adjacent parking structure minutes later in an older but stout black SUV in good condition. Two miles away, he pulled into a garage, changed the vehicle's license plates, and headed for the nation's capital.

An hour and a half later, Cole and Michele were in the queue to board their flight to San Francisco. Their passes were scanned, and as they stepped onto the plane, a steward stopped them, speaking quietly. "Excuse me. Are you Cole Huebsch?"

"Yes."

"We have extra room in first class this evening, and we'd like to upgrade you and your guest."

"That's not necess—"

Michele cut him off. "We are very grateful..." she read his nameplate, "Adam." He led them to their seats and handed each of them a glass of chilled champagne before takeoff. They clinked their glasses together, and Michele said, "Here's to whatever's next!"

The black SUV double parked beside a nondescript gray rental car outside of the parking garage used by APAG executives. The drivers of the rental and SUV switched cars, and the SUV drove away. The slim tattooed man kept a close eye on the parking garage exit. When a distinctive tan extended Audi sedan drove out of the structure a half hour later, the tattooed man placed a call.

A half-hour later, Nichole Sebastian sat in the back of her Audi. Another wave of thunderclouds was sweeping through the area, and the car's wipers worked in rhythm to keep the glass clear. She spent most of the drive returning emails and texts, but the last five minutes or so, she sat quietly with her eyes shut, trying to figure out how to replace Dexter Carter. She thought her driver a dullard, which is why she didn't mind him hearing her end of calls. But she didn't trust him to carry out the work that Carter had done for her. She cursed Agent Huebsch under her breath for throwing a wrench into her well-oiled machine. She was still contemplating her next steps when she was thrown sideways; the right side of her head would've smacked against the passenger window if her side airbag hadn't worked the way it was intended. Her head still whiplashed violently right, then left, and she was disoriented. She heard the muffled groan of her driver as he struggled to untangle himself from the front and side airbags that had protected him. That's when she noticed the black SUV that had t-boned the left side of her car. Its shattered grill had melded with the side panel of her car. But it made no sense. They were less than two blocks from her home on a quiet street. *Who would drive so fast here? Had they lost control on the slippery pavement?*

Someone exited the other vehicle and stepped to her driver's door. Four concussive bangs shattered the window, and the night and blood painted the rich light leather interior of Sebastian's car. She screamed as her driver, her bodyguard, slumped sideways in his seat. The killer was dressed in dark clothes and had a hoodie pulled over their head. They walked around to Sebastian's side of the car and pointed a pistol through the tinted windows at her. "Open the door. Now."

The windows weren't bulletproof. Sebastian had never worried for her own safety. She'd felt untouchable. Until now. She unlocked the door, and it was yanked open. "Out," the killer commanded. Sebastian stepped out and stood shakily on her three- and one-half-inch heels. She hadn't felt fear in years, but she cowered now. She started to beg for mercy when she saw something in the assassin's eyes. Something familiar. Something she could use. She was the best at negotiating any deal, and a spark of confidence grew in her. She opened her mouth to make an initial offer when she was stunned by a quick strike. Before the pain registered, she tried again to make her opening proposition, but no words came out. Then she felt an excruciating pain in her throat and the panic that comes when you can't breathe. She

CHAPTER FORTY-TWO

clutched at her throat and looked at her killer, who had stepped back and pointed the handgun at Sebastian's head. The gun shook unsteadily, and Sebastian felt she still had a chance, right before the trigger was pulled and her life was ended. The killer reached out as the CEO slumped to the wet pavement, grabbing her rare pearl necklace in a gloved hand and ripping it free.

A gray rental car paused at the corner, and the driver leaned across the front seat to open the passenger door. The killer slid in, and the car drove off as lights came on in the nearby houses.

The slender tattooed man drove three miles from the murder scene, stopping briefly as they crossed the Potomac. The killer looked at the large orange pearl, awash in light from a street lamp. Its flame pattern seemed to flicker and come alive in the killer's palm, and they could feel warmth and seduction slowly moving up their wrist and forearm. The killer clenched their fist and threw the pearl necklace over the bridge's railing and into the river. The car started moving again, keeping to the posted speed limits, before pulling into an unattended lot without working security cameras. A different rental car sat alone in the shadows. The assassin said something to the driver, then got in the rental, retrieved the keys from under the seat, and drove four blocks away before parking under a streetlamp on a quiet residential street. Then, fists rained down upon the dash, fast and heavy, thump, thumping like a heart at its limits until the strength leeched from the arms. The assassin sighed and leaned over the steering wheel, resting head on forearms. Their body shuddered, and a sob escaped their lips. Tears welled. Big drops forming one at a time.

A hot tear of shame slid haltingly from the right eye, trickling down the cheek and dropping to the floormat. From the left, a drop of bloodlust ran a parallel track down the other cheek. From the right, a tear of horror, followed by a drop of pride from the left. The tears ran faster then, the single tear becoming a torrent...a flash flood of conflicting emotions. Regret followed by self-respect. Anguish trailing righteousness. Fear and self-loathing followed by strength and self-awareness. Doubt, then uncertainty, and white-hot anger after empathy. Every emotion flowed through their tears, every emotion save indifference, until the assassin was drained.

The sobbing and moaning ended, and a hollow emptiness remained. Silence filled the car, except for the sound of breathing that went from ragged to steady. Strong, slender hands wiped away the tears, and they lifted their head from the steering wheel. The assassin took a deep breath and started the car, the engine's faint tremble a sign of life. A hand adjusted the rearview, and the assassin locked eyes with those in the mirror…one chestnut and one sky blue.

Cole was three hours and thirteen hundred miles into his flight to San Francisco when he woke with a start. He thought at first it was turbulence. When he looked around the cabin, he noticed nearly everyone else was asleep, and the plane ride was gentle as a lullaby. He had fallen asleep while reading, with the lamp, still focused on his hardcover. When sleep wouldn't return, he picked up the book again and got lost in its pages, escaping his worries for a while.

Chapter Forty-Three

A week later, Cole sat at his desk early in the morning, sunlight filtered by his window blinds lighting up his office. He and Michele had grown closer the past week, sharing their hopes and dreams and bottles of lush red wine. He rubbed his forehead and noticed he didn't feel a bump there any longer. His face and the rest of his body had healed as well. *No outward scars, at least*, he thought, but wondered if the toll he paid emotionally these past weeks would ever really be forgotten.

He had the Washington Post webpage open, and he was reading about the tragic death of Nichole Sebastian. It quoted the local police calling it a robbery gone wrong, and noted that her melo melo pearl necklace, valued at more than half a million dollars, was gone. It showed photos of Sebastian at charitable galas, dressed in an array of fabulous designer gowns, but always showcasing her necklace. The article pointed out the extravagant gifts she had made to nonprofit foundations, and the major boards she had served on. The Smithsonian, the American Red Cross, the National Gallery of Art, and more. The reporter painted Sebastian as a kind of Mother Teresa in three-and-one-half-inch heels.

Cole shook his head in disgust. His eyes wandered to the portrait Weezy had gifted him. The bold colors and block letters and the image of him he couldn't see until he somehow let go and saw the unseeable. He thought about the note Weezy had taped to the back of the painting....

Nobody ever really did anything for me before, and I never saw many people who could tell the difference between right or wrong or who gave a shit which was which. You and Li remind me of Batman and Robin...or maybe Batman and

Batwoman. Anyway, keep fighting the good fight, and don't let ol' Weezy down! If ever you need a hand, just give me a ring. BM

He remembered the portrait and note Weezy had given to Li. *If ever you need a hand, just give me a ring.* He thought about the SUV stolen in Baltimore that was used in Sebastian's murder. Li had been in DC in the early morning hours of the day Sebastian was killed. She had motive, means, and more. Cole drummed his fingers on his desk. He was on the verge of calling Li in for a conversation when she appeared in his doorway.

"Do you have a minute?"

Cole nodded. Li came into the office and sat across the desk from Cole. "I got a call from Linda's attorney late last week. Linda had a last will and testament and she remembered me in it. She actually left me everything she had, which was quite a bit. Her photography business must have paid pretty well. More importantly, she left me a note." She pulled it from her pocket and read...."

> *Dear Li,*
>
> *I am so sorry I wasn't strong like you. I know it might seem like I'm a weak person to take my own life, but I just can't face all the ugliness I see. The world I view through my lenses is beautiful beyond words, but when I pull the camera away from my face, the brutality of reality smothers me. But please know that you were always beautiful to me. And if I was a weak person, please at least know that my love for you was strong, stronger than any other emotion I have ever experienced. I hope someday you can forgive me.*
>
> *Love, Linda*

Tears were streaming down Li's face as she read the letter, and she brushed at them before carefully folding the letter and sliding it into the pocket of her shirt.

Cole was torn. Part of him wanted to comfort Li, and another part was determined to tell her to close the door so they could have a private conversation. Their eyes met then, his denim-blue and hers chestnut and

CHAPTER FORTY-THREE

sky blue, and the truth of what happened to Nichole Sebastian was shared between them. He was about to ask Li a hard question when Li asked him a simple one of her own, "How are you?"

And Cole remembered a long-ago conversation with Gene Olson and the old adage: *Don't ask a question you don't want the answer to*. Instead, he got up and walked over to his window. He opened his blinds all the way and squinted out at the brilliant waves crashing against the shore. *Like lemmings from the sea.* Li couldn't see the look on Cole's face that conveyed both the joy and sadness that was his life as he answered. "I'm livin' the dream, Li. Livin' the dream."

A Note from the Author

Writers write to be read, and our readers make us or break us. If you like *The Killer Speech*, please write a short review on Amazon, Goodreads, and/or Barnes and Noble. And if you want to learn more about this book or upcoming author events and news, please visit kevinkluesner.net. You can contact me from there, and I will answer any questions you have. Thank you!

Acknowledgements

Thanks to all the readers who take a chance on writers new to publishing. The warm reception and encouragement I've received from you through library talks, books clubs, and through my website (kevinkluesner.net), provided the energy to make this second book possible. I'm especially grateful to all those who've left positive reviews of my debut novel, *The Killer Sermon*, on Amazon, Barnes and Noble, Goodreads, and other popular book sites. Established authors tell me more reviews stimulate more buzz and more readers, so I'm unabashedly asking you to please take the time to review *The Killer Speech*. And reach out to me on my website. I promise to respond to every email. Thanks to my family and early readers, and to the "Dames of Detection" at my publisher, Level Best Books.

About the Author

Kevin Kluesner holds both a BA in journalism and an MBA from Marquette University. He's worked as the outdoor writer for a daily newspaper, taught at both the undergraduate and graduate level, and served as an administrator of an urban safety net hospital. The Killer Speech is his second novel in the FBI agent Cole Huebsch thriller series set in Milwaukee and Wisconsin. Kevin might be the only person to claim membership in both the American College of Healthcare Executives and the International Thriller Writers. He lives in New Berlin, Wisconsin, with his wife Janet.

SOCIAL MEDIA HANDLES:
　Kevin Kluesner | LinkedIn
　Kevin Kluesner | Facebook

AUTHOR WEBSITE:
　kevinkluesner.net

Also by Kevin Kluesner

The Killer Sermon

CPSIA information can be obtained
at www.ICGtesting.com
Printed in the USA
BVHW041519180423
662564BV00001B/105